There was a quick little tilt of confidence to Patricia's chin, and a set of triumph to her lips as she rose from her chair and looked about upon them with a smiling challenge in spite of her white face. In the soft candlelight of the room with the flicker of the waxen flames across her lovely face, and her silver garments, she looked more than ever like a thing of moonlight, and John Worth looked up at her, his heart bursting with the beauty of her. Then she flung her challenge, sweetly, simply, almost carelessly, as if it were a matter of course.

"I'm just announcing my engagement," she said calmly. She saw them sit up greedily for more, saw the relief and proud satisfaction beginning to dawn in her mother's face, saw Thorny, leaning forward with a voluptuous look in his eyes, saw his white matched teeth gleam almost with a snarl of conquest. . . .

Grace LIVINGSTON HILL

AMERICA'S BEST-LOVED STORYTELLER

PATRICIA

LIVING BOOKS®
Tyndale House Publishers, Inc.
Wheaton, Illinois

This Tyndale House book
by Grace Livingston Hill
contains the complete text
of the original hardcover edition.
NOT ONE WORD
HAS BEEN OMITTED.

Copyright © 1939 by Grace Livingston Hill
Copyright © renewed 1967 by Ruth Hill Munce
All rights reserved
Cover illustration copyright © 1992 by Heide Oberheide

Living Books is a registered trademark of Tyndale House
Publishers, Inc.

Library of Congress Catalog Card Number 92-80579
ISBN 0-8423-4814-X

Printed in the United States of America

01   00   99   98   97   96
  7   6   5   4   3   2

I

THERE were lilies of the valley, a rich mass of them, growing inside the hedge, lifting their delicate waxen bells among the deep green of their sheath-like leaves. John Worth made sure of this before he lifted the latch of the wrought-iron gate and stepped within.

It was not easy to see the flowers from the street for the hedge had grown so tall it was far above his head, though he was full six feet. The hedge was thick and firm, an impervious wall of green. One had to stand close to the gate and look carefully to find the fairy bells among the green.

He noticed as he paused to close the gate behind him that the grass had been sedulously cut about them. Or was that fancy? He stooped and picked a single stem with the perfect exquisite flowers strung like pearls on a thread of jade and held it shielded in the palm of his hand as he passed on up the path toward the mansion.

It was early for an evening call, not yet eight o'clock. He realized this with sudden acuteness as he drew near the house which was as yet hidden by thick foliage. He had had his reasons for not adhering strictly to the social

1

custom of the big town where he had been raised. Mainly, his time was short, and he wanted to make sure of the evening if possible before anyone forestalled him. But now that he was here he wondered if he had been wise?

A drifting sound of voices from the house, the purr of a costly motor gliding up the driveway beyond the line of hemlocks, a girl's laughter ringing out harshly from one of the upper balconies, struck him like successive blows. He had not thought of possible guests! It would have been better to have waited for the darkness!

Yet he would not turn back now.

The pavement curved about a fountain playing softly in silver spray above a marble-rimmed pool where cool lilies, white and pink, floated exquisitely. Marble benches stood beneath the copper beeches and high pines that sheltered the spot; and beyond, the path curved again to the low rising steps of the terrace.

Suddenly the house looked down upon him as some great personage well established upon his throne might look upon an intruder!

Two girls in diaphanous evening frocks of jade and coral were leaning upon the iron grillwork of a frail balcony just outside a second story window. They looked like flowers against the rugged gray of the stone masonry.

Another laugh rang out with a more perceptible note of hardness as they turned to go back into the room. They had not noticed his approach.

Something cold and alien seemed to blow across his face. Involuntarily he pressed the little flower he held as if it had been a talisman, but went steadily on up the steps to the terrace, until he stood before the door. His shoulders were erect, his step as firm, as if he had been accustomed to tread that way, and to stand before such portals daily.

As he waited to be admitted his lips took on a stern set, and his eyes were as if he were going into battle.

The door swung open silently. He turned, to realize that a man in livery was standing before him questioningly. His lips seemed stiff as he spoke her name.

The servant looked him over appraisingly.

"Miss Patricia is giving a dinner tonight," he explained with a questioning lift of one eyebrow. "Is— Mr.—?" He consulted the card Worth had laid on the silver tray. "Is Mr. Worth one of the invited guests?"

Something desperate flamed in John Worth's face.

"No, I'm not. But I *must* see her!" he said firmly.

"Perhaps, later in the evening," suggested the servant delicately. "I might enquire if it will be convenient—?"

A sick wave of despair surged over the young man. Later in the evening! As well give it up now! "No!" he said determinedly. "Wait!"

He brought out his fountain pen and reaching for his card wrote a few infinitesimal words on its back.

"Take that to her!" he said briefly.

He was led to a small reception room. The heavy velvet curtains at the doorway were drawn aside giving a vista of the dim lovely distance; a pillared aisle almost like a cathedral, with rooms opening beyond; a noble staircase dividing half way up and leading either side to a gallery screened by Moorish lattice; below the gallery a great fireplace in which logs were burning brightly, for the spring evening was cool.

More people were arriving, with a sound of high strained voices as they greeted those who were just coming down after removing their wraps, and their chatter blended with the soft twang of stringed instruments being put in tune behind a screen of palms.

There was sound and color and an arrogant life there to which he had never belonged.

"There's Thorny!" he heard a voice exclaim.

A general laugh, hard and knowing, followed, like the laugh that had come from the upper gallery multiplied by many voices.

Thorny appeared, tall, slender, confident, well-groomed, his perfect teeth like matched pearls flashing gorgeously as he smiled. There was no denying that Thornton Bellingham made a stunning appearance.

John Worth studied him furtively from the shadow of the curtain. He was not much changed. A shadow under the jaded eyes perhaps, fine dark restless eyes with long effective lashes.

There were those girls whispering again outside the curtain.

"Yes, Pat's mother told Aunt Fran! She said Pat had practically promised to announce her engagement to-night!"

What a fool he had been to come!

"Hot stuff, darling, but there won't be any great thrill about it, will there? We've all known it was coming for the last three years! I can't see why she let it drag out so. Stage stuff, I call it—"

The voices drifted by and mingled with the general buzz and laughter.

John Worth sat still and waited, turning cold to his finger tips with the futility of his errand.

Patricia had been called to the telephone. She had been awaiting the arrival of the last guest, a man whom she had met at the country club that week, who had done some notable flying and got himself into the newspapers. She had arranged to place him by her side at the dinner. Thorny would not like it of course, but under the circumstances he would make the best of it.

She had seated Thorny far down the table at her mother's side. It was her own dinner and she had arranged all the details.

The recreant guest was on the telephone. He had been in an accident and his car was disabled. It happened too far from a telephone to let her know sooner. It was impossible for him now to get there in time for dinner. Might he drop in later in the evening and make his apologies?

She turned from the telephone in dismay.

Rapidly she went over the list of her guests with a wild hope of finding another one who could be placed at her side at the table. But no, there was a reason for the placing of each one of them. She could not change now. It was going to be most awkward. And there wasn't anyone else whom she could call upon at this last minute. It was too late! She felt as if the walls of a great stone prison were slowly closing in about her heart to crush her.

It was just then, as she turned desperately away from the telephone that the butler approached her apologetically with John Worth's card in his hand.

"Miss Patricia, there's a gentleman in the small reception room insisting upon seeing you for just a moment."

"I cannot possibly see anyone now," said Patricia firmly. "Didn't you tell him, Barker?"

"Yes, I did, Miss Patricia. I suggested some other evening, or perhaps later in the evening, but he said no, and sent you this. I'll send him away if you say."

Patricia, frowning, took the card and read:

"I have never before been in a position to come. May I see you for just a moment about something that may be important to us both? I must leave tonight."

Wondering, she turned the card over and read John Worth's name.

Startled she turned the card back, reread the message, and the frown on her brow relaxed. A soft glow came into her eyes. She was suddenly lifted out of her perplexities and put back into her childhood. In a flash she saw a wooded hillside under a stormy sky, with anemones blowing like frightened children in the grass at her feet. And off in the distance across fields and fences, a small shingled house, weatherbeaten and gray, and a boy with eyes like a young knight, standing in the doorway with his mother, while all about the dooryard valley-lilies clustered closely, their perfume filling the clean wet air.

John Worth! After all these years!

A servant was approaching, and her perplexities dropped down upon her once more. Dinner was about to be served and she was lacking a guest!

Then a sudden thought struck her. John Worth! Why not ask him? He wouldn't likely have a dinner coat of course, and that would make him conspicuous, but what of that? She remembered him at school as often wearing coats that showed too much of his wrists. Thorny would be angry too, but Thorny's lips were sealed for this evening at least. Her mother wouldn't like it either, but what else could she do? The other man had failed her. Anyway her mother wouldn't remember who John was, that he used to live in a little frame house on the hillside, and bring honey, and strawberries and wild grapes to the house to sell sometimes when he was a small boy.

She turned to the servant with sudden determination in her face.

"I'll see him!" she said. "I'll be back in a moment. I think the last guest has arrived. Dinner can be served almost immediately."

The servant bowed and left her, and with a heart

wildly beating, like a condemned criminal under expected reprieve, she turned and made her way swiftly through a sun porch to a door at the far end opening into the small reception room where John Worth was waiting. As she entered she caught the faint fragrance of valley-lilies on the air and wondered. Was it her imagination?

2

WHEN Patricia Prentiss was a little girl there had been a battle royal between her father and mother concerning the school she should attend.

George Prentiss was a kindly, grave man with a great ability to make money, and a few old-fashioned ideas to which he clung stubbornly. For the rest he let his wife have her way.

Mainly his old-fashioned ideas were three in number. He did not believe in drinking intoxicating liquors. He had always attended church regularly in the same old church where his father and mother, and their fathers and mothers had attended church, and he always would, even though the denomination and most of the congregation had abandoned the old plain structure and built a fine new edifice, selling the old one to a small undenominational group, who were utterly beyond the pale socially. George Prentiss had allied himself with the minority and stayed in the old church, with the undenominational group.

And, finally, he believed that the public school was the only proper place in which to secure an education.

In the matter of liquor, his wife had more or less come off victorious. It was the first battle of their married life, and she claimed that life would be a desert drear if she couldn't have cocktails at her parties, that people all did it nowadays and she would die of shame if she couldn't do as others did. It had been a long steady conflict, but gradually she had dominated. Little by little liquor was served at the Prentiss table at social affairs. Usually the head of the house absented himself from the town, when he knew what was to be, and he never drank himself, when he was forced by circumstances to be present.

In the matter of church attendance Amelia Prentiss made several decisive gestures in the direction of a fashionable and formal place of worship. George went with her once and balked. It was not his idea of a place to worship God, and he would not go there again. She might do as she liked, but he would continue to worship where he always had worshiped. No amount of argument sufficed to move him, and finally, his wife, not keen on going to church herself, settled down to long restful Sabbath mornings in bed, to be ready for lovely, stately, social teas in the late afternoon, and Sunday evening musicales.

But when it came to the matter of where to send their only child to school, George rose right up and planted his foot down on principle. No, Patricia should not go to Miss Delicia Greystone's Select School for Girls. There might be girls' schools that were worth going to, but this one was not. Patricia should not be trained to be a little empty-headed snob. She should go to a good honest public school the way her father had done, get a little idea of the way the world was made up of all kinds of people, and not think she was "it."

It lasted a week, that battle, and cost so much in courage and pain and sleeplessness, that George Prentiss resolved he would never fight another, no matter what was involved. But he won. Amelia shed plenty of tears, cast reproach upon him, and even said he had deceived her when he married her. That she thought he was a man of refined feelings and high ambitions, and it seemed he was instead wedded to low uncultured things. That he was even willing to have his charming angel-child herd among the canaille in the public schools, where she would acquire low tastes, worse language, and the manners of common people. She wept so copiously that several times George Prentiss had to leave the house and walk out in the country to the old farm which he still owned, to get near to sky and trees and realize that he wasn't after all the low-lived criminal that Amelia had been trying to make him out.

But when he returned, his spirit rested, and his vision cleared by a sight of the sky and the green trees and grass, with a touch of the old home fraught with sweet memories, he would come into the house with his jaw set firmly, reminding his wife of the days when she used to contemplate him from afar and wonder if he wasn't a bit too set in his way to make pleasant company for life.

On one such occasion she eyed him through the evening meal between scant conversation, and finally remarked with the advent of the dessert she knew he liked:

"Well, I've made arrangements for Patricia to enter Miss Greystone's school Monday morning. She's not to lose her grade by the transfer. In fact they've agreed to guarantee that she will pass as usual in the spring. She is to have dear little Gwendolyn Champney as a seatmate, and be in the same grade with Thornton Bellingham. They are giving our child every advantage possible, and I'm quite delighted!" she finished with complacence. "She'll be free from that awful public school at last!"

Patricia sitting in front of her untouched dessert listened aghast, her eyes fixed on her mother's exalted countenance. Her mother was eating away at the thick meringue on her fat orange custard pie, and omitting to watch the expressions on the faces of her husband and child.

Patricia could usually be counted on to behave quietly like a lady, and not intrude into the general conversation unless asked a question, but on this occasion she was too deeply stirred to remember her manners, and suddenly her wide lovely blue eyes brimmed with great tears, a look of desperate panic went over her beautiful little face, and she broke forth in an awful and most unwonted rebellion.

"Oh! I don't want to leave my lovely public school!" she burst out in a scream of fear. "And I *won't* go to that silly old Greystone School. I won't! I won't! I *won't!* I *never* won't! They're all sissies and dummies that go to that school! Oh, daddy, I can't go to an old stuck-up school like that and have all my own school laughing at me and saying I couldn't keep up with my class!"

She finished the end of her sentence by jumping down from her seat and hiding her face in her father's neck where she stood and wailed her heart out.

Her father's arm went comfortingly, firmly around her, and his voice came soothingly into her ear.

"There, there, there! Daddy's little girl! Of course you shan't go to that silly old stuck-up school. Of course you're going to stay in your nice fine healthy public school. Don't you worry. That's one thing your daddy will see to, that you stay in the public school where he got his education. Nobody is going to cheat you out of that!"

"And I don't wanna sit with that old Gwendolyn, *ever!*" she went on. "She makes faces at me, and calls me 'old publicker.' I *hate* her! She copies her zaminations off other girls' papers too. Betty Brower told me."

"Of course you don't want to sit with her," thundered her thoroughly aroused father. "Her father's a crook, and her mother's a fool—!"

"George!" said his wife angrily. "Just please to remember that you are talking about one of my very closest friends!"

"Well, I'm sorry for you if you can call that painted piece of emptiness a friend!" sneered George Prentiss, "but I'm hoping my daughter will come up in the public school with a little more discernment than you got in that precious private institution where I understood you couldn't even graduate, my dear! I certainly don't intend to run any risks with Pat."

"I certainly wish you would call Patricia by her name! Not by that dreadful boyish nickname, *Pat!* I despise it!" said Patricia's mother furiously. "You just encourage uncouthness by calling her that. And she's coming up with no manners at all in that awful school you insist she shall attend. Her language is simply impossible, calling respectable children dummies and sissies! It is unspeakable! I'm afraid to have her speak before my friends lest she'll say something utterly common."

"If the friends you've been speaking of tonight are the ones you mean, I don't think they'd know the difference!" said her husband. "That Champney woman grew up in the back country and to my special knowledge went to a little red schoolhouse three miles away from her ramshackle home. I know that for a fact, for one of the men in our office went to the same school. And as for the Bellingham dame, I doubt if she ever had very many intellectual advantages, if one can judge by the expressions she uses."

"George! You are unspeakable! Can't you realize that

a young child ought not to hear her father talk that way?"

"Well, how about her mother? She isn't a babe in arms, and she's old enough to realize that the children you are urging upon her as playmates are second grade."

"Now what do you mean by that, Mr. Prentiss? Who, I ask you, is second grade? Patricia knows better than that. She knows they are superior children. Who, I ask you, are the children who attend Madame's select dancing class?"

"Dancing class!" snorted the father. "Oh, if you are counting the children whose brains are in their heels and toes, perhaps you might carry your point, but from all I've heard Pat say I don't think she admires them very much."

"Now, Mr. Prentiss, you're utterly mistaken," said his wife severely. "Patricia, why don't you speak up and tell the truth! You do love the dear little girls and boys who go to dancing class with you, don't you, darling?"

"No!" sobbed the child. "Only Betty Brower, and she's moving away!"

"Well, I certainly am thankful for that! Little low-lived thing! George, you don't in the least realize what low-lived plebeian tastes Patricia is acquiring. But darling—" addressing the weeping Patricia again, "you do like that dear little Thornton Bellingham, you know you do, don't you, darling?"

"No!" said Patricia, "he's a *sissy* and a bully!"

"Oh, *my dear!* You mustn't talk like that. Remember the pretty box of candy he brought you the other day! And his mamma says it was entirely his own little idea. He asked if he might buy it for you!"

"He ate every piece of peppermint out of it, and all the candied cherries!" sobbed Patricia remembering a new grievance. "He's nothing but a little *pig!*"

The mother turned a cold disapproving expression toward her husband.

"George, I hope you perceive what an unprofitable conversation you have started!" she said in a haughty tone, that promised a fuller explanation later in the evening.

"Unprofitable?" said her husband. "To whom? You? Yes, I can see that. But you're mistaken about who started it. It was you, I think, that introduced the subject of schools by stating that you had been making arrangements for Pat to go to the Delicious woman's school, after I told you in very plain language that never should a child of mine darken her doors! I just want to make a single statement and then I'm done with the subject. I still mean what I said about that, and Pat is going to continue to attend the public school! It was good enough for her father and it is going to stay good enough for his child till she graduates. After that if she wants to take up with some of your tommyrot-hifalutin-schools, she can go her own gait, but she'll have to earn the money for it herself."

So Patricia grew up in the public school, much to her mother's shame, who never ceased to lament and mourn about it, and to blame her child loudly for every fault she could find, laying them all to her training among common people.

Patricia herself adored her school, secretly feeling elated that her lines had fallen in such pleasant places. She loved the great school yard where every child was wild and free, and the rich and the poor partook alike of the joys of all the games. Her mother would have fainted in horror if she had known that her adored infant went hand in hand with two "mill" children of foreign parentage, through the thrills of crack-the-whip and here-we-go-round-the-barberry-bush! Though once when

Mrs. Prentiss was passing the school precincts at recess hour and caught a glimpse of the rough-and-tumble games, she advised her daughter to remain inside the schoolhouse during recess, and wait for her exercise until after school.

But Patricia grew up with most democratic ideas concerning other children, and sweetly, humbly made herself of no reputation. When the days of dancing school arrived and Patricia's mother reveled in the cunning dance frocks she bought her, Patricia discovered to her disappointment that not everybody in her beloved class at school had dance frocks and went to Madame Marchand's dancing school. She began to plan in her loving heart how she could extend the privileges of refinement to the others not so well favored. Once she was discovered by an eagle-eyed teacher down in the corner of the school yard teaching Jennie McGlynn how to lift the tips of her faded calico skirts and touch her toes lightly to make a courtesy, and she certainly would have seen to it that Jennie and her kind were supplied with pretty organdie frocks and bright sashes from her own ample store if she had had her way.

But she early learned that her mother disapproved of these less fortunate children, and she was not to bring them home or encourage any intimacies whatever with them, and daily the lines of her social world were more and more definitely defined before her rebellious eyes.

At this juncture desirables from other private schools were introduced into the scheme of things, at parties and social affairs connected with the dancing school, until Patricia had a fairly wide circle of acquaintances for one so young.

Sometimes she talked them over with her silent father, days when her mother was off playing bridge and her father got home early to read the evening paper. And now and again he would listen and snort when he heard some name of which he did not approve.

"Gwendolyn Champney?" he exclaimed one day, looking up from his paper. "Wherever did you get to know her? She may be all right herself, though I don't see what chance she stands, for her father's a crook and her mother's a fool! It isn't her fault of course but I'd just as soon my daughter didn't make a special friend of the daughter of a crook!"

Patricia would listen, and study her father thoughtfully and consider her world. She adored her father, and as she grew in wisdom, she began to realize that daddy's ways and mother's ways were far apart; for the most part she felt that daddy's ways were better. But even at that stage of the game she was far too wise to let her mother know how she felt.

Very often on Sunday morning Patricia went with her father to church, to the little old-fashioned plain church where a plain worshipful people gathered. The minister was a young man with a kindly smile and a way of making holy things exceedingly plain and easy to be understood. So Patricia, listening, and watching her father from time to time, grew up with a sort of God consciousness, and thought her small thoughts as in the sunlight of His knowledge.

After a time she also became a member of the Sunday School of that same little "behind-the times" church, and so long as the hour of its meeting remained in the early morning she enjoyed its privileges, for her mother rose so late that she did not discover how her child was occupying the morning hours. But when some hapless superintendent finally changed the hour to afternoon, the child found it difficult to attend.

Not that she had learned much, beyond the emphasis of God-consciousness, for her teachers had not all been either wise or well taught, but it answered very well for a sacred background as she stepped on into her checkered life, with her quiet reserved father on the one hand and her aggressively worldly mother on the other hand. She often longed for something, but she didn't quite know what it might be.

For the first few years boys didn't enter into the scheme of things at all for the little girl. They were all "children," but dancing school and her mother's constant questioning gradually enlightened her.

"And were the boys nice to you, darling?" her mother would question her when she came home from dancing school. "Did the really nicest ones ask you to dance with them?"

"Who are the nicest ones, mother?" Patricia would ask solemnly.

"Oh, you dear little silly!" her mother would say. "Surely you know who are the nicest ones. Little gentlemen. Like Thorny Bellingham. He is one of the very nicest, you know. His mother is my very best friend, and they live in the nicest house in town."

"I don't think he is nice at all!" Patricia remarked thoughtfully. "He pinches the girls when the teacher isn't looking, and he trips all the girls that dance with him. I'm sure I hope he doesn't ask me. I don't like him. He makes ugly faces at Mary Todd and I saw him bite her finger one day. He just set his teeth down hard on it and made the blood come, and Mary cried!"

"Who is Mary Todd?" said Patricia's mother. "Isn't she quite a common child? I think her mother is a professional dancer or something. I don't see why they allow her in the class at all. I shall have to speak to Madame about it."

"Well, I don't like Thorny, anyway!" said Patricia firmly.

"Oh, but my dear, you mustn't say that. His mother is your mother's best friend, and he's only a child, you know."

"Well, I'm only a child, too, but I don't go around biting people," she said. "I don't think he is nice at all! I won't dance with him either."

"Oh, my dear! That's what comes of your going to that common public school!" bemoaned the mother. "It's just what I thought would happen! I really shall have to speak to your father about it. He must be brought to see his duty and send you to a proper school."

With a gasp of alarm Patricia shut her lips and resolved in her child-heart never to say anything more against Thorny Bellingham and the days went on with Patricia still in the public school.

3

PATRICIA had seen John Worth for the first time when she was just a little girl in the third grade at school.

He had been a tall slim boy, taller than any of the boys in her grade. He came into the school room and was given a temporary seat just across the aisle and one form ahead of her own. There was a window opposite his seat and his clear profile was sharp against the morning light. She could not help but notice his expression. He had a nice dependable face, for just a boy, with well-cut features and strong firm lips. He seemed different from the other boys in the room, perhaps a year older and somehow very true and straightforward. Perhaps that was what made his eyes seem to have pleasant lights behind them like the glow of lamps. Once he turned his gaze in her direction and she caught a friendly look in his face, and the lamps seemed to blaze out with quick radiance. There was cheerful interest in his glance.

He was only there about two hours, writing, taking an examination. Then the teacher called his name. He was sent for from the principal's office. Patricia watched him as he walked across the room to the door. He walked with a quick firm tread. He was wearing brown corduroys and a flannel shirt. He had dark brown hair well cut and a little curly. Patricia knew as she looked at him that he wasn't a boy to be afraid of. He wouldn't play tricks on you, nor try to trip you. Not with those lamps behind his eyes.

He didn't come back again after he went to the principal's office. Days afterward she heard someone say he was in the fourth grade, and that was upstairs. She scarcely ever saw him.

But she did not forget his face. The other boys she knew were just boys in her mind, careless, thoughtless, childish boys. But this boy had looked as if he had a spirit behind his face, a spirit that thought and weighed things like a man, only he didn't seem old, nor what they called sissyfied. He had a merry twinkle in his eyes, and though there was a gentleness about him, she had once seen him in the schoolyard thrashing a big bully who had been tormenting a smaller, younger boy.

The next year she was upstairs herself. Not in his classes of course, for he was a year ahead of her. But sometimes during study period they sat in the same room, separated by the length of the room. Whenever she happened to notice him he was hard at work study-ing, not just sitting there gazing about him and fooling the way so many of the boys did. It made her want to study harder herself to see how hard he was working.

Sometimes John Worth's class would recite while Patricia's class was sitting in the back of the room studying, for the school was crowded that year, waiting for the new building which was in process of erection.

Patricia would always raise her eyes from her book whenever he recited. She liked his clear accent, the touch of Scotch on his tongue that always claimed attention at once. He had what the little girl afterward learned to call a "scholarly" tone. And he made what he said interesting no matter what the subject. He defined his words and gave his answers in such simple terms that it was clear to them all, even though the study was one that they had not as yet taken up. So Patricia made a point of listening to every word John Worth said, and once after she had been watching him so, he gave a quick puzzled look toward her as he sat down, as if, like words that had been spoken, he had felt her gaze upon him.

It was only the minutest instant that their eyes met, and no one else noticed. But she suddenly saw those lamps that were behind John Worth's eyes lighted, bringing that illumination to his face. Briefly, his lips trembled into a fleeting smile and her own lips smiled shyly in acknowledgment. Then the boy bent to pick up a paper that had fallen to the floor, and instantly he was back in regular form, his gaze turned toward the teacher. But somehow Patricia felt that she knew John Worth a little from that time, although he had never spoken to her, nor she to him, and he did not look at her again. They were just children.

One morning in the springtime Patricia came into the kitchen in search of her mother whose voice she could hear. She wanted to ask something about an errand her mother wanted done. But Mrs. Prentiss was quite occupied talking to a boy with a basket of beautiful wild strawberries on his arm. She was picking over the top berries and inspecting them.

"They're not very large," she said in a cold critical voice. The little girl hated to have her mother talk in that offish way to people she considered her inferiors. Patricia gave a quick glance toward the boy just as he lifted his gaze to his customer's face.

"Wild strawberries are not usually very large," he said earnestly, "but they make up in flavor what they lack in size." He said it quietly, quite respectfully. And Patricia recognized him at once. It was John Worth! And with quick sympathy and a desire to cover her mother's coldness, she hurried forward, looking at the boy with a shy smile.

"Oh, hello!" she said in a friendly tone.

The boy looked up, and then the lamps in his eyes blazed forth with their sudden beautiful lights.

"Hello!" said the boy brightly, a kind of surprise in his tone, and gave her a friendly smile.

Mrs. Prentiss looked up in astonishment.

"Patricia, what are you doing here?" she said severely. "I thought I sent you on an errand."

The little girl looked up with quick apprehension, scenting the disapproval in her mother's voice.

"Yes, but I wanted to ask you about it," she answered quickly. "Oh, mother, aren't those perfectly lovely strawberries!" and her beautiful eyes and smiling face turned toward the boy and his basket again.

"Taste them," offered John Worth, holding out his basket pleasantly.

Eagerly Patricia reached and took a beautiful berry from the top of the heap.

"No!" screamed her mother.—"Don't taste those berries, Patricia! They haven't been washed yet!"

But the berry was already inside the little girl's mouth and her pretty red lips had closed over the sweet morsel.

"Patricia! You are a naughty girl!" stormed her mother angrily. "Didn't you hear me tell you not to taste them? You can't tell who picked them, and they say pickers always have horribly dirty hands. Now perhaps you've caught some terribly low-down disease! Go to the door and spit that berry out, quick!"

The little girl with a grieved look toward her mother went over toward the door, her heart filled with shame.

But the boy spoke quietly, almost as if he were an older person.

"They are quite clean," he said. "I picked them myself this morning, and I washed my hands very carefully before I went out." There was a sound of protection for her in the boy's voice, and Patricia swallowed the berry instead of spitting it out, though her mother was too annoyed to notice that.

"Be still!" she said to the young huckster. "It is not your place to answer back! Patricia, go up to your room and stay there till I come!" And then to the boy again:

"I don't think I care for any berries this morning. I prefer to do my buying from hucksters who are not impertinent."

The boy's face flushed, and the lamps in his eyes winked, almost went out, and then blazed up again. The boy straightened up to his full height and lifted his head with dignity, young though he was.

"I'm sorry," he said. "I did not mean to be impertinent. I wanted you to know that the berries were all right, but I will not trouble you by coming again."

"Wait!" said Mrs. Prentiss sharply. "I didn't say you were not to come again. On the contrary I think I would like some of those berries every day while they last. I remember that they make unusually fine jam, wild strawberries. Perhaps you may leave those today, too. I think I could use them after all. But remember, I won't stand for any answering back!"

Patricia, going slowly up the stairs with tears running down her cheeks, heard it all for the kitchen door was not closed tightly. It made her feel ashamed. She wanted to rush back and tell her mother that she was talking to one of the finest boys in the public school, but she knew that would only add fuel to the flame of anger already started, so she went sadly up to her room.

A few minutes later her mother came, having delayed to discuss honey, when he could bring it, and the possibility of getting fresh peas and seckel pears in their season. Though if she had noticed the set of the boy's shoulders as he left the kitchen door, she might have had her doubts as to whether he would ever return again.

"Well," she said as she breezed into her little daughter's room, "you certainly are doing credit to your public school training! Coming out into the kitchen and addressing a little hoodlum from the back country with that elegant expression 'Hello!' I certainly am ashamed of you, and I shall have to speak to your father about this! Haven't you learned yet that you mustn't speak to strange boys? Had you ever seen him before that you dared to address him so intimately right before your mother? A young scapegrace with bare feet? I ask you, had you ever seen him before?"

"Oh, yes," said Patricia. "I see him in school, though he's not in my grade. I only see him once in a great while. But he's not from the back country, mother, he's considered one of the best scholars in his grade."

"Well, I'm sorry for his grade then. That speaks well for your school that they allow a barefoot boy to come to school!"

"Oh, he is not barefoot when he comes to school," protested the child. "He wears nice shoes like any of the boys."

"And so that's a specimen of the public school children, is it!" went on Mrs. Prentiss, ignoring her daughter's explanation. "Well, I certainly shall make your father understand how you are mixing with common people, and saying 'Hello' to them as if you were a child of the street."

Patricia's lip trembled.

"But mother, Gloria says 'Hello' all the time. All the

girls do. Even the girls in dancing school, I mean. It's what they say now. It's considered what they call smart and up-to-date!"

"Be still, Patricia! Don't you take to answering back. I suppose you learned that in your precious school, too, where your huckster-playmate learned it. Upon my word, we are coming to a pretty pass, hobnobbing with farm children!"

"Well, but I don't!" said Patricia earnestly. "I never spoke a word to him before. I just see him in study hour, across the room, and of course he's seen me, and heard my name when I was reciting. I thought it wouldn't be polite not to speak to him in my own house."

"Polite!" sniffed the lady furiously. "As if you had to be polite to a little hoodlum like that. Now, Patricia, I want it thoroughly understood that you are not to do that again. If he comes here with honey or fruit, just understand he is a menial like any of the delivery people from the stores, and you have nothing whatever to do with him. If I find you in conversation with him again I shall have to refuse to buy of him any more. Do you understand?"

Patricia's head drooped.

"Yes, mother," she said meekly, but she stood for a long moment looking out of the window thinking, realizing that this was something she could not understand. She shrank from appearing unfriendly if she should happen to meet John Worth about the house unexpectedly. But she mustn't ever be around when he was there, or she would lose him a chance to sell his wares, and she realized that it was probably important to him to sell them, or he would not be going about trying to dispose of them. How complicated life was growing. So many things she must not do that she couldn't understand, because they seemed to her things that were really right to do. And they all seemed to center around her darling school, and the dear little church where she and her father liked to go. Why was it so? Why couldn't mother and father be alike in their ways of thinking? She sighed deeply, and her mother, passing her door again, heard and looked annoyedly toward her.

"For pity's sake, don't stand there mooning about nothing! Get your hat and go on that errand at once! It's almost an hour since I told you about it. And wash your face! You've got tear stains all around your eyes. So ridiculous, weeping because I refused to let you get intimate with a child who is far beneath you. I'm afraid you have low tastes. That's what it does to be continually in the company of common people! I declare you get more and more difficult! If this keeps on we may have to move to another suburb. Perhaps then we could select a suitable school and there would be some hope of your growing up with a few decent manners."

Patricia caught her breath and went swiftly to her wardrobe to get her hat and depart on the errand. But her heart was sore as she walked along the street, with the sunlight flecking through the young maple leaves from the arching trees above. She felt somehow as if she had been the cause of bringing unpleasantness to the nicest boy in school, and it made her very unhappy. The worst of it was that she couldn't in any way make up for it. There wasn't a way of explaining it or apologizing to John Worth without being disloyal to her mother. And Patricia had a very strong feeling of loyalty to her family.

The next winter Patricia was ten. One day when the creek was frozen and the skating wonderful, Patricia had permission to go skating with a group of girls who went to the same dancing school. She was never allowed to go to the creek with her own schoolfellows. There had been a grand battle before she even learned to skate, until her father took matters in hand and taught her himself. Then grudgingly the mother consented, provided the companions might be of her choosing.

That day they had gone down to the creek together, Gloria Van Emmons, Katherine MacShane, Sylvia Vane and Martella Rankin.

"I do hate to have you little girls going down to that horrible creek alone. Seems to me there might be some nice boys to go down with you," said Patricia's mother as they started gaily off.

The other girls laughed.

"Oh, we don't want any boys!" they said with a knowing wink, and a grin at each other. "Anyway there'll be plenty of people around the creek. The skating is swell!"

"Well, I wish you girls would stay on this upper end of the creek. Don't go down where the whole village is. I hate to have you knocking around with all the loafers of the village!"

Gloria Van Emmons giggled and called rudely from the gate:

"Okay, Mrs. Prentiss," and darted on ahead.

Patricia wondered what her mother would think of such informal address. Most of the girls at the public school would have been more courteous, she thought. But she went on her way, happy to be off skating, though she wasn't especially fond of these girls.

They were half way down the hill to the landing where they intended to sit down and put on their skates, when a large snowball struck Patricia's shoulder and another knocked her hat off, while a third smashed into the back of her head and made her so dizzy she lost her balance and toppled over in the snow.

"There they are!" cried Gloria with a giggle. "That's

Thorny Bellingham and Terence Gilder with his gang. I knew all the time they were coming, but I didn't want to tell your mother, because I didn't know who Thorny would bring with him. And it's lucky I didn't. Your mother wouldn't have stood for Terence. His father keeps the tavern down at the cross roads, but he's a swell guy, he always brings candy, and he can skate all around anybody else I know. Come on, Pat, be a sport and get up. You don't want them to think you're a softy!"

Patricia sat up and looked back angrily. She hated Thorny! She was almost sure he had been the one who had thrown the last snowball. She felt dazed with the sting of it, and large icy fragments of it were sliding down inside her collar and slipping down her back.

The boys came on with a rush. They were approaching from the direction of the Prentiss house. Patricia suspected that her mother must have had something to do with their coming, or at least with their knowing just where to find the girls.

She struggled dazedly to her feet and gave her head a little shake, but she did not smile, nor respond to the noisy greetings of the new arrivals. Instead she stood at one side to let them pass, indignant scorn upon her, her young eyes flashing.

"Hello, Pitty-Patty, what's eating you?" asked Thorny leering up into her face. "Want yer face washed, Pitty-Patty?" He stooped and gathered a great handful of snow and rushed down the hill at her as if to carry out his threat.

Patricia in a flash saw what he was about to do and dodged his onslaught so skillfully that Thorny was thrown off his balance and went down the hill, rolling over and over from the unexpected counter and cutting a long jagged gash on the back of his knuckles on a stone as he fell. It was little more than a deep scratch, but it brought the blood and it was painful. Thorny with a howl clasped his injured hand and knew not that he was weeping great splashing furious tears. When the sting of the pain was more bearable, he lifted his voice in words; choice epithets, the worst he had been able to learn so far in his young life, and applied his maimed hand to his mouth. Sucking furiously, he unfolded himself from the earth, and made as if he would come toward her again.

Patricia meanwhile stood her ground, her frightened young chin held steadily, haughtily, though it was all she could do to keep her lips from trembling. She had seen enough of Thorny to know that he would stop at nothing to wreak his vengeance upon her.

After a surprised, swift, admiring glance at her the little audience took up the fight, this time aimed at Thorny.

"Cry-baby, cry! Cry-baby, *cry!*" they hailed him, pointing the finger of scorn, albeit ready to run themselves should Thorny recover his poise too soon.

Thorny turned his bleared anger toward them at once.

"Aw, shut up, you fool kids!" he roared. "I'm not crying. That's just—just—perspiration, that's all!" he said, mopping off his cheeks with his dirty hands. Then, discovering the red streak, "It's just sweat and *blood!*" he shouted. "See *there!*" he hunted out a grubby handkerchief and mopped it over his hands and face and held it forth all bloody. "See what that little old cat did ta me? She's a little devil, she is!"

Patricia was surveying him with contempt, and suddenly Thorny caught her glance and writhed in his naughty young heart. He'd get even with her!

He struggled to his feet and dashed down the hill a few steps to Gloria.

"Come on, Glory. I'll go with *you!* I ain't going ta have anything more to do with that little cat. She's a regular panther-cat, she is. She's a—a—a—!" he searched his mind for the right adjective to couple with cat.

"*Hell-cat!*" he shouted, as Patricia turned and walked with stately tread back up the hill.

The girls were greatly impressed. They giggled.

"Oh, Thorny!" Gloria applauded. It sounded very grown-up and sophisticated to her. "Say it again, Thorny! That'll make her awful mad!" Gloria was ordinarily proud to call herself a friend of Patricia's, but she couldn't resist the temptation to get in with handsome twelve-year-old Thorny who had never looked at her before.

"Say it again, Thorny!" she urged eagerly, grasping his none-too-clean hand fervently.

And Thorny said it again, screamed it, several times, standing half way down the hill looking back at his former dancing partner as she walked across to the path that led up to her father's house, paying no attention whatever to the epithets that were being flung freely up the hill after her now, amid an admiring audience of her own companions.

Suddenly it grew very still, ominously still down the hill there, but Patricia did not pause, nor waver, nor turn to look. She walked steadily on, swinging her skate shoes by their strap as nonchalantly as if nothing had happened.

Thorny could not have done what happened next if there had not been a worn beaten path from the top of the hill to the bottom, made by many young feet who had gone that way for the last few days. Quite silently and cautiously he stole back up that hill after Patricia. Before she was at all aware he was upon her. The little company of admirers who had heard him announce his intention stood below in breathless silence waiting to see if he could accomplish it.

Deftly, as he reached her side, Thorny leaned forward and snatched the strap of Patricia's skates from her, almost whirling her from her footing. Then he turned and dashed down the hill.

Patricia did not cry out. Instead she stood there for an instant and gazed after Thorny appalled. Those were her new skates, a recent gift from her father, the skates she had so longed for, and this was to have been the first time she had worn them since trying them out in company with her father. And now, they were in Thorny's power, and there was no telling whether she would ever see them again! Or, if she did, whether they would not be broken, dulled, spoiled in some way. He was perfectly capable of it, she was sure, and he would stop at nothing to have vengeance on her.

For just that second's time she surveyed the young hoodlum and then her firm childish lips set themselves, and her eyes flashed fire! That should not happen! Thorny should *not* spoil her lovely skates!

A quick glance about her showed her a handy weapon. A long branch of an oak tree, broken down and flung by the side of the path. There were dried brown leaves still clinging to its twigs, and particles of ice.

With a quick flashing movement like a bird she swooped and caught it up, then plunged down the hill after Thorny. Her motion as she went was still like a bird in its flight. Her feet scarcely seemed to touch the ground, so swiftly they went. She seemed to have no fear of losing her footing; it was as if she could not fall because she was skimming over the path so fast. It was just like flying.

Suddenly the little audience below looked up and saw her coming. They all stopped and cried out.

"Look out, Thorny! She's coming!" breathed the girls in exquisite fright, backing away from her path.

"Beat it, Thorny! Pat's *coming!* She's got a big stick! Beat it! *Beat* it!"

Thorny dropped the strap he was holding and obeyed. He ran so fast down the hill that when he reached the bank he rolled right out on the ice in his haste, and had much ado to pick himself up. His adherents scattered widely away from oncoming vengeance, for they all felt they would be more or less involved this time. And it frightened them a little. All of them. For Patricia was a girl whom they respected and admired, even if she did go to the public school. Perhaps that made it still more fearsome to alienate her, because it was rumored that people who went to the public school had all kinds of courage. Besides, Patricia's father had a strong arm when he was roused. Some of them had experienced it.

By the time Patricia had reached her skates, stooped to recover them, and lifted her head again to look about, across and up and down the creek, there wasn't a hide nor hair of one of them. They had utterly vanished.

She looked steadily for two or three minutes to make sure they were not hiding in the bushes near by, and then she found a comfortable seat on the bank and sat down to change her shoes. After all, she was out with her skates, why not enjoy them? It was not often she got permission.

It gave her satisfaction to reflect that her mother had schemed to get Thorny along with them, and then it had all been his fault that she had been ill-treated. If her mother could just have seen what happened, maybe, *maybe* she would get over the idea that Thorny was an ideal companion. Perhaps she would tell her mother all about it when she got home. Or would she? Wouldn't her mother just think her child was prejudiced because Thorny didn't go to the public school? Well, perhaps she *wouldn't* tell her mother, but she would surely tell her father. He would understand why she didn't like Thorny.

When Patricia had her shoes fastened, she stepped cautiously out upon the ice, keeping her eyes out for a possible ambush of enemies. She skated in a wide circle, nonchalantly, trying the ice, her circle widening until she started up the creek. Should she follow them, or take an opposite direction?

Well, she wasn't sure which way they had gone, they had scattered so quickly. They might have hid in the thick undergrowth and slipped along the bank. They might be anywhere, of course. But she didn't want them to think she was afraid of them. She was, terribly afraid of Thorny. He was ruthless. But he mustn't know it or she would be in his power. If he knew she dreaded him he would torment her all the more.

She circled around to the place from which she had started and picked up her oak branch. She would take that with her, just in case.

So with the branch held before her like a hockey stick she started skating, her body bending gracefully, making strong quick strokes with her skates, and exulting in the ring of steel on ice.

There were many marks on the ice of skaters who had been here in the middle of the creek, yet Patricia came upon nobody, and she could not be sure whether her companions of a few minutes before were ahead of her or not, or whether they had climbed the hill out of sight and gone down another way. But she held her head high and skated on.

Off in the distance she could hear far voices, laughter, calling, but as she went on up the stream they grew more and more dim, until at last she could hear nothing.

She knew that today the village people were having

some sort of informal contest on the ice, old and young together, and that all her own school companions would be down the other way. But that was the way her mother had forbidden, and Patricia usually tried to mind her mother.

Then suddenly she heard a voice:

4

"I wouldn't go up that way any farther," it called. "The ice is weak up there! It isn't safe"

"Oh!" said Patricia, curving about to look at the speaker. That was John Worth! She smiled shyly.

And then suddenly she heard an ominous crack.

"Come away from there!" cried the boy sharply. "No, not over there. Here, this way! Hand me the other end of that branch," he commanded.

Patricia could sense the thinness of the ice beneath her skates, and fear possessed her. But she was a courageous little soul and she trusted John Worth. With one hand outstretched she held out the branch till the boy could grasp it and pull her to safety. Then she lifted a suddenly white face and frightened eyes.

He grasped her mittened hand in his strong one.

"Let's go."

Patricia glided along by his side, her skates ringing with his, in perfect time.

Patricia had never skated this way before, in step with one her own size. Her father was so much taller that he had had to suit his strokes to hers when he was teaching her. And the girls who had been out with her had been so jerky and uncertain in their movements that she had preferred to go alone. But this was like poetry of motion. The boy was just a little taller than herself, and his strength seemed to guide her and bear her along. This was real team work. She was breathless with the delight of it, and her face was wreathed in smiles.

"Where were you going?" the boy asked at last when they were moving along steadily down the middle of the stream. He was looking down at her as if she was something rare and precious, something that it was his privilege to restore to its native environment.

"Why, I started out to skate. I was with some girls, and then some boys came along and were disagreeable. I don't know which way they went. I don't want to find them anyway. I didn't like the way they acted."

He smiled down upon her as if he might have been somebody very much older than herself.

"Well, if I were you I wouldn't go any farther up the creek today. Besides the ice being treacherous in some places, there are a lot of bums up that way. I don't think you ought to up there alone, anyway. I'd go with you if I could, but it's time I went home. My time's up and there's some work I'm supposed to do now."

Patricia smiled up at him again.

"Oh, that's all right," she said cheerfully. "I wouldn't want to bother you. I think I'll just go home now. I've had a lovely skate, and there's some homework I must do for school tomorrow."

"I think perhaps your friends went around the island and down by the village. I thought I saw a bunch of kids going along that way but I wasn't near enough to identify them. I'd like to help you find them if I could before I leave," said the boy with a troubled look.

"But I don't want to find them," said Patricia earnestly. "I only wanted to know where they were so I could keep away from them. That Thorny Bellingham stole my skates and threw them down the hill. I don't want to get anywhere near him again. And besides I think I ought to go home now."

John's face looked indignant, and he murmured stormily, "Say, some day I'll get that guy. I'd like to give him what he deserves!"

They glided over to the bank near the path that led up to her home, and John Worth knelt down on the ice before her and unlaced her skate shoes for her, then helped her on with her house shoes and smiling politely was about to skate off. But Patricia looked up at him shyly.

"Thank you for being so nice," she said childishly. "It's been a lot of fun."

"Oh, that's all right," said John Worth, embarrassed, "I liked it a lot, too."

Their eyes met warmly for an instant, and then the boy put on his woolen cap and swung away up the creek.

Patricia stood there for a minute or two watching him. Watching his straight young shoulders, his head held high, his graceful glide on the skates that seemed so much a part of him. What a nice boy he was! How kind he had been! Why couldn't Thorny Bellingham have been like that? She sighed, and picking up her skate shoes trudged on up the hill.

That was all. She didn't see John Worth again except passing in the hall at school for many months, but the memory of that time she skated with him for ten or fifteen minutes, shyly, almost silently, stayed with her always, and became one of the pleasant memories of her childhood.

When her lagging feet had reached her own home, her mother met her at the door with a relieved look.

"Oh, you've got home at last! Well, I'm glad! I've been so worried! Did dear little Thorny find you? He said he would look after you, but I was afraid he would miss you."

A look of swift anger passed over the little girl's face.

"He found us all right!" she said indignantly. "He threw hard snowballs down the hill and hit the back of my head so it *hurt!*"

"Oh, now, Patricia, don't be a baby!" said her mother impatiently. "You know perfectly well he didn't mean to hit you. He was only trying to have a little fun and surprise you."

Great tears suddenly welled into Patricia's eyes.

"He was *not* joking!" she cried out indignantly. "He *meant* to be horrid! He called me Pitty-Patty, and he knows I hate that. And then he tried to wash my face in the snow. I don't mind when some of them do it, but he's just mean. He never cares how he hurts."

"What had you been doing to him, Patricia? Answer me that! I'm quite sure you had done something first or Thorny Bellingham would never have been rude to you. Remember his mother is my best friend and she is bringing him up to be a real little gentleman. Tell me what you had done to him! I'm sure you did something to him first. I can't understand why you have taken a prejudice against a respectable boy!"

"He is not respectable!" said Patricia stamping her foot, the angry tears coursing hotly down her cheeks. "He is just as mean and sneaking as he can be, and if I hadn't dodged him as he rolled down hill," Patricia could giggle in triumph now at the memory, "he would have had me down and there's no telling what he would have done."

"You made Thorny Bellingham roll down the hill? Patricia, you are a naughty girl! To be rude to the boy mother sent after you to take care of you! That is terrible!"

"I'm glad I did!" said Patricia. "He was awful! If you'd seen him you would have known what he is! And then afterward when I started away he ran behind me and snatched my skates away from me, and threw them down the hill into the snow!" Patricia's eyes were snapping angrily now.

"It all sounds to me very babyish for a great girl of ten years old," said her mother coldly. "And where are they all now, those children you went to the ice with? Where is Thorny?"

"They ran away and left me!" said Patricia with a voice almost as cold as her mother's. And she turned haughtily and stumped sorrowfully up the stairs.

"Stop! Patricia! Stop right where you are!" commanded her mother harshly.

Patricia stopped and looked sadly around.

"You come right downstairs and go out and find those children and bring them back into the house with you. I've got some nice hot cocoa and little cakes and sandwiches ready for you all, and I certainly am going to find out all about this performance. I'm sick of having you act this way about those nice well-brought-up children! Go out there and find them. Go down the street after them if necessary! Only bring them back here! Tell them I have a nice little tea-party all ready for them. And if I find that you are at fault, young lady, you certainly are going to apologize to Thorny Bellingham!"

But Patricia stood firmly on the bottom step of the stairs.

"I can't go mother. They are gone! They ran off and left me. I followed up the creek after I got my skates on but they weren't anywhere. And anyway, I can't ever apologize to that bad Thorny! He was awful, and I hate him! I never want to see him again!"

The storm finally ended in Patricia being sent to bed weeping, and later Patricia's mother called up Thorny's mother to say that she was so sorry that the children had had some kind of a misunderstanding, and she did hope that dear little Thorny hadn't been hurt. Mrs. Bellingham took it all very sweetly, saying that it was quite all right. Poor Thorny had a few scratches of course, but they would soon heal up and she did hope her friend would be able soon to influence her husband to allow their dear little Patricia to go to a respectable school where she wouldn't get such bad examples of sportsmanship and behaviour as she was getting in that terrible public school!

Patricia heard a little of the telephone talk, and her sad little heart grew more and more belligerent toward Thorny Bellingham. Why was it that her mother couldn't understand what a bad boy Thorny was? Softly she cried herself to sleep.

Late that evening after his wife had retired Patricia's father came in and sat by her bed and held her hand. She woke to find him sitting there, and to feel the comforting warmth of his hand on hers.

They didn't talk much, for fear of waking Patricia's mother, but Patricia's father asked her all about what had happened, and why she hadn't been allowed down at dinner, and she told him brokenly in whispers the whole story, ending with a terse sentence or two of John Worth's part in the tragedy. A well worded question brought out the whole thing.

Patricia's father patted her and comforted her, and whispered:

"Never mind, father's little Pat! It will all come out right in the end!"

Then he wet a towel and washed her face, dabbed it dry, kissed her, and went downstairs to bring back a lot of nice little sandwiches and a glass of milk. Patricia went to sleep again all comforted and happy.

After that Patricia didn't attempt any more to tell her mother anything that Thorny had done. It wasn't any use. Her mother would only blame it all on the public school. But Patricia often thought about the wonderful time she had had skating with John Worth, and wished that it could happen again sometime.

THE first year John Worth was in high school he began to be identified with the school teams. He was looked upon as one of the best pitchers they had, and all his athletic work was good. Now and then Patricia would hear the high school girls talking about how he had struck out this or that formidable player. When at the end of his second year they made him captain of the basket ball team enthusiasm ran high.

By that time Patricia was in high school herself. Many a time she longed with all her heart to be able to stay to the baseball games or come out to the evening games in the gymnasium as the other girls did and watch all that went on. But Patricia's mother drew the line at evening affairs connected with the public school. They were not for her child. The evening was the time for social affairs, parties, with well-selected children of her own class. So Patricia had no part nor lot in the school spirit that rejoiced over winnings and mourned over losses, and cheered lustily for their school wherever they went.

But secretly she was glad that John Worth had taken his place among the best, and she wished she might be a part of it all. Once or twice it is true she lingered after school for a few minutes, especially when she was sure her mother was engaged with her club meetings or her bridge parties, and hovering near the edge of the ball grounds watched a play or two. She was always glad to sight John Worth among the team. But such stolen moments brought her no touch with the players, and little of the thrill that came to the other girls, huddled joyously on the grand stand, cheering for their favorites, wearing their colors, and waving pennants with vigor.

She was growing taller now, and distinctly lovely in appearance, although of that she was hardly yet aware. She was not a vain child, merely eager to have her part with all the others in the interests of her beloved school. She was at all times more interested in the school than in anything else. The constant parties to which her mother subjected her meant little to her, because she was not fond of the company she met there. Little by little, she was trying to withdraw herself from them.

Her first open rebellion was occasioned by a party at Thornton Bellingham's on his fifteenth birthday, and Patricia did not want to go. It was a long time since the occurrence on the hill above the creek, and the incident was only a childish affair of course, but Patricia had never forgotten the look on that boy's face as he came at her. It seemed indelibly stamped upon him, a look of deviltry, almost of hate, and she had avoided him as far as possible ever since.

Of course he was no longer in the little boy's prep school where he used to be when they had their snowfight on the hillside. He had been away three years now, during school sessions of course, and they had not been thrown together, but now he was home for his birthday and his mother was making a grand affair out of it.

"I shall not go!" announced Patricia decidedly when she received the invitation. "I don't like him and I don't want to have anything to do with his old parties!"

"Patricia!" exclaimed her mother horrified. "Not go! Of course you'll go! Thorny Bellingham's mother is my dearest friend. You know that perfectly well. It would be insulting to my friend for you to do that. I can't see how you can be so disagreeable as to say things like that."

"I'm not disagreeable, mother," said Patricia. "I don't see how that's insulting anybody either. I'll write a very nice polite note and thank her for the invitation, and tell her that I have another engagement. There's nothing insulting about that. I have another engagement, anyway, that I wouldn't miss for anything. It's a meeting of our Sunday School class at the church, and I promised to help get ready for a rally that's going to be held pretty soon."

"Your Sunday School class!" sneered the mother. "What's that got to do with things? Nothing from that little old-fashioned Sunday School has any claim on you. Give them some money and tell them you can't come, you have something more important on hand!"

"But I haven't, mother! I *want* to go to that meeting. I *like* to help them. I don't like Thorny, and I don't want to go to his party."

"Patricia, I'm ashamed of you!" said her mother. "To think you would carry your childish dislikes all through the years. That's ridiculous! You're both almost grown up now and you'll find Thorny very much changed. I saw his picture the other day when I went over to call on his mother, and he's stunning looking. He's grown handsome, although I always thought he was one of the prettiest little boys I ever saw. He didn't really need to get any better looking."

"I don't like pretty boys!" said Patricia gravely. "I like

boys that have some character in their faces. Thorny always looks as though he liked to eat better than anything else!"

"Patricia, that's coarse of you! Do you realize that you are no longer a child? You cannot afford to let your childish prejudices hold through the years that way. Thorny is your natural friend in every way. His family and yours are close friends. He is brought up under the same ideas, he is your equal in manners and education— that is, you should be his equal if your father hadn't had such absurd ideas about making you go to that bourgeois school among the canaille. But of course we will have that remedied when you graduate from high school. Your father promised that you might do what you liked after that, and I intend to see that you have all the educational opportunities possible to make you Thorny's equal. And then, my dear, there is another point which perhaps you are too young to appreciate. Thorny's family are wealthy, as wealthy as your father, and you will both inherit good fortunes. There is nothing like money to make people akin. You will be invited to the same places, have the same traditions, the same tastes, and will in all probability be the closest of friends, so I advise you not to do anything which will make your future friendship embarrassing. You will go to his party of course. You will write your acceptance at once, or I shall see that your father does something definite immediately about removing you from that ridiculous school."

"Mother! You couldn't do that now, when I've only two years more before I graduate!" Patricia's voice was all of a tremble.

"I *couldn't?* Oh, you think I couldn't?" Mrs. Prentiss' voice was cool and dominating, and very assured.

"Watch me, and see what I can do, if there is any more demurring about that party."

So Patricia sighing deeply, wrote her acceptance to the invitation, in cold little stilted phrases, and assented apathetically to all her mother's plans for the dress to be worn on that occasion.

She was very beautiful, and always exquisitely attired, although she herself would have liked plainer, more youthful frocks than the ornate and sophisticated ones of her mother's choosing. Her mother of course laid all her reluctance toward the party and the sophisticated garments, to her being a product of the public school, though she might have been greatly surprised if she could have known how many of her daughter's fellow students in that school wore just such trailing robes of glory and sophistication at their parties.

When the hateful day arrived, Patricia went to the party. The committee at the church had to get along without Patricia's wistful presence, while she was swept away to an undesired evening in the world. A mere meeting in a little old-fashioned chapel should never bind Mrs. Prentiss' child to an engagement that would hinder a brilliant affair. Patricia was attired in a long full white tulle dress that touched the floor all around. It had an abbreviated top strapped on with bands of tiny pink rosebuds sewed to narrow black velvet ribbons. The girdle was an assorted collection of black velvet loops and long stemmed tiny rosebuds. The same rosebuds garlanded her dark hair, fastened with a small knot of the velvet. It was a charming costume, and Thorny's mother in conference with Patricia's mother, beforehand, had seen to it that a charming bouquet of sweetheart rosebuds set about with a frill of quaint lace paper, had gone to Patricia that afternoon, with Thorny's card. Not that Thorny himself had anything to do with the sending. He was merely told it had been done. Thorny hadn't seen his erstwhile enemy now for sometime, and he only made an ugly face when his mother told him about the flowers, for he was not at that time any more enamored of Patricia, than she was of him.

Patricia herself, on receipt of the flowers, was most contemptuous of them, especially when her mother told her that she would have to wear them, or carry them.

"Well, I certainly will *not!*" said Patricia firmly. "What would I want to let him think I liked his flowers for? I don't like him and he doesn't like me, and why should we have to act as if we did?"

"Patricia! Have you no politeness, no courtesy at all? When a young man sends you flowers to wear to his party have you no sense of gratitude? It certainly shows that the young man has no such dislike as you are attributing to Thorny, since he sends you such charming flowers."

"Young man!" sneered Patricia. "He's nothing but the same old spoiled Thorny he always was. And as for the flowers, his mother probably made him send them! He probably didn't want to send them any more than I want to wear them!"

"Patricia, you are simply unspeakable! The sooner you get out of that terrible school, and that impossible church and Sunday School, the better. As it is I'm afraid it's already too late!"

Patricia gave her mother a despairing look.

"All right. I'll carry them. But I won't wear them. They aren't the kind to wear anyway. They are supposed to be carried."

Patricia went off to her party with an independent little toss of her head, but a sorrowful frightened feeling in her heart. She would have to watch her step tonight. If anything went on that didn't altogether please Mrs.

Bellingham it surely would be reported to her mother, and then there would be another battle royal with dad, and how long would it take to tire dad out and make him give up and send her to a private school after all? If she couldn't graduate with her beloved class, if she had to have her own commencement come off without her, while she took her place among the dummies in Miss Greystone's Select School for Girls, she would *die!* She would simply pass out with shame and humiliation!

So all that evening she trod the hours with care and discretion. Not once did she try to lay down that awful little dub of a sissy bouquet and lose it or hide it. All the evening she carried it elaborately, posing it so that it would show how well it matched the garlands on her dress. She even curtsied low with a deft sweep of her long skirt, before Thorny as he stood near his mother, and no one else in immediate proximity, and said with pleasant husky tones:

"Thank you so much, Mr. Bellingham, for your darling flowers. They are just too quaint and lovely for words."

And Thorny lifted his handsome head and fetched forth his cocksure smile and said in a new prep school voice he had acquired since he had been away:

"Oh, hello, Pitty-Pat. Glad you like the weeds!"

Then his eyes came to dwell on her fresh young loveliness, and in a kind of surprise he added, "They're not half so charming as the girl who carries them!" and prepared to devote himself to his old enemy for the evening.

But Patricia had no such plan. All the technique of formality she had learned at dancing school she drew upon now, and Thorny was surprised into setting up an active campaign for her company. If he had had his way he would have danced every number with her. But

Patricia had been clever. She had thought this thing out. Not entirely by herself either. Her father had had a hand in it.

Patricia had come home from school by way of her father's office that first afternoon after the invitation had come, and coaxed her father to walk home with her. Then on the way she had made her plaint to him. Did she have to go to that old party? Did she *have* to dance with that awful Thorny?

Her father talked it over with her gravely. "I don't like Thorny any better than you do, little Pat," he said, looking down into her earnest eyes, "and I don't like the dancing part either. If I'd had my way you would never have gone to dancing school, you know. But—you know how your mother is—and I had crossed her about your school. I didn't see that I could make a fuss about the dancing. But maybe I should have."

"No, daddy," said the little girl earnestly, "it doesn't really matter. I don't mind the class so very much. But I do hate dancing with that terrible Thorny. Why, daddy, he used to step on my feet every time we had to dance together. He just did it on *purpose!*"

"Well, let us hope he's too grown up for that now. He was only a little devil then. Perhaps he's learned some politeness. But of course, little Pat, I suppose you would have to dance once with him if he asks you. I guess that's what's expected, for the host to dance at least once with every lady present. I really don't know much about it myself. I never liked dancing and I used to stay away from such things the few times I ever got invited. But you know, Patty, *we* weren't rich people then, and *I* didn't get invited much to such things."

"Well, I guess I'm like you, daddy," said Patricia, comfortably nestling her hand in her father's. "I don't mind the dancing if I could do it by myself, but I just can't bear that Thorny. And some of the rest of the boys aren't so pleasant, either. Besides, I'll have that long dress on, and I'll maybe fall right down on the floor."

"Oh, no, you won't. You'll sail in there and act like a little princess. You'll remember that you're father's little girl, and are going to do just as well as you can, and then when you've got through this one party maybe there'll be a way out somehow. Maybe there won't be any more dancing parties after Thorny goes back to school. Anyway, maybe he isn't so bad as he used to be. He's growing up now, you know."

"Maybe!" said Patricia doubtfully. "I don't expect it, though."

"Then there's another thing, little Pat. Perhaps you can get your little program card pretty well filled up so Thorny won't have a chance to ask you but once."

"Yes, I know," said Patricia thoughtfully. "There's Eddie Bridgeman. I suppose he'll be there. His mother's in the club. He's not so very interesting. He's what the girls call a dub. But sometimes I feel sorry for him. He's kind of awkward and doesn't seem to know what to do or say. I'll make him put his name on my program."

"Do you think he will like that, Pat? Wouldn't he ask you of his own accord?"

"No," said Patricia decidedly, "he would be scared. He always stands around till the teacher tells him who to ask. I'll just smile at him as soon as I see him and say, 'Eddie, don't you want to put your name down on my program?' I think he'll be glad. I don't think he likes to come to the class, but his mother makes him. He gets awfully red when he has to ask a girl."

"Well," said the father with a worried look, "I don't like your having to ask people to dance with you. It isn't a lady's place. But after all you're only a little girl, and I guess it won't matter if it's to protect you against

Thorny. If you say so I'll have a talk and try to get mother to let you decline the invitation. Of course she'll be awfully upset, she's so fond of Mrs. Bellingham."

"No," said Patricia, "you can't. It's too late. Mother made me write my acceptance right away this morning, and I guess by this time she's mailed it. And anyway, daddy, I guess it would make too much discussion. I do hate to have you and mother argue. She always wants me to go to a private school, and daddy, you won't ever, *ever* let me have to do that, will you? I do love my school!"

Reassured about her school Patricia swallowed down the necessity for going to the party and began from the first to plan to evade Thorny as much as possible.

So Patricia at her first big party was sweet and smiling. She danced that first dance with Thorny, because he asked her right before his mother, and Patricia knew that whatever was done in the presence of his mother would be reported tomorrow morning to her mother, so with fear and trembling she stepped forth into what she dreaded.

Thorny was not the awkward little hooligan that he used to be in the early days of dancing school. He did not step on her feet, and he did not fall all over the room as he used to delight to do. He had acquired a mature technique and a grace that made him what was called a good dancer. But he grappled her possessively from the start, and held her too close. How she hated this contact with him. How she despised the way he looked down into her eyes and pressed her to him! She was suddenly appalled at the disgust that filled her. Somehow, somehow she had got to get through this gesture and acquit herself graciously, and yet how could she stand it? She loathed the way he held her hand as if it belonged to him, the closeness of his daring handsome face, the hotness of his breath in her face. She had never experienced anything like this in her life, and she wanted to strike him. Yet she knew she must do whatever she did like a lady. Thorny's mother was watching her, and would report to her mother.

"God, won't you please help me now," she prayed as she closed her eyes briefly, and drew back a little and away. But Thorny only pressed her body closer to him and swept her on.

Patricia held herself aloof as much as possible, and endured it with as sweet an expression as she could, and when at last the number was over and he made as if to keep possession of her for the next dance, she laughed and tossed her head gaily.

"But we can't," she said happily, "it's promised. My program is all filled up. I just saved this first one for you in case you wanted it."

"Let's see!" said Thorny rudely, snatching at her dainty little program card. "I don't see how you got them all filled up when you didn't have the cards till you got here."

"They're not all written in yet," said Patricia amusedly, "but I've promised them."

"Well, that doesn't make any difference," said Thorny loftily, "this is my party and I intend to dance every dance with you. I can do what I like at my own party of course. I'll just tell any fellow that comes that he can go chase himself away, I'm going to dance with you. Except Harold Charlesworth of course. He's my roommate at school and he's visiting me. If he wants to dance with you he can have one dance."

"Really?" said Patricia archly. "But only if _I_ like. Besides, I haven't met this roommate. And besides I've promised practically all my other numbers."

"Here he comes now," announced Thorny as a tall bored looking fellow came toward them. "Hey! Chas!

Meet my girl! Isn't she a humdinger? I'll let you dance once with her, but that's all. She belongs to me. We were practically brought up together, you know."

Patricia looked young Charlesworth over coolly, and then as Eddie Bridgeman shyly approached in response to her signal, she lifted her dainty chin and taking Eddie's correctly stiff young arm she bowed laughing and swept away. There was one thing about Eddie, he would do as he was told, and he would not dare to hold her in a close embrace. Patricia was doing the princess act now, remembering what her father had said, and being wise and naive and charming all at the same time.

Thorny and his chum stood looking after her with puzzled glowers upon their faces, until Thorny's mother sent for him and reminded him that he had duties as host to other girls as well as Patricia, and he must make haste to fulfill them.

By means of smiles and wiles, and finally twisting her ankle just the least little bit, Patricia contrived not to dance with Thorny again that evening, and only to dance with his guest Harold once. But by so doing she only managed to make Thorny become all the more anxious to absorb her exclusively. When at last the evening was over and she could get home and think things over, she didn't know whether she was pleased or not at the way it had all turned out. For though she hadn't had to dance with him but once during the evening, still the once bitter enemy seemed to have turned into an over-eager friend and admirer. It was all a terrible bore. Patricia acknowledged to herself that Thorny was even better looking than he had been as a small boy, that his eyes were handsome, and his teeth sparkled like jewels, and his smile was most flattering when he had looked at her, still she liked him no better than she had when he was a small boy. He was still selfish, she could see that. She still had the feeling that with all his admiration he was only being nice to her now because he thought she was pretty, and Patricia was not a vain little girl. Her head was not turned by his attention. She was glad he was going back to school in a day or two. She did hope that something nice would develop during the interval that would send him off to Europe, or Alaska, or California for the vacation time, anywhere so that he would not have to stay around home and be flung in her face daily by conniving mothers. Patricia did not want to grow up too soon, and be in training for the proper selection of a husband. All the hints about nice boys, and culture, and making friends in her own class, and the importance of money, made her dread to grow up, made her turn from her mother's world with loathing.

Sometimes she would talk it over with her father, on the rare occasions when he was at home and her mother was away for some social or club gathering. And her father would listen, and watch her, and sigh, and say, "Oh, little Pat, I'm with you. You have the right idea. I wish your mother didn't set her heart on things so much!"

Such cheer was enough for the time being to brighten her heart. If daddy agreed with her then surely when she was older they could work something out together.

So she went happily on through her school days.

PATRICIA seldom saw John Worth any more except afar. His last year in high school was her third year and he was seldom in evidence. He didn't seem to be in athletics any more. Once or twice she had lingered to watch the start of a game, and he was never there. Then one day she heard one of the girls say it was too bad John Worth couldn't play that spring, that it was likely they wouldn't win many games without him, he had been so much better than anybody else on the team. And when she asked why he didn't play they looked at her astonished. Didn't she know that John Worth was working now? Oh, yes, he had been working ever since the late fall. He worked on Miller's farm, was a hired hand, or something like that. Even in public school it seemed that there was such a thing as caste.

Oh, yes, some of the other boys worked after hours, but their work was confined mostly to delivering papers, or driving the delivery truck for one of the grocery stores during Christmas holidays when the rush hours were on. But that was mere fun of course. And that was at holidays. That did not class a high school boy as a menial.

John Worth had to milk the cows, and groom the horse. He had to get up before daylight to do these things. He had to feed the chickens and clean the chicken house and the stables. He had to plow and plant. He had to weed and hoe and help harvest wheat and corn. Just a common hired-man! And still in high school! The girls said it was a shame, and the boys put on superior airs, even some of the public school boys.

Yet John Worth seemed just the same. He was always neat and clean and well groomed, even though he still wore corduroys and a flannel shirt. His hair was always handsome and carefully brushed, and his hands, though tanned and strong, were as well cared for as if he did nothing but play the piano all day. He still walked with an upright bearing, a spring in his step, and that light in his eyes that set his face apart from the others. It was almost as if that light behind his eyes were a symbol of something in his soul that was guiding him.

One girl said she had heard that John Worth's father was very sick, and couldn't go in town any more to business or whatever he did, and that was why John was working, to help out. He was only working part time of course, because he was going to finish high school, and he never seemed to miss a day, but he went to the farm the minute the afternoon session was over. She said she had heard that he was going to work at Miller's farm full time as soon as he was graduated.

Patricia thought about that several times. It seemed so hard that a nice boy like that had to go to work before he was done high school, and didn't have a minute to call his own, couldn't play ball any more, or even skate perhaps. It seemed too bad. And Thorny, spoiled conceited Thorny, had all his time to himself. She had heard through Gloria Van Emmons that Thorny had flunked his spring examinations and was going to have to have a tutor and take them over again in the fall. If that was so he would probably hang around home all summer and bother her a lot. How she wished it were Thorny that had to work on Miller's farm, and John Worth that lived in the town. But then of course she wouldn't see anything of him anyway. He was an older boy and very studious, and her mother wouldn't consider that he was in her class.

So the days went on. Patricia's studies grew harder, and she had to work with all her might. She mustn't flunk her examinations. She would never be allowed to go on an extra year. Her mother would rave at the school system and keep saying "I told you so!" to daddy. For the honor of her father and her school she must do well and graduate.

The spring was coming on apace and commencement was in the air. John Worth was to graduate. He had been selected to give the valedictory address, and it was generally conceded that he was the best scholar in the school. Too bad he couldn't make use of the school scholarship which would have given him a free year at college.

"I should think they'd get along somehow and let him go to college," said Doris Price. "A boy as bright as John simply ought to have college."

Patricia as she listened wondered just how "somehow" was, and wished there was a way to provide that how.

But John Worth went and came and held his head as high and smiled as cheerfully as before, although there was a serious look in his eyes now that had not been there before. But Patricia noticed when she met him one day that the lamps behind his eyes were still lighted when he smiled, just as they had been ever since she had known him.

Patricia's class was coming into notice now, holding meetings and electing officers. Patricia herself was an officer, treasurer of the class. She kept her accounts with scrupulous care, and took her duties seriously. Her mother laughed at the idea that she had to stay after school for a class meeting. She said it was absurd, that a public school had no class, and why should it take on airs like a college. But Patricia's father took her part, and showed her mother that she had been honored by the office and must do her part of course.

"Nonsense!" said Mrs. Prentiss. "Treasurer! What honor is that? You are as blind as your child. Don't you see that it's very plain why they made her treasurer? They know her father is rich and will make up all deficits. They know what they are about."

But Patricia was allowed to attend her class meetings in peace.

"After all it can't last much longer! Only one year, thank goodness!" Mrs. Prentiss said to her friend Mrs. Bellingham.

"Well, I must say you've been very patient," said the Bellingham woman. "I wouldn't have stood for what you have, allowing a girl as beautiful as Patty to be commonized by attending that impossible school. I certainly wouldn't have stood for it a day. There are things about that school that will cling to that child all her life. It gives her entirely too democratic an outlook. Why, they tell me that one of the graduates this year is nothing more nor less than a hired man on Miller's farm, and he, my dear, is the one they have selected to give the valedictory address. Imagine it! Giving the highest honor of the school to a mere hired hand on a farm!"

"Oh, my dear! How dreadful! But you see that's something I hadn't heard. Thank you for telling me. I don't suppose Mr. Prentiss knows that. That may make some difference. I shall tell him as soon as he comes home tonight."

But to her dismay when she told Mr. Prentiss he gave her a mildly surprised look.

"Why, my dear! What's the matter with that? I clearly remember hearing your father tell me that he himself hired out to a farmer in his youth in order to get money enough to finish out a year of college."

"Mr. Prentiss, you are utterly mistaken!" said the good lady in an irate tone. "My father never was a hired man! It is strange how you are willing to try and drag your family down."

"There is nothing demeaning in honest work. It is often uplifting to get back to the soil and down to primitive conditions. In fact I can think of nothing that would be better for that little prig of a paragon you are always talking about, that young Thorny Bellingham, than to send him to a farm for a couple of years. Let him learn to plow and plant and sow and reap. Let him milk the cows and tend to sheep and chickens. Perhaps it might put some sense into even that pretty little sissy boy."

"I think you are too insulting, Mr. Prentiss, talking that way about the son of my dearest friend. I think it is contemptible the way you always try to get the better of me."

Mrs. Prentiss got out her small elaborate handkerchief and began to wipe her eyes neatly, dabbing at them, so that her make-up might not be impaired. Her husband looked at her with cold despairing eyes, at her florid complexion enhanced by brick red rouge and blue black shadows under her eyes; at her sleek head that was too childish in its outline for a woman of her years; at the brisk ruddy wave of her hair, hair that he knew was already graying softly before she had it so deftly treated, and he thought back to the days when he thought he fell in love with her. When her hair was a ruddy gold and her gray eyes gay, not hard and cold as now. When her father had been a poor man, and the neat print dresses she wore had seemed beautiful to him.

He had been glad to be able to give her beautiful expensive garments such as she was wearing now, but as he looked back those days seemed so much happier, Amelia so utterly more desirable! That time was not so many years removed from the time her father had worked on a farm. Oh, Amelia had climbed too far on his money and rising position, and now she was insisting that his little girl should climb too, into an artificial life that money could buy, but true worth could not always attain.

He sat there regarding her sternly, sadly, not answering at first. Just letting her talk herself out. And as he watched her he sighed.

Patricia had come into the house while they were talking, and hearing her mother's loud excited voice, tiptoed softly into an adjoining room to listen a moment and see what it was all about. These were the days when Patricia was always quaking lest her mother would somehow manage to get her out of her school before she graduated.

Patricia stood across that adjoining room in the hall doorway, and looked through the partly open door from the library into the sitting room where they were. She could see her father plainly from where she stood. He was sitting in his old leather chair that he liked so much; he wouldn't let it be put out of the sitting room even though it was shabby. His head was resting against its back and his eyes were straight ahead studying Amelia, sadly, hopelessly, dejectedly. The late afternoon's sun came in at the window beside him and shone across his face, showing deep furrows in brow and cheek and heavy lines about his eyes that always looked like cheery crinkles when he smiled at his little girl. It suddenly struck Patricia that he was getting old, and was tired of it all, and sorrowful. It came to her that he must be as unhappy about the way life had turned out as her mother was. Her mother wanted a showy luxurious life, an imposing home, and a pliant daughter and husband who would contribute their all to her purposes and have nothing that they wanted for themselves. In fact she resented it that their desires were not as hers. And on the other hand her father wanted a sweet quiet home where peace and harmony reigned. He wanted tender words and loving deeds, and he admired real things. And money alone could not buy such things as he desired.

Patricia in that moment, with that image of her father stamped upon her heart, slipped away, feeling that she had suddenly grown up, and had comprehended things that were too great for her to understand or remedy. Sadly she stole upstairs and sat in her own room for a long time trying to puzzle it out. Why did homes get that way? Why did fathers have to feel sad about what mothers did and said? Life was certainly a most perplexing thing.

But the rising sound of her mother's angry voice continued belowstairs, and the little girl, suddenly bowed with grief over that hopeless look in her father's eyes, flung herself down on her knees beside her bed and burst into soft tears.

"Oh God!" she whispered into her pillow. "Did you mean things to be this way? Aren't there any fathers and mothers who are happy and like the same things?"

And downstairs the battle went on.

George Prentiss did not attempt to give his usual angry retorts to the things Amelia said. He just sat and looked sadly at her, and for once Amelia said all that was in her heart at the time, without interruption. But at last she became aware of the silence, like a stone wall that seemed reared between her conversation and her husband. She looked up from her delicately attended weeping to see why her words seemed fairly to rattle back into her face, and she caught that look in George's eyes, that patient, hopeless look, and she became all at once incoherent. At last she managed to stutter out:

"What—what are you sitting there looking at me like that for? Wh—what do you *mean?*"

He gave a deep hopeless sigh.

"I was just thinking how different you were from the girl I married," he said, getting up and going over to look out the window.

Amelia was flabbergasted.

"Different?" she screamed. "Different! And I'd like to know what you think *you* are? You were real spruce and good-looking, and you seemed to want me to have what I wanted. You don't think I'd have married you if I'd thought you'd look the way you do now? Going around in baggy trousers, and insisting on not getting your hair cut often enough, and sticking to an old shabby leather chair around with my nice furniture, making me ashamed so that I don't dare bring my friends into this room at all. You don't think I'd have married you if I'd known you were going to be like that, do you?"

"Perhaps not," said George Prentiss sadly, not turning his head to look at her. "Perhaps it would have been better for you if you hadn't. But it's rather late to talk about that now, Amelia. I'll take the old chair upstairs to that little back room and sit there, if you would like that better."

There was great weariness in his voice, and humility, and Amelia was suddenly silent, almost as if she were ashamed. Then George Prentiss turned about and looked her sternly in the eye, as if there were still one point on which he was firm.

"But there's one thing, Amelia, I will have. No matter what you think or want in the matter. Pat has *got* to have this last year in high school as she wants it! I won't have her interfered with! She shall not have disappointments in connection with it. She has only this one more year to go there, and it's not going to be spoiled by any more fool nonsense. There'll be doings in the school, gatherings, and plays and parties and the like. Picnics sometimes too, and games, and the child has got to be free to attend every one of them if she wants to. She isn't a girl who will overstep her privileges, and her wants are very simple, and usually very safe. I don't want her school life interfered with from now till she graduates, and I don't want any other fool nonsense got up like parties in your circle to interfere with what she wants to do there. The same goes with regard to her church obligations. It isn't much to ask, is it? And after all she's part my child, and certainly I'm paying for what my family has. I feel that I have a right to make such stipulations, and I'm making them. And I don't want to have to battle this over again, either. I want it understood that this goes! And what's more, I mean every word I've said!" Then he turned and stalked out of the room, and did not look back to see what Amelia thought of it. There was something decisive in his attitude that kept her silent as she watched him walk away.

Amelia looked after him with a hard determined glitter in her eyes, and her lips set in a stubborn way that did not mean George's victory would be an easy one. But she knew that her former tactics would no longer work as they had been working of late, at least not on those subjects upon which he had declared himself. She

must by guile work her will some other way. So it was
that when the matter of the spring picnic of the junior
class in high school came up for discussion she knew her
time had come to spring some new method on her
family.

7

THE spring picnic of the junior class was an annual
affair. It marked the appearance of the class, as a class,
into the official program of the new year. It was the first
recognition of the school that a new class of seniors was
about to step upon the carpet. That a fresh group of
young people was about to enter upon that serious
business of being seniors and undergo the final polishing
of their educations preparatory to stepping out into the
world to begin life. It was in their minds a most important affair, and had been talked about with great enthusiasm ever since the Christmas holidays.

Patricia had taken little or no part in all these discus-
sions, knowing not whether she would be permitted to
attend. So far she had not been counted in on their
festivities, because almost always she had had to say that
she couldn't come out evenings, or her mother had
something else planned for her. These admissions were
always made with lowered head and averted eyes, humility in all her bearing. They had been the one great
trial of her school days.

So when her father told her the next morning after his

talk with Amelia that she was to feel free to attend everything that went on, if she wished, a great radiance came into her face, and she trod as it were on air on her way to school. And when she announced to her most intimate mates that she was coming to their meeting, and going to the picnic, and the play, and all the doings of the class, there was great rejoicing, for Patricia was a favorite, and not one of them considered her a dummy or a flat tire or any of the other derogatives current at the time. They put the blame where blame should be, on a mistaken family whose word was law.

So Patricia with great joy began to tread the normal path of a high school junior and to make her pleasant plans for the different events. And not the least among them all was the class picnic.

It was an all-day affair in the woods, with games and fully planned amusements. Patricia entered into it as she had scarcely ever entered into anything since her very little girlhood, and her father rejoiced to see her bright eyes and sparkling face. He felt condemned that he had not sooner asserted his will, and gained her freedom from the constant home surveillance of class prejudice.

When her mother first heard of the picnic she cast a withering glance at her daughter and ejaculated in a cross between a snort and a hiss, "A picnic!" As if the affair in question might have been something in the nature of a scorpion, or other deadly beast.

Patricia was engaged in telling her father some of the delightful plans, with eager eyes and a voice full of throbs, and did not notice her mother. The father looked up with a quick warning glance that stopped Patricia in the midst of her sentence, but unfortunately it also reminded Amelia that she must invent new methods immediately. So she set her lips thinly and went out of the room, where she would not be expected to enter into the talk at all. But she did not go so far that she would be out of hearing.

It was thus Amelia first learned that her child was prominent in the plans, and discovered that a most unattractive young boy from a side street in the village was associated with her in preparing certain lists, and posters, and two girls whose fathers were anything but prominent citizens were on the same committee with her. When these facts first came to light in Patricia's eager talk with her father the mother almost forgot her new resolves, and started into the other room to make a wild protest. Then something she heard her husband say warned her that she would get nowhere with him that way, and sent her back to make other subtle plans. And the next morning, after Patricia was gone to school, she hurried over to her friend Mrs. Bellingham, to have a friendly visit with her, and incidentally discover what day Thorny's school closed, and when he would be coming home.

But Patricia went happily on her way greatly relieved that her mother was not interfering.

Later that day Mrs. Prentiss indited a letter to Thorny.

Dear Thornton:

Your mother tells me that you are coming home somewhere near the fifteenth of May, and I'm wondering if you would mind helping me out with something that is worrying me.

Patricia's school is having a picnic on that Saturday, and they seem to think it is quite important that she attend. We haven't encouraged her attendance at such affairs of course, but she thinks it is a duty this time.

You will understand of course that I shrink from sending her into the woods without some proper person to look after her, and there would be naturally no one in her class whom I would feel like calling upon. So I am wondering if it would be possible for you to go with her and keep an eye on her. There are so many possibilities in the wilds of a woods. I am sure you will understand how I feel, and how grateful I shall be if an old friend of Patricia's can spare the time to attend her.

But whether you find it possible to do this or not, may I ask you to keep the whole thing to yourself, for Patricia is very proud, and would, I am afraid, be hurt that I felt someone must attend her, so I am trusting to your courtesy not to tell her.

Thanking you in advance for your trouble, and hoping this will not be a burden to you.

Very sincerely,
Amelia H. Prentiss.

In a few days there came a response from Thorny.

Dear Mrs. Prentiss:
O.K.! I get you! I'll be on hand if possible.
Yours, Thorny.

Mrs. Prentiss, with a little shudder over the form of expression, hastily destroyed Thorny's note, and with a relieved look on her face went forward with her plans. She surprised her daughter greatly by seeming to enter into all her preparations for the picnic, suggesting chicken salad and angel cake for the lunch baskets, and offering to prepare a basket herself. Patricia was so happy her face was fairly radiant. It seemed to her that heaven had smiled upon her at last and her mother was doing all the beautiful things she had always wished she would do. She was a forgiving little soul and utterly ready to forget all the unpleasantness of the past. Mother hadn't understood before perhaps, she thought. Now she understood. It was going to be a wonderful year, this her last year in high school. Daddy had made mother understand at last.

"We might have the gardener carry down a freezer of ice cream for you," suggested her mother. "I suppose they really expect you to do something pretty nice for them, since you are probably in better circumstances than anyone else in the class."

"Oh, no, mother, thank you!" said the girl, shrinking from the thought. "I wouldn't like to do anything like that. They would think I thought I was better than they are. They would think I was proud. No, everybody has a part in this. We take up a collection for things like ice cream. I couldn't do a thing like that!"

"Nonsense! That's ridiculous!" said her mother sharply. "I think you really ought to do something like that. I'm sure your father would be entirely willing to get the ice cream or anything you wanted to give them."

"But no, mother, you do not understand. They would not like it. I am just one of them."

No, she didn't understand. It was ridiculous for common people to have sensitive feelings like that and she didn't believe children of common parents felt that way at all. However, Mrs. Prentiss did realize that if she was to carry her point it must be done subtly, quietly, so she put aside her suggestions and let her daughter have her way.

There was another clash of both tastes and wills, when it came to a matter of what Patricia should wear on the eventful day. Patricia had selected a plain little chintz dress with small blue flowers sprigged over it, corded with blue. Her mother, mindful of the young escort, who was to arrive "unexpectedly," wanted her to wear an elaborate pink dimity with lace ruffles and a flowered ribbon sash, or else a smocked white silk with pink ribbons, but Patricia utterly refused both even to the verge of tears.

"No, mother! It wouldn't be good taste. Not for the woods!" she protested. "All the girls will wear gingham or chintz. We couldn't have a good time in the woods dressed up in silk and lace ruffles. I want to be free to sit down on the grass or a log, and not have to look after my clothes."

"But dear, you could take a rug along to sit down on," pleaded her mother.

"I don't want to be hampered with a lot of baggage," said the girl stormily. "I've got to be like the others or I don't want to go."

"Well, I can't understand why you want to go anyway," said her mother with a sigh. "Of course you're not like the others, and I don't see why you want to imitate them. I should think you would like to show them what pretty things you have. Things they seldom have the opportunity to see, you know. It might be a real pleasure to them."

The child looked at her mother in astonishment.

"Why, mother, they all have pretty things, just as pretty as mine, but they don't wear them in the woods. I can't see why you think they are any different from us. They all have nice homes, and always look pretty wherever they go. I wish you'd come to school sometime and see them. I'm sure you would get a different idea of them. They are lovely girls and boys."

"No!" said her mother sharply. "I don't care to see them. I know where some of them live and that is enough. Little back streets and two story houses. No, I don't wish to go to that school at all. I don't want my friends to think that I am in sympathy with your going there. I suppose I may have to go when you graduate, *if* you graduate there, though I'm not even sure I'll be willing to do that, unless it is to show how glad I am that you are done with them all."

"Oh, mother!"

"Now don't 'Oh-mother' me! I'm sure it's enough that I'm willing for you to go to this terrible picnic, without your trying to force me into that obnoxious school. All right, wear a calico dress if you insist. I'm sure I hope none of my friends have to see you on the way. But you may as well have your own way for this once. Perhaps you'll learn reason after a while. I'm sure I hope so."

So the days went by and there was no more discussion about the dress, or the plans. The only thing that surprised Patricia was that her mother took such a deep interest in the lunch she was to carry. She even went to the city and bought a lovely new lunch basket. If Patricia had known who was expected to carry that basket she would have been in utter despair.

Patricia was just starting out the door when Thorny arrived. She gave a little gasp when she saw him.

"Oh," she said as he came smiling up the steps with his usual "Hello, Pitty-Pat!" "Oh, I'm sorry! But I have to go away today, Thorny."

"Yes, I know," said Thorny indulgently, "I heard you had a picnic and I got here just in time to carry your basket, didn't I?" He reached over and took firm possession of the new basket.

The girl gave a despairing look at it and hung on.

"Oh, no thank you!" she said. "I'm carrying this myself. It's not at all heavy. And of course I couldn't take you with me anyway. This is a class affair and positively no one else is invited."

"Oh, that won't bother me a little bit," said Thorny, holding on to the basket. "I'm great on crashing parties.

Got it down fine. They never question me at all. You see, they're always glad to get me, I'm so good-looking!" Thorny's air was inimitable. Three of the high school girls who had stopped for Patricia giggled admiringly, but Patricia herself looked stricken. Besides she hated his frank conceit. Even if it was a common joke with him that he was good-looking, it never seemed funny to her. She couldn't bear to have him accept it as if he knew it and presume upon it. And she couldn't have this one perfect day, the first really independent school frolic, spoiled by having Thorny along.

"But really, Thorny, we voted not to have anyone outside the class along. Not even any seniors! You can't go, Thorny! *Positively!*"

"My dear, never say can't to me!" said Thorny shaking an impressive finger in her face. "Can't is only a stimulus to my ego. I'm a crasher by nature, and I like nothing better than to crash in where I'm not wanted. But I'm not anticipating much trouble here. My native town. These hicks wouldn't dare say me nay. Come along, Pitty-Pat, and we'll paint the town red. That's all right, Mrs. Prentiss. I'll look out for your child. You don't need to worry!"

He waved a gay hand to Mrs. Prentiss who appeared suddenly at the door, smiling.

"Oh, is that you, Thorny? How nice. I wasn't sure you were home yet. Now I shall be relieved. I'm so glad you are going to the picnic. Now I shall not have to worry about Patricia. I always think there are so many dangers in the woods, things like snakes and tarantulas. It is so good to have a nice boy along!"

She cast a withering glance toward the three high school girls.

Patricia was almost in tears. Her day was spoiled! And what could she do? She walked with downcast eyes, ashamed before her school friends, hurrying out to the sidewalk where another group was gathered waiting for her to come. It was useless for her to try to get rid of Thorny while her mother was about. Oh, if only her father had not gone to the city that morning! He would have understood, and he would have done something to help her out of this dilemma! She tried to think rapidly what she could do. It wouldn't do to set the other boys on Thorny; that would only precipitate a big row, for the high school boys would delight to put Thorny in his place. Whatever she did must be done with as much courtesy as possible. But she waited until she was down the walk and out on the street before she attempted anything. Then, safely behind the sheltering hedge she greeted her schoolmates as gaily as she could in her tense state of mind, and turning to Thorny who was walking by her side she said pleasantly:

"Now, I'll take my basket, please, and thank you for bringing it down so far. Sorry we can't invite you to go with us, but this is strictly a class affair, you understand."

She reached a determined little hand toward her precious basket and there was a quick stillness in the group as they watched her, admiring her courage, for they all knew what Thorny was.

But Thorny quickly swung the basket around behind him and laughingly shook his head.

"Oh, no!" he said. "You don't get this basket away from me! I know there are too many good things inside of it for me ever to be willing to give it up. Sorry about your exclusiveness, but it can't be did this time. You'll have to take me along, because, my lady Pitty-Pat, I'm going anyway, and you'll find it a hard job to get rid of me, as the thistle said to the lady's dress! I'm quite sure there isn't a hick man present who would care to come to blows with me over it, is there?"

He looked around on the glowering youths who stood fully able to handle him, and taunted them with his handsome grin.

One of the taller boys, a halfback from the football squad, spoke out, looking at Patricia.

"Do you want us to handle him for you, Pat?" There was menace in his tone, and his glance went quickly, significantly around the group of his fellows.

She gave the boy a quick rewarding smile.

"Thank you, Bert, but I don't think that'll be necessary. The boys of our school are too courteous to do anything like that of course, and I'm quite sure Thorny will understand and not bother us."

"Guess again, pretty-Pat!" sang out Thorny. "If you mean you think I'm going to give up and go home you've got another guess coming. I'm sticking around."

Patricia gave him a look which ought to have made him see that he would get nowhere with her that way. Then she lifted her firm little chin a bit haughtily, looking very much as she had looked that day on the hillside when she stood alone against Thorny's attack. Then she walked quickly on ahead with Charles and Helen Ayres, a brother and sister in her class who were rather shy and undemonstrative. And as she swept past Thorny she said in a cool clear voice that could be heard by the whole group:

"Oh, all right. I can easily get along without that lunch basket, Thorny, if that's what you want."

The rest of the group burst into rollicking appreciative laughter, but Patricia with head held high walked straight on.

Thorny with a grin and a sneer sauntered along beside Della Bright, a girl who seldom had any notice at all, and who was tremendously flattered by Thorny's attention, even though she knew he was not popular among her classmates.

The little procession paused several blocks farther on to gather up a group who were waiting there for them, and then went on for another group before they turned across the meadow path and down the hill toward the woods.

All this time Thorny walked placidly with Della Bright, ignoring Patricia, laughing and talking as if he had always been a part of the group, telling stories of his feats in school athletics and studies, talking so loud that those ahead could not miss it if they tried. Now and then he would ostentatiously open the clasp of the pretty basket he carried, and poke an investigating finger inside, coming forth with a sandwich, or a piece of chicken or a carefully wrapped bit of cake, which he generously divided with the half frightened but giggling Della.

Patricia on ahead ignored him utterly. If Thorny was determined to try and annoy her she would not let him spoil her day. Let him have the lovely lunch. Everybody would understand and someone would share with her, she was sure. Or she could go without. She didn't feel as if she would ever want any food anyway, she was so annoyed and angry that Thorny had crashed in and spoiled her perfect day. Would it always be so? Would every promise of a perfect day be spoiled by someone?

And had her mother known that Thorny was coming? She put that thought resolutely from her. She could not bear to think her mother had deliberately planned to do that. Yet her mother was very determined to have her intimate with Thorny. Why?

Something cool and lovely met them as they entered the woods. It had always seemed to Patricia, when she thought about Heaven, that there surely must be a wood there, because here it was so quiet and sweet and peaceful, like the entrance to great delight. It was only a childish fancy, she supposed, and she had never told anybody about it. Her mother would never have understood. Her mother was practical, and liked fancy artificial places better. She had never approved of the woods for her child, there seemed too many dangers lurking there. It made Mrs. Prentiss shudder to think of worms and snakes and creeping things. It was too dark and cool for her taste, too. She felt it must be unhealthy. But her child loved it. Yet she had never had much of it. Her mother had generally managed to substitute a trip to the movies, or a picture gallery, or a store for any trip she tried herself to plan. So she could count only a very few times she had experienced that thrill of entering the cool quiet depths, of visioning a quick twirl of a stealthy squirrel darting to a higher branch and looking down with questioning beadlike eyes, of hearing the high far note of a wood robin, of discovering hepaticas and wood anemones and jack-in-the-pulpits lurking under tall ferns with a drift of maidenhair fern not far away. It was to Patricia the most wonderful place in the world, and now as she entered the green shadows, trod on the velvet moss, and penetrated farther to a floor of pine needles, she forgot about Thorny. Even Thorny couldn't spoil the long-anticipated day for her. There had always been a Thorny or his like in her life to spoil every lovely experience. She reflected that probably it was so with everyone's nice times.

So, basketless but happy, she entered her Eden and walked as if under an enchantment. And Thorny might career ahead and pose as carrying on a flirtation with any of the other girls he chose, or shout out execrations upon all woods in general and this one in particular when he happened to step into a hole and turn his ankle slightly, or he might take the center of the stage in the immediate foreground and tell in blatant boasting of his achievements at school. It could not dispel the beauty all about her, nor spoil Patricia's joy in the day. It wasn't pleasant, of course, to think that the rest of the class might be offended at her for bringing such an alien element into their festive day, but by this time most of them understood that it had been none of Patricia's planning. They laid it all at her mother's door. But neither did the girl enjoy that thought. She didn't like to have her mother despised by her mates. She wished her mother wouldn't do silly things and bring wrong elements together and misjudge nice pleasant plain people, but she didn't want others to blame her. She felt in her heart that if her mother had only had the privilege of attending a public school all these discrepancies in her character might have been rectified. It was her mother's misfortune that she had not had the privilege of such a school in her childhood.

So, offsetting the disadvantages of the day, Patricia felt that she had the full sympathy of her class. They liked her and admired her, and were taking her into their heart of hearts today as they had never quite done before. She felt their new loyalty about her like a pleasant garment, and it filled her with a sweet elation she had never known. There had always been that little element of doubt in her mind before. But today the fact that she had deliberately left the pampered "prep school kid" and walked off with the stupidest and most unattractive brother and sister in their whole class had done a great deal to convince them that she was one of themselves. She knew now that they were her friends, and she was greatly glad over it. So in the light of that knowledge she trod the sacred precincts of the wooded aisles and was glad.

Thorny was ahead there nibbling into that wonderful

basket, discovering the choice tidbits that her mother had evidently put in for her to feed to Thorny, gobbling down a whole glass of fruit cup that he had rooted out of a corner and smacking his lips over it. But what did she care? She had for the first time since she entered high school a sense that her class and she were one, and nothing else mattered.

8

A committee of their class had selected the place for them to gather for their games, and for eating their lunch, and arriving there they surveyed the vaulted arches of great forest trees above them with satisfaction, then stacked their baskets and wraps under a convenient tree and drifted away in groups. Some of the boys went to gather wood for a fire on which coffee was to be brewed and marshmallows toasted, others to make arrangements for games that were to be a part of the program later in the day, some to set up the target for archery, and to prepare a spot for quoits and other games. Everybody was on some committee. Patricia headed a small group to gather wild flowers and arrange them on the table, which another committee was to spread and set for lunch.

"I shall have nothing but a bag of oranges and a box of candy to contribute to the lunch table," said Patricia to her associates, with a bitter glance at the handsome Thorny grubbing again in her basket.

"Why don't you let the other fellows go after him and get it away?" suggested Helen Ayres excitedly. "They could, easily. He's eating it all up from you, Pat. I just saw him take out a whole handful of chicken salad. There won't be anything left fit to eat. Charles could go and tell the boys to organize and get him before he knew it. They could easily get it away."

"No!" said Patricia. "I wouldn't want it after he's mauled it all over. Let him have it. There'll be enough for everybody. I'm not very hungry myself any way. Let him have it. Let's forget it. What are those blue flowers over there? Aren't they hepaticas? And oh, see the spring beauties!"

"I know where there is some birch bark," contributed the somewhat diffident Charles. "I've got my knife. I could make a birchbark box and you girls could fill it with the flowers."

"Say, that would be great!" said Patricia with sparkling eyes. "And we'll lay some of those small lacy ferns around the bottom to look like green doilies. Come on, Helen. We'll have to work fast, for they'll begin to get hungry before twelve o'clock, I'm sure, and I want it to be the prettiest table ever!" cried Patricia, leading the way to the banks of flowers. Soon they were hard at work.

But Thorny, and the basket, and Della Bright had drifted away to the top of the hill and Patricia was glad for now she could the more easily forget them.

The table cloth was charmingly decorated with a lovely mass of wild flowers in a birchbark container in the center, all wreathed about with a beautiful pattern of small ferns. In between there were substantial piles of sandwiches of all kinds and sizes, chicken, lamb, ham, corned beef, cheese, lettuce, watercress. It seemed as if there was no end to the different kinds of sandwiches that had been provided. Patricia, looking them over, rejoiced that her elaborate basket would not be missed, even if Thorny ate it all up.

The three decorators surveyed their handiwork with satisfaction and then decided that it would be nice to have the dish of olives surrounded by a wreath of violets. So they hurried off to the place where they knew they were plentiful and began to pick, handling the great lovely blossoms delicately with pleasure in their luscious growth.

Suddenly, just behind them as they stooped was Thorny's voice.

"Hey, you two, Chick and Helen, aren't those your names? They want you back there! Something about the arrangements. Quick! They're in a hurry!"

Charles straightened up with a troubled look toward Patricia, his mild, homely, pleasant face full of worry. And Helen gave him a look of hesitation. Then suddenly Thorny, scowling ominously at the two, stamped his foot and waved his arms at them.

"Scram!" he said. "I want to talk to Pat." And they gave him a frightened look and scrammed.

As they hurried away Patricia suddenly sprang to her feet and took in the situation, then lifted her chin and looked haughtily at Thorny.

"What's the idea?" she said coldly.

"The idea is that I'm about fed up being treated like the dirt under your feet, Pat," said Thorny indignantly. "I'd have you to understand that I came to this old picnic to take care of you, and I think it's about time I had a little of your company. Come on over to that tree with the moss on it and let's sit down and catch up on our acquaintance. You certainly don't think I enjoy the company of the rest of this hick crowd, do you? Come on, let's eat our lunch now!"

"Oh," said Patricia in a cool little voice, "haven't you

eaten it all up yet? Don't let me hinder you. Just go over to the tree by yourself and eat it all. I assure you I don't want any of it. I'm going to eat with the class!" and she made as if to pass him and walk highheaded back to the lunching place. But Thorny put out a hard young hand and caught her.

"Not on your life you don't get away!" he said fiercely. "Pat, you're mine and you might as well give up at once and acknowledge it. We've been pals ever since we were little kids of course, but I'll say you've even improved. I haven't seen a girl since I've been away that can come up to you in looks and that's a fact. There! Will that please you? Say, those eyes are hot shot! And I'm aiming to take those lips and make them mine. Watch me!" And suddenly Thorny flung his arms about her unsuspecting young body and drew her close to him in a fierce bearlike embrace that nearly took her breath away. And then his hot lips found hers and poured passionate kisses upon them until she was almost strangled.

Bewildered and frightened beyond anything she had ever felt in her life, taken off her guard and limp with horror, she could do nothing at the first instant. Blindly she struggled, gasping, trying to scream but unable to get a sound across because he held her face so close to his and kissed her so fiercely that her breath came only in jerks.

He had her in such an embrace that her arms were pinioned to her sides.

"Stop! Stop!" she gasped. "We're—only kids! And—I *hate*—you!"

But now her strength and sense were coming back to her. She began to kick his ankles and shins.

"You little handsome devil!" said Thorny between his kisses, returning her kicks with a lashing out of one of his own heavily shod feet. "I'll teach you to fight me! I will! You're *mine,* now, and I'll make you know it and own it,—yes, and *like* it before we're done. Do you know that?" and then his face came down and smothered her again with his tempestuous fondling.

Struggling, turning, gasping, Patricia at last got one hand free and let it fly at Thorny's face in a blinding blow, scratching at his cheeks and eyes. Freeing her own face at last she let out a terrific scream. True, it was stifled and cut in two at once by Thorny's hard hand clapped over her mouth, but she had got one finger in his eyes and he was blinded himself.

She was like a young fury now, getting her other arm free, beating him about the face, and giving him all he could take, especially directing her blows about his eyes, till suddenly with a howl of pain he put one hand up to guard his eyes and she struggled free. Turning she fled with all her might away from him, not staying to see in which direction she was going, not looking back to see if he were following. She dashed across the mossy ground, screaming as she went.

But it happened that she was going in the opposite direction from all her comrades, who were at that moment engaged in a rollicking game in which they were all shouting and laughing and screaming at the top of their lungs, so they did not hear her. But she went on and on, climbing up a hill, stumbling over roots of trees, and logs, once caught in the branches of a low-hanging tree, but struggling on.

She had stopped screaming now, but the tears were raining down her face, and she was crying softly, sometimes groaning as she stumbled against a log or a treetrunk.

Then it occurred to her that Thorny might be following. Yet she dared not look behind her. She must get out of the woods, into the open, into the road somewhere if possible, where she could call for help if he came.

Then suddenly she fell prostrate across a big root of a tree, and her whole being was shaken with the shock of the fall. Now if he came she could not hope to get away. Her strength was utterly gone. She was trembling in every nerve. She was frightened beyond anything she had ever experienced. For a moment or two she dared not try to look around. He might even be just upon her. It would be like him to creep up and take her unaware. He had always been that way, selfish and ready to take anyone at a disadvantage. A memory of the way he had held her in that close horrid embrace, the feel of his hot wet lips against hers, his quick excited breath upon her face made her shudder. Oh, she would die if he ever caught her and did that again.

She was not a girl who had been used to petting parties. She was only filled with inexpressible horror at the awful contact she had had. Why did people want to kiss unless they loved one another? How could they bear to go around hugging one another? She shuddered again, and then that horror lest he was stealing up to her quietly grew so strong that she had to look around. Slowly, very quietly, she looked back to see if he was coming.

No, he was not in sight. And the way was fairly open. There did not seem to be any covert where he could be hiding.

With stealth she drew herself up from the ground and looked about her, and then up. She seemed to be about ten feet below the top of the hill, and there were great open spaces up there, a field perhaps, a meadow. If she could only gain that, get out into the wideness where there were no obstructions to fall over, no roots to hinder, no bushes to hide, perhaps she might get away home. She felt as if she would never go out again if she once gained that stronghold. And oh, what would her mother say now? Surely she would see how mistaken she was about Thorny! At least her father would see, and he would do something definite about it to protect her. Surely her mother would never think it was right for a boy as big as Thorny to kiss a girl that way, as large as she was, and do it against her will, again and again. Oh!

Shudder after shudder went over her as she slowly tried to rise and creep out of the place where she had fallen.

Blinded by her tears she stood up and slowly gained the top of the hill, reaching at last the shelter of a great tree where she could lean against the trunk and peek out to make sure Thorny was not anywhere about. If she could only have known that Thorny was still seated on a log trying to get the dirt out of his eyes that had been rubbed in along with the violet stems and anemones when Patricia turned upon him, what a comfort it would have been to her just then.

When she turned to look about her at the top of the hill she was not just sure where she was. In a general way she knew that the village where home was should be behind her, beyond the woods from which she was emerging, but she did not want to return that way. She was utterly humiliated and filled with shame over what had happened. She did not want to meet Thorny again—*ever!* And she dared not go back through the woods lest he would be there, and insist on taking her off again. There was no telling what kind of explanation he would give if she went back. She trembled at the thought. So there was no more picnic for her that day. Thorny had managed to spoil it forever, even the memory of it.

They would get along without her. Nobody would

likely miss her very much. Or if they did they would think she had gone off with Thorny. In fact that was the worst thing they could think, but perhaps she could explain to them sometime that it had been because she wanted to get away from Thorny that she ran home. Anyway, that wasn't something to settle now. She had to get away from here right away, because there was no telling how soon Thorny would come plunging up that hill after her, and she felt that that would be the end of her forever. With another swift glance down the hill, and a quick scanning of the meadows, she turned toward the left and hurried along the edge of the woods. Somewhere ahead ought to be the road, and if followed eventually it ought to lead to home. And if it should be that Thorny had figured out already that she would take the road and go toward home, at least there might be people passing in cars to whom she could cry out for help.

So, breathless and trembling she hurried along, stumbling over uneven places in the way, and once actually falling down again. She was so tired, and so sorrowful, that now she did not try to rise, but just lay huddled there in a discouraged little heap and began to cry. Long shuddery sobs that shook her whole young body, tears that flooded her face and hung jeweled drops on her long eyelashes and rained down her pink cheeks with a healing tide. She must get these awful shudders and tears out of her system before she attempted to go home.

And what was she going to say when she got there? What would her mother think? Oh, if only mother would stay late at her all-day club meeting, then she could have the day to herself to rest and think up an explanation; perhaps she would never even have to explain. When she tried to think of words to make it all plain she couldn't find the right ones, not words that she dared utter before her mother. Not words that would explain how she felt about the way Thorny had treated her. Her mother would think she was something vile and awful to have such thoughts, if she tried to tell her how terrible Thorny had been. Her mother would say that if she hadn't been to that low down school she would never have put such an interpretation on Thorny's actions, that, of course, Thorny was a nice decent boy and wouldn't have any idea of doing anything wrong. That all boys of that age liked to kiss nice well-behaved, pretty girls, and that Patricia was acting childish to think that there was anything so very terrible about being kissed. That all pretty girls expected to be kissed, and were proud of it. They felt that it only showed that they were growing up and getting more attractive, and that Patricia was a silly little goose to get all excited because that delightful boy Thorny had chosen to kiss her. If she had only been trained in a nice private school like Gloria Van Emmons she would have understood and known how to accept a little attention now and then. Why, Patricia could fairly hear her mother's voice saying these things, and suddenly it seemed to her more than she could bear, to have her mother like that, not understanding. How could her mother be so blind as not to know what Thorny had become? Oh, perhaps her mother thought that was all right. Perhaps she thought that all boys and men were like that. If that was true Patricia felt she never wanted to have anything to do with boys again. But she knew it wasn't true. She knew that the boys in her school wouldn't have dared crush her in their arms that way. They always treated her with respect.

Oh, perhaps some of them would be rough and silly with some of the girls, and perhaps they might get like Thorny when they were older, but the ones she knew best in her class were either sober, serious, studying hard, and very shy with girls, or else they were all absorbed in athletics and had no time for anything else. Not even those she knew in the senior class were loudmouthed and silly like Thorny. Maybe they weren't as good-looking as he was, but they treated the girls with respect. Why, there was John Worth. Of course it was true he never even went to their parties—though she knew several of the girls had invited him, and wanted him— but John Worth would never behave that way if he did go with the girls. He was a boy you could trust. He wouldn't take advantage of a girl and try to kiss her and hug her the minute he got alone with her. Look how nice he had been to her, just a little girl, that day on the ice! Of course he had been only a very young boy then, and she a very little girl, but he had acted like a gentleman. She knew in her heart that he was different. Oh, why couldn't Thorny have been different, if she had to be such friends with him because he was the son of her mother's friend?

How long would this have to go on anyway? When Thorny grew older, and she grew older would her mother think she could go on making dates for them, forcing them on each other? How dreadful!

Then the tears came again, a perfect avalanche of them, and terror mingled with disgust and hate for Thorny. Somehow, she would have to take a stand against him, and *make* her mother understand! Yes, even if she had to tell it all to her father. Poor father! And let him in for a terrible argument with her mother. She visioned what it would be like and shrank away, shuddering into her little sopping inadequate handkerchief. Then her face was down again in her hands, and a little cool breeze stole across her forehead and touched it softly. And something else, cool and silk-like brushed across her hot wet eyes, and soothed and comforted her burning skin. It seemed so tender, almost like little fingers gently pitying her, that she opened her eyes, and there were little white blossoms, touched with pink, a perfect little flock of them, dancing in the breeze close beside her and softly caressing her face at the whim of the wind.

She gave a little nervous laugh of relief, and nestling nearer touched her lips to their coolness, and brushed them with her finger tips. Dear little flowers. Dear little lovely creations of God doing their best to comfort her!

Lying there so near to them she studied all the little delicate pink veins in them. She felt as if God had sent them to help her through this hard time. Did God understand? Did He care? Sometimes in the little unfashionable chapel where she and her father went Sundays, she had heard people pray as if God cared for everybody, especially for those who loved Him. Her mother's teaching had always carried the implications that God cared of course for the very poor good people who couldn't help themselves, but that people who were well off, like her father and his family, could look after themselves. They didn't need God because they were well educated and had plenty of money, and moved in the best society. Her mother had never actually said that in so many words, but all her upbringing of her child had implied that, and Patricia had gathered that, and wondered, and had not been able to harmonize it with the things she heard at the chapel. But she had never dared talk to her mother about it because that question of hers would surely be charged to the little plebeian church that her father allowed her to attend.

But now as the little flowers continued to whisper soft things to her, lying there in the grass at the woodside, she came to a swift conviction that the chapel people were right, and that God did care for His own.

It was very still there with just the whispering flowers around her face, and a sweet bird up in a high tree top singing an occasional song of lonely far-off cheer. Someone was working over in a distant field. She could hear the ring of a hoe touching a stone now and again. When she opened the fringes of her eyes a tiny crack she could see a figure in blue overalls, working with brisk quick movements of arms and body, keeping time with the hoe. It was quite far away, but it was reassuring. If Thorny should suddenly appear she could scream and that workman would hear her. She was not absolutely all alone.

So she lay still for a little. At least she did not need to hurry home. Perhaps if she waited long enough her mother would not think to question her about the day, and she could keep the whole dreadful happening to herself. Anyway she could close her eyes again and just rest a few minutes and try to think what she should do. She must remember that some explanation must be given to her classmates, too, for they would wonder at her absence, and there was no telling whether Thorny would go back to them at all! She must work out the whole matter so that she need not be ashamed.

But lying so, with the little still breezes all about her, and that bird singing a lullaby above her, with the reassuring hoe chiming in now and again like a bell, she fell asleep. For she was really very tired, what with the excitement, and the fight with Thorny, and the unaccustomed climb.

It might have been a long time she had been lying there, she was not conscious of time and its flight, but she awoke suddenly to the sound of a low rumble above her, and—was that a step she had heard? Was somebody coming?

9

PATRICIA sat up sharply giving a wild look about her and frantically rubbing the sleep from her eyes. Then she looked up. This strange place! The woods, the wide field, the little pink frightened flowers at her feet! Ah! Now she knew where she was! She had run away from Thorny, and this strange lassitude upon her was from her struggle and the climb up the hill!

But the sky was overcast! A storm! The clouds were heavy and dark, and that was thunder unmistakably! And lightning! A vivid quiver darting down the sky and cleaving a blue black cloud in half!

And those footsteps that were coming! Oh, could it be Thorny? She suddenly rose with new strength and darted her glance about wildly. There had been somebody working over to the right, in the field.

Her eyes went to the distance where the man had been and then she saw him, running toward her. But that wasn't Thorny! A vivid flash of lightning lit him up. This man had overalls, blue overalls. With mingled relief and fear she watched him, her clasped hands over her heart, her eyes wide with dread. But there was something strangely familiar about that run, head up, shoulders poised easily, arms flexed, running with long easy strides, not a motion wasted. Like an athlete! Somewhere before she had seen this man run!

Then suddenly he was almost upon her and she saw his face. Another long frightening gash of lightning in the sky, a crash of thunder, that seemed to roar and blaze between them; it lit up their faces, and Patricia's face broke into a welcoming smile.

"Oh! It's *you!*" she said with relief, and her eyes were bright with friendliness and welcome.

It was John Worth!

"And it's *you!*" said the boy. "What are you doing away up here? Weren't you at the picnic?"

"Yes, but—I ran away!" Then she laughed. It had been just this way the last time he came to her rescue, down by the creek. Their eyes met and understanding was in his face.

"It wasn't Thorny, this time, was it?" He laughed pleasantly. "He wouldn't be in on this picnic of course."

"Why, yes," said Patricia, "it was. I told him he wasn't invited, but he came anyway."

"He would!" said John Worth with a frown. "He's that way! I'm surprised the other boys stood for him."

"Oh, I'm afraid they thought I brought him, and they were trying terribly hard to be polite. But of course they didn't know what happened. I was picking violets and he came and sent them all off and then he tried to kiss me, and I hated it!"

Patricia's face grew dark with the memory of it.

"He—is—awful! So, I ran away!"

"Wait till I get a chance at him!" said John Worth with an ominous glint in his dark eyes. "I certainly will give him his! But—that didn't just happen, did it? Weren't you lying here quite a while? I thought I saw something white down on the grass, but I didn't identify you till just now. At least I wasn't just sure who you were till I got here, but I saw a storm was coming and I thought I'd better find out what it was that was lying here before it began to rain. Where are the rest? Were you to meet them somewhere?"

"Oh, no, I'm on my way home. I didn't want anybody to know I had gone, so I rested here a few minutes, I'd run so hard up the hill. And I guess I was rather frightened. Maybe I went to sleep. Then I heard thunder—"

Suddenly another crash rent the air, and the lightning covered the whole heaven with brilliancy.

Patricia stood quivering with her hands over her eyes.

"Oh!" she said in a trembling little voice. "There is going to be a storm! I must go home!"

"I should say there is!" said John Worth coming quickly over to her. "Come! Quick! There's the rain!"

He held out his hand and caught hers.

"Let's go!" he said and with a quick motion drew her arm within his own. "You can't get home till this is over! I'll take you to my home! It's not far. All set?"

They started out across the field, but suddenly the very windows of heaven seemed to open and let down a torrent. Patricia stumbled on, blinded with the rain, and almost fell once or twice, except that John's strong arm held her steady. But when they came to the plowed ground, he halted her and stooping picked her up in his arms and ran on, over the furrows that seemed so endless and so unnavigable to the girl. Her face was against his broad breast, she was sheltered partly by his shoulders, and she felt as safe as if she were at home.

She was panting and breathless, what with the wind and the rain and the running, but she felt as if suddenly a strong shelter had come down above her and put her into a quiet haven. The wind might blow, and the rain had soaked her through, but she was not chilled because strong young arms were about her. The thunder might crash and the lightning glare, but her eyes were closed against John's shoulder, and she was not afraid any more.

Suddenly it came to her what a difference it made which boy held you. Now if this was Thorny she would hate it. His very touch, even if it were to shelter her, was unpleasant. Too possessive. But John was carrying her as her father might have done, or her brother if she had had one. There was something about John that made him seem dependable even in the midst of peril. He was only a boy but he took the responsibility of a man. There was a gentleness and courtesy about him, even in his overalls, that made one trust and rest.

So Patricia, only a little girl yet herself, thought her sweet bright reasonings and was comforted. John Worth was standing to her now for an angel of mercy, and she tried not to remember Thorny's unpleasant intimacy.

She nestled there out of the frightening world, and John Worth sheltered her by the slant of his body and the length of his arms enfolding her. She felt so glad she was not down there in the woods during this awful storm, with Thorny trying to take care of her. Somehow she felt that if she had been left in a strait Thorny would have fled and left her to find her own way home as best she could. Thorny gave no impression of being a gallant gentleman.

John Worth's stride was buoyant even in this storm. He did not seem to be puffing and panting with her weight.

And then while the thunder still rolled and the lightning filled the whole sky with a sheet of glorylight, they arrived. He set her down on a small porch that had a little seat on either side.

It was a plain little shingled house below the side of a wet green hill. Behind and beyond the house were those long black plowed furrows they had just come through so safely, which she never could have crossed alone she was sure. And there were wet trees bending in the blast, and a clean smell of freshly washed vegetation.

Then almost as soon as her feet touched the porch floor the door opened and a sweet-faced woman stood there, reaching out tender soft hands to draw her inside the room, where there was a fire burning in an open grate. Someone was sitting in an easy chair beside the fire, with blankets wrapped about him. He had a face like John Worth's, only older, and tired looking. She remembered that she had heard that John Worth's father had been sick.

"Well, well, son, who is this ye've brought me?" John's mother said, as she looked smilingly into the girl's face. "A wee bairnie come in out of the storm, is it? A wee birdie that couldn't fly away to her own nest in a wild wind like this!"

There was a pleasant burr on her tongue, and a lovingness about her touch that made Patricia glad. What a mother! That must be what made John Worth different from the other boys. He had a mother like this!

"Why, mother, this is Patricia Prentiss," said John. "The girl I told you I skated with a few minutes once."

"I mind," said the mother, giving Patricia another loving smile and a little pat on her arm. "And now, come away, my bairnie, and we'll get you dried and warm. There's a cauld wind and we don't want you to get sick from coming to visit us. You're verra welcome. My lad has told us all aboot you, has pictured the braw hoose where you live and we're honored the noo ta have ye enter our wee bit co-tage."

She led Patricia into an inner room opening from the

larger one. She opened a closet door and took blankets from a shelf and set a chair for her.

"Noo, you tak off yer wet things and wrap ye in yon blanket. It's all clean from the wash and the sunshine, and laid away in wee bags of lavender. It's soft and warm, made from our own lambies in Scotland, a part of my ain dowry, and kept for special occasions like today." She smiled as she hung the blanket over the back of the chair.

"Take off yer bit frock with the bonnie bluebells on it, and I'll iron it dry for ye. It's na sa verra wet."

"Oh, no," said Patricia gaily. "John covered me up with himself as far as he could reach. I think he must be very tired. He carried me all the way over that awful plowed ground."

"John's a hearty lad," said John's mother, "he'd tak it all in the day's stride and think nothing of it. You're only a slip of a thing, you know, and John's used ta hard worruk. That's it. Noo, I'll pit the blanket aboot ya, an you slip off the rest of yer things an' give them ta me. I'll hev them right an' dry in a trice."

Mrs. Worth took the limp chintz frock and smiled.

Patricia answered her smile with one as bright and full of gratitude.

"Oh, but I don't want you to go to all that trouble for me. Let me hang them about the room. They'll soon dry," said Patricia. "I'm making a lot of trouble for everybody."

"Yer makin' a lot of pleasure for us all, lassie. It's like havin' a bit o' sunshine come inta the room on a dark day. And feyther'll be wantin' ta see ye. It's hard days for feyther, shut away from the worruld, and John always tries to bring brightness home with him when he comes. You see feyther's always been active and traveled aboot the worruld much, an' he taks it hard to be shut away all the time. Not that he says much aboot it, ye ken, but his eyes will light up when someone comes in ta break the monotony. Noo, wrap the blanket aboot ya close, and drop doon on the wee cot for a minute and rest ye. I'll soon be back wi' yer garments. I'll tak the bit shoon too, an' set them by the oven wi' the door open. They'll soon be fit and right. Noo, mak yersel' at home, lassie, till I return."

Mrs. Worth vanished shutting the door quietly.

Patricia, wrapped in the wonderfully soft blanket, sat down and looked about her, greatly intrigued by everything.

The room was spotlessly clean. The windows shone even with the dashing rain upon them. There were thin old muslin curtains. They were edged with delicate crocheted lace starched crisply and tied back with a band of themselves. The floor was wide boards, their cracks filled and painted gray, there were braided rag rugs scattered about, some pieces of fine old furniture, a quaint bureau, a little sewing table with lovely drawers, a small but beautiful old desk, two or three chairs, one an old-time rocker. And there were pictures on the wall, photographs of people with strong dependable faces, sweet womanly faces with gentleness and peace written in their eyes. Like John's mother, Patricia thought. She got up and went over to the wall to study them. There was one of a sweet old lady with a little muslin cap on, white hair smoothed down, parted in the middle, sweet wise eyes. She was older than John's mother. And there was a girl in the next frame. She looked like John. It must be a picture of John's mother when she was young.

There were others, too. She went around the room picking them out, wondering who they were, tracing resemblances. And there was a whole row of John's pictures. Some when he was a baby, with little tendrils of curls framing his round cheeks and wide wondering eyes. Patricia studied those until they were stamped upon her memory. When at last she turned away she felt as if she had known John Worth since babyhood. She went back to those pictures again after she had studied the rest.

There was one, a wide rambling old stone house, foreign in its look, and very old. Quaint, her mother would have called it and tossed it aside as worth little. But Patricia looked long at it. It had a home look. She wondered if that was where John's mother lived when she was a little girl. She asked her when she came back with the little pile of pretty garments neatly folded over her arm and the slender slippers in her hand.

"Oh, how quickly you did them!" said Patricia turning to meet those kindly eyes that looked so much like John's eyes. "But I am so sorry to have made you all that trouble!"

"It was a pleasure, dearie. You know I've always wanted a little girl's pretty things to fuss over. My wee lassie went home to Heaven when she was only two years old, and John was well nigh three. I didn't begrudge her to the Heavenly Feyther, but my heart was yearned toward a little lassie ever since, and so it has been pleasure to handle your bonnie clothes and make them fit for you! But now, I'm fearin' ye didn't get a bit nap at all. You look wide awake."

"Oh, I couldn't lie down," said Patricia, "it was so interesting. Won't you tell me, is this picture yourself? And that row over there, are they John?"

"Right you are, lassie. These of me were taken over in the old country, before I met feyther. And those two pictures above, they were my own feyther an' mither. And this," she pointed to a little frame on the bureau "was my wee bairnie." Her voice was full of unshed tears.

Patricia looked at the picture for a long minute, and then she said, her voice very tender:

"I didn't know about the baby. I'm sorry. And you are such a lovely mother! She's missed a lot, not having you!"

"Oh, but she's been with the Heavenly Feyther!" said the mother with a sudden bright smile. "And—I shall go to her some day. Then we'll have each other forever. But whiles I like to see a pretty lass like you, and think what my wee Margaret might have been if the Feyther had chosen to leave her here awhile. Noo, get yersel' dressed, lassie, and come you out to eat a little supper with us. Then John'll find a way to be taking you home when the storm is over."

"Oh, but I can walk home by myself," said Patricia. "John must not take any more trouble for me. That is, I can walk home if you will just point out the way to the highway. I think I'm a little turned around now. This house is not very near the road, is it? When I came I didn't do much looking around."

"It's quite a walk, dearie," said Mrs. Worth. "My lad will be glad to see you home, but we'll wait a little till the storm is by. Noo, here's a comb an' brush. And here are towels and water. Just make yourself at home. I'll run out and look after my scones. We'll have a bit supper as soon as you're ready."

Patricia hurried with her dressing and was soon ready to go out. But before she opened the door she went over to the row of John's pictures, and studied them again. Then she sighed.

Such a nice boy he was, with such a sweet mother! Why couldn't Thorny have been like that? Would she have to be bothered with Thorny all her life, or had she angered him and was he done? She sincerely hoped he was angry and would never come again, although she knew if that was the case she would have to account for it to her mother, and she and her father would have an uncomfortable time of it until Thorny was placated and brought back. Oh, why did mother like a boy like that?

Then with one more long look at John's pictures, and a lingering glance at the dear old house in Scotland, she went out.

She could see through the door of the living room out into the kitchen, where John's mother was stooping down to the open oven door and a delectable odor of hot gingerbread filled the air. She was very hungry and suddenly she realized that she had had no lunch. She had gone all day on excitement and now the odor of the cooking made her ravenous. She stood in the kitchen doorway looking at the big pan of gingerbread that Mrs. Worth was cutting into lovely squares, deftly placing them on a big platter. She looked up and smiled and Patricia smiled back shyly.

"That looks wonderful!" she said with eyes aglow.

"You want a piece now while it's hot, don't you, lassie? My lad likes it best when it's hot, too."

She plumped a generous piece on a pretty china plate and handed it over.

"There! Take that in the room there and sit by the fire with feyther. He wants to pass the time of day with ye."

10

PATRICIA took the plate gratefully, and went in to the fireplace, looking down at the wonderful velvety shining brown crust. It looked better than anything she had ever eaten in her life.

"That's right, lass," said John's father, smiling her a welcome and pointing to a low rocker on the other side of the hearth, "come, let's get acquainted."

Patricia sat down and then looked doubtfully down at her gingerbread.

The kind eyes of the man smiled at her.

"Eat it up, lassie, while it's hot," he advised. "It's best that way. Mother will bring me a bit presently. You're not to wait on me. I'm an invalid, I'm sorry to say, and they baby me."

Patricia smiled and began to eat the delectable cake, and reflected that here was a man her father would enjoy knowing. Would she dare to tell him about him sometime?

Patricia found it easy to talk with John Worth's father. He had kind twinkly eyes, and he seemed glad that she was there.

Then John stamped up on the porch, wiping his feet hard on a mat outside, and came in with a brimming pail of milk.

"Had to come in this door, father," he explained apologetically. "It's fair a flood at the back door. But it's lightening up a little now. It won't be long before the storm is over. Will your mother be worrying, Pat?" he asked anxiously.

Patricia gave him a quick smile.

"No, not worried," she said thoughtfully. "She thinks I'm with people—a person—who will take care of me."

John grinned comprehendingly.

"I see," he said. "Well, you are, you know. I promise you that!"

"Yes," said Patricia, "and a great deal better than—any of the others." Her eyes met John's and a quick little message passed from eye to eye. "I'll never be able to thank you for the way you did it."

He gave her the look an old friend gives, as he passed out into the kitchen with his pail of milk.

Patricia sat there thinking what a nice time she was having, and hoping she wouldn't have to spoil it all when she got home by explaining everything.

Suddenly she looked up and found John's father's eyes upon her kindly.

"I think it is beautiful here," she said with childlike frankness. "I should think you would be very happy here, all shut in from the rain and the world."

"Oh, I am," smiled the invalid. "Of course I would like to be well and strong again, and go out and work for my beloved ones, but since I may not, it is good to be here with them."

"It is very homelike," she said. "I like this house."

"But you live in a very beautiful home, they tell me."

"Yes, I guess so," sighed Patricia reflectively, "but it

isn't a home like this. We never sit down by an open fire and just enjoy it. My father has to be away a great deal on business, and my mother likes the house all kind of cleared up and empty as if you always expected a lot of company and couldn't act like yourself. Of course it's my home, and I like it all right. But this house is so cosy. I like it here. Is that building in the picture up there in Scotland?" Patricia pointed to a large photograph of a columned structure hanging over the mantel.

"No," said Mr. Worth, "that's in this country. That's my college where I used to teach."

"Oh," said Patricia with a sudden surprise in her eyes. This, then, was the explanation of why John Worth was such a brilliant student in school. But she did not say anything more, for John and his mother came in bearing trays.

John put his down on a small table and pulled out a beautiful old mahogany table, lifted its leaves, spread on the cloth his mother handed him, and quickly the table was set.

"Couldn't I help?" Patricia asked hesitantly. "I'd like to."

The mother's face lighted up.

"Yes," she said brightly, "bring in the scones. They're in the big blue platter on the kitchen table. There's a holder by them. Better use it. The platter is pretty hot. I like my scones piping hot."

Patricia came back carefully carrying the big platter of scones. She hadn't known what scones were when she went after them, but there they were, a heaped up platter full, steaming hot and delicately browned. They were most inviting.

There were thin slices of cold chicken on another smaller platter, and Patricia, as she sat down, thought of the great slices of breast of chicken that had gone into that elegant lunch basket that Thorny had probably finished by himself. It wasn't conceivable that he would share with anybody else if he could help it.

John brought his father's chair up to the table. The mother brought in the teapot, and they all settled into a sweet reverent quiet with bowed heads. Patricia bowed her head too. This was something quite new to her, but she liked it. And then the voice of the father was raised in a beautiful blessing that included her also, "the young guest in our household." Her heart thrilled as she heard the petition.

"Grant that the young guest in our household may early learn to know Thee as her Saviour, and may have a gracious and a lovely life of service before her, so that everywhere she goes all who see her shall notice the glory in her face and take knowledge of her that she has been with Jesus."

When the blessing was over and the heads lifted, Patricia's eyes were all dewy with the wonder of it. She felt as if she had been listening at the door of Heaven. She raised her eyes and met the eyes of the boy upon her questioningly, as if he were wondering how she would take that, whether she might have disliked it, as if he were ready to resent it if she did. But she met his glance with one full of appreciation, a look that fully entered in to this bit of worship by the way, and his own face lighted with gladness. It seemed to the girl that now some special bond had come between them, a kind of recognition of a strange lovely kinship that she would never forget, no matter if time went on forever without their meeting again.

Patricia thought that she never had tasted such food before. She thought the scones delicious, and the rich creamy milk was cold and delightful. There were stewed apples, too, in great translucent quarters, golden and clear, big glass dishes of them, and more gingerbread to eat with them. Patricia was ashamed at the way she ate and ate and could not get enough.

When the meal was over John went to the shelf at one side of the room and brought a big worn Bible to his father. As if it were a daily custom right after the meal, and while they were still seated at the table, the father shoved his chair back a little and began to read. His voice was very sweet and strong and gentle and the words seemed new and real to the girl as she listened in wonder. She had no experience whatever with which to compare this. She had read, of course, of family worship in old times, but it had not meant a thing to her. Was this what it was?

> "And as Jesus passed by, He saw a man which was blind from his birth."

The steady voice read the words as if it were telling of a happening the reader had seen. Patricia's attention was caught at once and riveted. It was an old story. She had studied it for Sunday School of course. But never had she heard it read with such clearness, such understanding, as if it were a matter of much moment, a matter that concerned people today. It had never seemed before to her that the Bible had anything to do with today. It had only been a kind of traditional tale that people used in forms of worship to a dim and distant God. Now it suddenly came alive.

This was a real blind man, whose blindness might be like something in herself. It had never occurred to her that such a thing could be possible. She was not blind. Yet, was she, perhaps?

"Jesus answered, Neither hath this man sinned, nor his parents: but that the works of God should be made manifest in him."

Did that mean that God had let him be blind so that someone should be able to understand what God could do?

Her eyes grew larger, and more thoughtful as she listened to the old story of the blind made to see, and the mother glimpsing her now in shy admiration, caught her glance and wondered. "Bless her, dear Father, bless her and teach her," she prayed.

And Patricia as she listened, wondered where would be the pool of Siloam if she needed it?

The prayer that followed the reading was tender and intimate. Sitting there with bent heads about the table, Patricia almost felt she could see the loving smile of the Father as He listened. She never dreamed anyone could be so intimate with the great God. Afterwards she looked at John's father with wonder and awe in her glance. And then when he met her gaze with a pleasant understanding smile her lips trembled into an answering one, and there was a light in her eyes.

He had prayed for their "young guest whom Thou hast sent by the hand of Thy rainstorm to be among us for a few hours, and may it be given her to know Thee aright and truly, and to live her life as in Thy sight."

The words had thrilled her. They seemed to be graven upon her memory. Somehow they became a great wish of her heart, and afterwards when she was alone in her room she said them over softly, then wrote them down on a card which she laid carefully among her treasures. So when they had lifted their heads and that smile had passed between them, the girl by her smile was thanking the servant of the Lord for introducing her so to God.

She hoped he understood how it had pleased her, and seemed to lift her beyond the mere common things of life, and make her a friend of God's.

And then suddenly a ray of a sunbeam shot into the room, and looking out they saw a great rainbow brightly thrown across the clouds.

"Ah! The rain is over!" said the man almost regretfully. "It has been pleasant while it lasted."

The clouds were indeed breaking and the rain had ceased. The sunbeam glanced away again for more clouds were hurrying by, but they knew their time was short and they scurried in haste. A low distant rumble of the vanquished thunder seeming calling farewell, and Patricia remembered she lived in another kind of world and must go back to it again. Could she keep the fragrance of this one to take with her? Or would it fade like the little bunch of anemones that she had clutched as she came away from the woods, and now were lying in a wilted heap in her pocket?

She jumped up and began to pick up the plates.

"May I wash the dishes?" she asked, her eyes shining, as a child would ask to play a game.

"You may help me," said the mother. "John usually helps, but he'll awa' ta bed doon the coo, and settle the chicks for the night before he tak's you hoom. And I'm sair loath ta let ye gang. I wish ye cud bide wi' us awhile."

"Oh, I'd love to!" said Patricia. "May I come again sometime?"

"Indeed ye may, lassie. We'll all be right glad ta see ye."

"I'll come," said the girl with a sweet dreamy faraway look in her eyes, trying even then to plan how she could do it without interference from home, for she knew instinctively that her mother would not permit visits to people of this quiet plain sort, whose only link with her was through that hated school. But there would be a way. She would ask God to make a way for her. So she only smiled when she said, "I'll come!" so confidently.

Patricia wiped the delicate sprigged china carefully, and put it away where she was told in the quaint corner cupboard, as if it were part of a story book tale to be handled most tenderly. She let her touch linger on the last cup as though she were wishing it good-bye till she saw it again.

They started home in the summer twilight, with a sunset so quiet and brilliant in the west that one would never dream the storm that had been raging a few hours earlier. There was clear green like translucent jade, shot through with tatters of scarlet and fragments of coral fringed with bright gold; over against it a phalanx of purple with gold dashed along its rim; and behind it a delicate rose that peered through crevices in the soft and cloudy wall of gray that loomed, and then crept laughing out and reflected rosy lights into the clouds above.

"Oh, isn't it glorious!" exclaimed Patricia with clasped hands, gazing off, and taking deep breaths of the clean air, washed pure by the tempest.

It was a new world, like stepping into fairyland, or Heaven. The girl thought of both, and her eyes went to John's eyes as he stood there with his hands filled with lilies of the valley he had picked along the walk to the little white gate that closed the white fence hemming in their garden.

He held them out, and Patricia put out both hands and gathered them joyously in.

"All those! For me?" she breathed happily. "I never saw so many, together, not even in a bride's bouquet. Aren't they wonderful, just as if they had come from— another world!" she finished, and looked up with the sunset glow upon her face, and great contentment in her eyes.

"They seem like you, lassie," said John's mother softly, as she stood in the doorway, and knew she was voicing what her boy was thinking.

"I've always loved lilies of the valley," Patricia said. "I didn't know they grew in gardens. I thought they came from hot houses."

"Would you like to take a plant home?" asked the boy.

"Oh yes!"

The boy was down at once upon his knees digging.

Patricia put her face down and touched the flowers with her lips, then with her eyelids. Their coolness against her face seemed like a message from God, as if He knew what thoughts and feelings and hungers and longings had been stirred within her by this visit, and as if they were telling her He understood. She watched John as he dug.

"You are taking a lot of trouble," she said.

"I like to," said the boy with a warm smile.

"It's been beautiful, being here," said Patricia, "I thank you!" and her pleasure shone in her eyes.

They went down the walk together, the tall boy and the young girl, John carrying a goodly clump of lilies in a paper, while the mother stood in the doorway and watched them wistfully.

"Oh, God, my Father," she murmured with her eyes uplifted to the blue above for an instant, "she is lovely! But please don't let my lad be hurt by her, not in *any* way. Please, dear Father!"

The two young people reached the gate and turned, as John put out his long arm and swung it open. Then each of them waved at her with a happy little motion as if she were a part of their pleasant time, before they walked on down the hill, and out of sight.

John helped her down the roughness of the path, touching her arm gently with deference. Both of them were conscious that she was going back to her world out of his, and that it might be a long time, or forever, before they saw one another again.

"I've had such a lovely time," said Patricia thoughtfully. "I loved it all. Especially the end. Do you do that every night, or was it just a beautiful courtesy for me?"

He looked down at her from his tall height and smiled. "You mean the family worship? We do that every night and every morning. It is always a part of our day."

"Is that what you call it? Family worship. I've read of that but I didn't know people did it any more. I thought it was something of long ago."

"I think there are many people who still keep to the custom," said the boy thoughtfully. "They are Christian people of course. But I know that many so-called Christian people live worldly lives today, because they have gotten away from God."

"I think perhaps I only know worldly Christians," said Patricia. "At least, they are the only ones whose home life I know. My relatives and mother's friends. But I think it is a beautiful way to begin and end the day. I wish we did it!" She sighed deeply.

He studied her face furtively, and there was a moment of quietness between them. Then John spoke again.

"Of course you could do it by yourself," he said slowly.

Patricia's face was full of brightness as she looked up.

"I will!" she said with sudden resolve. "Of course I couldn't do it as wonderfully as your father did. He made the reading so plain and understandable. I never thought the Bible sounded like that before. But I could read a chapter. And I could—talk to God—although—I don't know Him intimately, the way your father does."

"But He knows you," said John earnestly. "He'll make Himself acquainted with you if you will let Him."

"Oh, I will," said the girl eagerly. "I'd like to know Him. But I never thought He had time to pay attention to just me. I've always thought of Him as paying attention to just the world at large, wanting everybody to do right, just in a general way."

"Don't you know what God says? He says 'I have loved thee with an everlasting love.'"

"But would that mean me?"

"Well, here then: 'God so loved *the world* that He gave His only begotten Son'—listen to that! He gave His Son! His *only* son!—'that whosoever believeth in Him should not perish but have everlasting life.' Isn't that for you? You belong to 'the world', don't you? And you'll find thousands of other verses that tell how He loves you and cares for you. You begin studying the Bible to find that out and see how many you find."

"I will!" said Patricia.

They were still again till they got down the hill and into the broad pasture below, that lay between them and the highway. Then the girl spoke again.

"Oh, I know I'm going to be very glad that I ran away from the picnic, and you found me and took me to your lovely home!" she said happily with a sigh of pleasure.

"Our house is a very plain shabby little house beside the grand one where you live," said the boy thoughtfully.

"But yours is lovely," said the girl looking up earnestly. "I think it is wonderful. You have things in your house that our house has not got."

He looked at her wonderingly.

"What, for instance?"

Patricia looked off at the sky thoughtfully, considering.

"Well, you have some lovely old furniture," she said slowly. "I loved that desk in the room your mother took me to. The wood is just satin-smooth. Of course we have some handsome furniture, but it's modern, and I don't feel that way toward it, as if it were something precious. It's just furniture, not all full of dear memories like yours."

The boy looked at her with his eyes suddenly full of something almost like worship.

"Do you feel that way about things," he said happily. "Just *things?* I do. I always like those old dishes we have. Mother used to tell me about them when I was a little kid. She told me how grandmother bought them, and was always so careful of them, saving them for her. It always seemed as if anything tasted better out of those cups with the little blue sprigs on them."

"Yes," said the girl understandingly. "I can see how you love them. And then you have pictures!"

"Pictures?" said the boy, puzzled.

"Photographs, I mean, but they are real. Of people, and an old house. I loved the old house. If I ever go abroad I'd like to see old houses like that. I'd like to see that special one, I think, because it seemed so much like a place where people were happy, and where children played."

The boy smiled.

"Oh, those! Yes, they are that way. I love them of course. I can just remember playing around there myself. But I wouldn't expect a stranger to see that in them."

"I did," said the girl thoughtfully. "I thought how nice it would be to live in a place like that with a great big wide yard, and mountains in the distance where you could watch them."

The walk seemed very short, down the highway after they climbed the fence from the meadows and John had helped her down the grassy bank to the roadside. They talked of pleasant things, like clouds and flowers, and old homes, even the cows and chickens he knew so much about. He could tell so many amusing little stories about them until it seemed as if his cows and chickens had each a personality.

Patricia had never had such a pleasant talk with a boy before. Either they had been shy and silent, or else they had been boasters and bullies like Thorny. But now Patricia forgot she was a high school girl walking with a senior. She had a feeling that she had known him a long time and that they liked the same kind of things, and could be real friends if things only were different.

They were coming into the village now, and would soon be at the Prentiss gate. Involuntarily Patricia's steps slowed as she remembered. Would her mother be home yet? She was sometimes late at the club when she was on the committee. She might have to stay and clear up afterwards today, as it was a sort of party meeting with guests. Oh, perhaps she wouldn't be home yet! For if she was and saw her walking with John Worth, what would she say? Very vividly Patricia remembered the awful experience several years ago when John Worth came to sell strawberries. What if that were to happen all over again? Of course they were both older now, but her mother wouldn't stop for that. If she happened to recognize John Worth she would be very angry. And especially since Thorny Bellingham wasn't anywhere in sight. That would be rather terrible. Oh, if only her mother wasn't home yet!

She grew very silent as they neared her home. She remembered that her father was not to be home until the midnight train from New York. She wouldn't have anybody to take her part.

The boy by her side studied her furtively. At last he said quietly:

"It's been very wonderful having you visit us today. I'm not going to forget it. I always thought you would be worth knowing."

"Oh, thank you!" said Patricia with her pale cheeks suddenly flaming happily. "I guess I felt that way about you, too. Only of course you were older and a lot wiser than I." She looked up with a sweet glance of humility. "It's rather wonderful to be walking home with a senior!" And then her cheeks grew pink again.

"Oh, but that sort of thing doesn't matter, you know," said the boy. "I always thought perhaps you were real, and now I know it. It's being real, that counts, you know. And knowing God. That counts most of all, I guess."

Their eyes met in a quick glad understanding.

But they were quite near to the gate now and they both realized it. Their steps lagged slower and slower. Patricia was trying to think what to do. In a moment the house would be right in plain sight, and she couldn't bear the thought that her mother might glimpse them and come out and be disagreeable to John, after the lovely way he and his people had treated her. She couldn't stand it. But the boy seemed almost to share her feeling, for his steps lingered too.

"Listen," he said in a guarded tone, as if even now someone might be upon them, watching, listening. "I'm not coming in. I think it's best not, don't you? But I'll set out these lilies. Would it do if I put them right here by the fence behind the evergreens? No one will see me here planting them, and it won't take but a minute. I have my knife in my pocket. And then if you want to move them somewhere else afterwards it will be all right, you know."

He smiled at her engagingly, and his eyes seemed to be pleading with her to agree with him.

"Oh," she said with a troubled look, "I could stay here till you have finished. Or perhaps *I* could set them out." She looked with a worried question at her useless little white hands that had never attempted such a task.

He smiled back and the lamps in his eyes flamed out.

"Of course you *could,*" said the boy, "but I like to do it, you know. Please let me finish. I like to think I am giving you these and fixing them just right so they will go on growing for you."

Her glance beamed in shy response.

"Besides," he went on, "I don't think it would be wise for me to come in, do you? Your mother might not understand. And there are things that can't really be explained in a case like that."

"I know," said Patricia suddenly sobered, a shadow coming over her bright look.

"Are you sure no one will object to the lilies being put here?"

"Oh, quite sure," said Patricia. "Nobody ever comes past here to look over the hedge."

"That's all right, then," said John Worth dropping down on his knees between the hedge and the tall evergreen trees with their plumy branches that hid the house completely. He began to dig rapidly with his knife. "I guess it would be better if you went into the house now. Your mother might be worrying about where you are. Perhaps she is telephoning all around the neighborhood by this time trying to find out if the others are home. And if you should go in now I could go right on working here and nobody would notice me."

"Yes, of course," said Patricia a little sadly, "but—it

doesn't seem quite polite to leave you this way. After you've been so kind, and I've had such a lovely time—"

"That's all right," said the boy dropping his knife and standing up, "you and I understand and that's all that matters, isn't it?" The look in his face made it seem as though he had said a great deal more than just those few words, and somehow she knew he understood how her mother would feel and wanted to protect her from unpleasantness. She answered him with a sweet wistful look, assenting to his words, and turned reluctantly to go.

"I'll drop in now and then and give these flowers a bit of attention sometimes, late, or early, while it's still dark and no one can see me. And—" he hesitated shyly, *"sometime* I'm coming to *see you,* when things are so— that—I can come—honorably!"

She turned back and her eyes met his with a glad light in them.

"I—shall be—*expecting* you—sometime," she said with a little tremble of happiness in her voice. She turned and slid out of the green shelter by the hedge and he could hear her quick steps on the walk up to the house. Then all suddenly there came a strident voice rasping on the quiet evening air and he shrank behind the trees in the deepest shadow.

II

"WELL, for pity's sake! Where did you come from?" said Patricia's mother sharply. "Mrs. Bellingham just got done telephoning me that you were all going to stay at a roadhouse where you had had to take refuge from the storm, and have dinner and a dance. I said you might stay if they would bring you back before ten o'clock. And now you come walking in alone! Where is Thorny?"

"I don't know, mother. I wasn't with Thorny when the storm came on. I didn't go to any roadhouse."

"Do you mean to tell me that you have been wandering around all this time since that storm came on without seeing Thorny, when he went as your special attendant?"

Patricia came into the house and tried to walk past her mother, but her mother caught her arm and held her.

"Answer me, Patricia! Don't try to evade me. Where were you during that awful storm?"

"In a pretty cottage, mother, quite near to the woods. There was a sweet lady there who made me welcome and gave me hot gingerbread to eat, and fresh milk. I've had a nice time."

"But what became of your escort, Thorny?"

"I don't know, mother, indeed I don't!" said the girl, her voice beginning to tremble. "He was very unpleasant. I was ashamed of him the way he acted to my classmates. And then afterwards he was awful! He came where I was picking flowers, and told the people I was with that somebody wanted them, and then he grabbed me and kissed me and hugged hard. I was so frightened I didn't know what to do. Mother, he was *disgusting!* You wouldn't have liked him if you had been there! I had an awful time getting away from him. He was just awful. I never will go anywhere with him again! I *hate* him! Mother, if you had seen him you would have hated him too."

"Nonsense!" said her mother sharply. "As if a kiss or two from a nice boy would hurt anybody! What a baby you are, Patricia! Don't you realize that you are a fairly pretty girl and you are getting to the age when nice boys will want to kiss you? It is time you grew up and began to act like a lady and not a child any more. You ought to be proud that such a nice, well-educated, well-mannered boy as Thornton Bellingham wanted to kiss you, instead of making such a fuss!"

"Mother! Please don't talk that way by the door. Everybody will hear you! Please come inside and shut the door."

"Shut the door? Why, you poor little silly! What is there in that that the neighbors shouldn't hear? I certainly am proud that Thorny honored my child by kissing her!—"

But suddenly Patricia pushed by her mother and fled up the stairs, bursting into wild noiseless sobs as she went, and in her own room flung herself face down upon her bed.

Oh, had John Worth heard her mother? Her mother talking about that shameless conduct of Thorny's as if it were all right! And now the whole horrible experience was down upon her young soul again, as if she could not bear the thought that it had happened in her life.

Suddenly her mother spoke from her open door.

"Patricia, get up and wash your face and behave yourself!"

Patricia caught her breath and got up. The lilies of the valley were still in her hand, and she clutched them to her side so that her mother would not notice them as she went toward the bathroom to wash her face. Oh, she didn't want her mother to bring them into the open and examine them and put a line of questions on them. But Mrs. Prentiss had eagle eyes, and she could ferret out anything when she was on the warpath.

"What is that you are trying to hide behind you, child?" she said sharply. "Is it your lunch basket?" Patricia winced. Now, she would have to be examined about that lunch basket. She sighed and lifted up the flowers in all their lovely freshness.

"Well, really, where did you get those lilies? It looks like a bride's bouquet."

"They were growing in the yard where the nice lady lives," said Patricia in a colorless young voice. Oh, if her mother would only forget about the lunch basket, and not talk about the flowers.

"Well, they're very pretty indeed," said her mother surprisingly. "You may put them down in my Dresden vase in the living room. I'm expecting callers this evening and it will be nice to have some flowers."

The door bell rang while Patricia was washing her hands and face, and her mother went downstairs. She hoped the flowers would be forgotten. She did so want to have them all to herself, at least for tonight. Besides, if the flowers went downstairs somebody would be sure to ask where they came from and there was no telling but John Worth's name might come out somehow in connection with the afternoon.

So Patricia washed her face and hands, then bent and laid her lips against the sweet waxen lilies in her drinking glass. She hung a clean towel where it would hide them from anyone casually passing her bathroom door. After that she went and stood at her window. She could catch a glimpse of the front gate if she put her face very close to the glass in the upper window sash and twisted her neck slightly. She watched a long time to see if John Worth was still there behind the evergreens, but the rosiness of the sunset was fading now, and there was no sign of him. Perhaps he had slipped out while she was washing her hands. She hoped and prayed that her mother had not seen him. It seemed too sad to think her day that was to have been so wonderful, and had unexpectedly turned out to be marvelous because of John Worth, might even yet be picked to pieces by her mother, and its joy utterly demolished by criticism and ugly commands.

But now came a command from downstairs. The maid came up to say that her mother wanted her to put on her pink dress with the white lace on the ruffles, comb her hair nicely, and come right downstairs and play a piece or two for the callers.

How Patricia hated to be exhibited in this way! It happened so often, too. It seemed to take all the joy out of her music, to have to parade it before people who didn't care a bit about music.

But in the hope of a brief reprieve from uncomfortable questioning, she was almost glad of it this time.

"Who is down there?" she asked the maid.

"The Warriners," said the maid. "I don't think they are staying long. Your mother said to hurry."

Patricia slid out of her crumpled picnic dress and into

her pink in a trice, reflecting that the Warriners lived in another township and wouldn't be likely to have heard of the picnic. She resolved to play as well as she could and as often as she was asked. Perhaps in that way she could distract her mother's attention for a time from the happenings of the day.

So she went downstairs looking very sweet and pretty, and played several times. And when at last they said good-night she slipped away unnoticed while her mother stood talking with them at the door.

She went out the side door and into the shadows of the yard, making her way by a circuitous route to the big evergreen trees by the front walk. She slid between their interlacing branches and arrived within the dim sweet aisle between the hedge on one hand and the trees on the other. Eagerly her feet found the way down the grassy path, and then, going carefully, she stooped and felt through the darkness, till her hand came in contact with the sharp crisp leaves of the plants. Her fingers brushing lightly the lily bells, brought forth that heavenly fragrance of the blossoms. Then her young heart thrilled to think those were hers and she could come down there sometimes and find them growing; that John Worth was going to tend them, at night and early morning when no one was about. It was something all her own that no one else knew anything about. It was pleasant.

"Good night, dear little flowers," she whispered softly, and then with another touch like a caress she slipped away among the feathery trees, around to the back door, and so upstairs, hoping her mother might forget her various grievances and let her go to her bed in peace.

But she had scarcely reached the haven of her room when her mother arrived at the door.

"Now, Patricia," she began severely, "I want to

understand this matter thoroughly. And first of all I certainly expect a little thanks for the nice basket of luncheon I took the time and trouble to put up for you. Weren't you surprised at the darling little strawberry tarts I put in, in those cute little paper cups with individual covers? And weren't those chicken sandwiches delicious?"

Patricia was very still for a minute looking out of the window into the night sky with a twinkling star winking at her as if it understood her dilemma. Then her mother spoke again.

"Well? You don't seem to have even any appreciation."

"I'm sorry, mother. I know the lunch you put up was very nice. Everything you do like that is always lovely of course, and I do appreciate what you tried to do for me."

"What I *tried* to do for you! Is that all you can say? Haven't you anything to say about how pretty the basket looked inside, how tempting it was, and how delicious everything tasted?"

Patricia was silent another moment and then she said:

"But mother, I didn't see inside the basket at all, and I didn't have a chance to taste anything that was in it! You remember you gave the basket to Thorny, and that was the last of it so far as I was concerned."

"Do you mean you deliberately walked away from him and wouldn't eat your lunch with him? Did you carry your animosity to that extent? I declare you don't deserve any consideration at all if you acted like that."

"No, mother. It was nothing like that. I asked Thorny to give me the basket, and he wouldn't. He downright refused! And when they all put their baskets together in a pile till lunch time, he wouldn't give it up, even then. He just carried it around with him everywhere, and he kept poking his fingers in it and bringing out a sandwich or a piece of cake, or a drumstick, until I'm very sure there wasn't much left in it by lunch time. And he went off with another girl and gave her pieces too. You see, I didn't get a single thing from that basket myself, so I can't exactly say I was surprised."

"You mean, of course, that you acted so disagreeable to Thorny that he was obliged to walk with another girl to make you jealous. Is that it?"

"No, mother, no. Why would I be jealous? I didn't want to go with Thorny. It was you who must have invited him. You see, the class had voted not to have any outsiders, and it put me in a very uncomfortable position, appearing to bring in someone none of them knew."

"And so you thought you would get it back on me by being disagreeable to Thorny!"

"Mother! No! Oh, you will not understand."

"No, I'm afraid I never will understand," sighed the mother in a deeply hurt tone. "That you should pick out the son of my very dearest friend to dislike is more than I can fathom. A nice, handsome, wealthy, dependable boy, and yet you scorn him! Just because your mother favors him, and wants you to have an escort who is from a good family, and has some social standing. Just to disappoint me!"

The mother's voice trembled, and Patricia's tears flowed copiously. She did love her mother in spite of everything, and she couldn't bear to hear her talk in that hurt tone. It was worse than her scolding.

Mrs. Prentiss went away at last and left her standing by that dark window crying. Slowly, sadly the daughter prepared for bed, thinking sorrowfully about the day, how eager she had been for it, and how almost everything she had planned had gone awry and been deeply disappointing. Yet there had been a bright ending when the storm came. She wouldn't have missed that experience in the Worth home, not for all the picnics in the world! And she had the dear valley-lilies!

Her mother came back just then.

"Patricia, where did you say that lovely expensive lunch basket is that I took the trouble to buy for you? Surely you didn't throw it away, or leave it behind in the woods."

"I don't know where it is, mother. Thorny must have it. I have not had it in my hands since you gave it to him."

"Now that is absurd, Patricia. Thorny wouldn't carry a basket as large as that around with him all day! You must know what he did with it."

"No, I don't know, mother," she said desperately. "I didn't see what he did with it."

"Well, you certainly are a careless girl, after I spent all that money to have a pretty basket for you."

"I'm sorry, mother. If you had given it to me I would have looked after it. But I could not get it away from Thorny, though I tried more than once."

"Well, I suppose there is no use talking to you as long as you go to that terrible school. You care more for that school than you do for your family. However, I shall be obliged to ask you to use your brains a little and remember where that basket is. And in the morning you and I will go and get Thorny and go back to those woods and find that basket! And you will apologize to Thorny, too, for the way you have treated him, understand that! I'm not going to have you insulting the son of my best friend."

Patricia stood very still in the darkness by the window in her little white nightdress until her mother's footsteps died away behind the living room door which closed sharply. Then forlornly she dropped on her knees beside her bed.

Patricia was in the habit of saying her prayers at night as she had been taught, but now it came to her that she had been hearing a different kind of prayer today from any she had ever said. She had heard a man talk intimately with God, and bring all his concerns and cares and interests to Him as if He were a real father. And John had said that she might do that herself, too. She caught her breath and brushed away the tears.

Tears on her face when she was daring to come to God intimately for the first time! Was that right? But yet, if He was to comfort her and help, if He was the loving, caring God that John had seemed to suggest, might she not hide her face on God's breast and let her tears tell Him just how sorrowful and perplexed she was? Her earthly father was always touched by the sight of her tears. Perhaps the Heavenly Father would care too and do something about it.

So with her head down on her clasped hands she prayed:

"Oh, dear Heavenly Father, won't You please straighten out this trouble about Thorny? Won't You please fix it somehow about that nice pretty basket so mother won't be so angry with me? Won't You please make me Your real child, and help me to live so I please You, and if possible my mother too."

She remembered her lilies and stole into her bathroom to set the glass in the open window. Taking one long cool stem of the flowers back to bed with her, she lay with it against her cheek, the sweet perfume soothing her to sleep.

About that time over in another street, a noisy couple of groups were wending their way home from the roadhouse where they had been dancing. They had had something much stronger to drink than water, and at least Thorny was exceeding gay with it all for he had not stopped with a few glasses, and he had reached the affectionate stage. The quiet shy girl who was his excited and half-frightened companion was in a stage between giggling and screaming.

"Oh, stop it, Thorny! I say, stop it!"

And then in real protest.

"Don't you do that again! *Stop* it!"

It wasn't so far away but that Patricia might have heard the echo of the screams if she had been awake, but she was sweetly sleeping and did not know.

12

JOHN Worth was coming swiftly down the street behind them when he heard the scream. He had been on
an errand into the city after planting the lilies, and had
had to wait for quite a lengthy answer to a letter his
father had written to an old friend about the possibility
of a part-time job for John next winter in case he should
be able to enter college. He had had to come out on the
late train and was hurrying because he knew his mother
would be awake until he came in.

And then he heard those three sharp screams!

That was Della Bright. Could she be out with Thorny
Bellingham! How did she get to know Thorny? She was
frightened! That was plain.

He dashed ahead and saw them, struggling there on
the sidewalk, Thorny giving a maudlin laugh now and
then, two or three others in a group a little farther ahead,
laughing inanely.

Yes, that was Thorny, and his mind reverted to the
few words he had inadvertently heard from Patricia's
door while he was patting the earth around the lilies.

Yes, that was unmistakably Thorny! The hound. The

cur! The *swine!* He could not think of words enough to call him. And poor backward stupid Della Bright was getting the worst of it. Thorny had her in his arms now against the fence, and Della was screaming and writhing away from him. Was this what Thorny had dared to do to Patricia, that she had told her mother was so dreadful?

He had wanted to give Thorny what he deserved ever since he was a youngster and had seen him tripping the little boys and girls from kindergarten, making them cry. He had wanted it more as the years went by and he saw the hateful, contemptible acts that Thorny perpetrated on others, always those weaker, less able to cope with him; and especially had he wanted it since that day when he and Patricia had enjoyed that brief skating time together and he knew that Thorny's torments had been dealt out to her as well. And now it looked as if here was his opportunity! Patricia's words to her mother about Thorny had sunk into his heart and stirred his deepest sense of outrage. So now he darted in and went to the rescue.

As he ran his mind reasoned it all out: he was doing this to help poor dumb Della Bright of course, but he was really doing it for Patricia's sake; and at last he was going to give Thorny that walloping that he had so long been promising him in his heart!

With well-calculated poise he took Thorny off his guard, just as Della, twisting away from him fell heavily to the sidewalk, screaming as she fell. Thorny lost his balance and fell with her, taking care to pin her beneath him where she could not get away.

But instantly John Worth was above him. He plucked him by a strong arm, clutching Thorny's collar and swinging him away from the girl.

"Get up, Della!" he ordered in a low tone. "Get up and run! *Scram!*"

And then as Thorny rolled over and attempted to rise with an angry roar, he pounced down upon him and pinned him with a strong young knee, administering the punishment that Thorny had had coming to him for many a day, and many a deed.

When John Worth was through with him there was no spirit left in Thorny. He lolled against a picket fence in front of a vacant lot and surveyed his suddenly blighted world with a more sober mind than he had had for several hours. He looked at his adversary impersonally, unable to find any of his usually voluble taunts wherewith to address him.

It was fortunate that the location of this brisk skirmish was at the outer edge of town, where the residences were few and far between, else Della's horrible screams would surely have brought the neighbors to the spot and John might have had to explain several things when it was discovered that handsome Thorny Bellingham was the young man who was being thoroughly chastised.

John Worth, when he was through with his victim, brushed the dust from his best suit and reflected on this. However, there hadn't been time to think about such risks when his duty plainly sent him to the rescue of Della.

Della had evidently "scrammed" in a hurry. And even the huddled group in the offing had disappeared into the shadows. Only furtive shuffling footsteps in the distance gave a hint of where they were.

John Worth stood away from his victim a few steps and watched him. He knew that he had not done him any serious damage, but he wanted to be sure that Thorny was sober enough to take care of himself before he left him. Then Thorny spoke.

"I say, you, you, wha's the matter 'ith you? Who gave you the right ta touch me? Don'tcha know who I am?

Don'tcha know who my father is? I c'n have you jailed fer this!"

"It doesn't matter who you are nor who your father is," said John Worth firmly. "If I ever hear of you treating a girl like that again around this town I'll see that everybody knows *what* you are! And I don't mean maybe, either!" And John Worth turned and walked down the country road toward his home. He wasn't sure whether Thorny knew who he was or not. It didn't matter. He had done what he thought was right. But he did not whistle as he strode down the road in the darkness. He was thinking about Patricia, the girl with the lovely eyes who had spent a little while at his home that afternoon. Thinking of how he had carried her to safety from the storm, as if she had been a young babe. Did a sweet little girl like that have to grow up among such friends as the low-minded cur he had just walloped? Just because he was the son of a rich man must she be friendly with him, and have his vile mouth kiss her sweet lips, even against her will? His heart was heavy with the thought.

As he drew near to the fence he must climb to cross the meadow he paused a moment with his hands on the top rail, and his head lifted, looking up to the starlit sky, his face very earnest.

"Oh, God!" he uttered in a low tone, "You'll take care of her, won't You? I did this tonight for her sake—and any others he might harm—but it's all I'd be allowed to do, of course. You'll take care of her, I know. She's Yours. I'm leaving her in Your hands. I know You want her kept safe!"

Then after a minute he drew a deep breath and sprang over the fence. Presently across the meadow his cheery whistle rang out to reassure his mother who would be sure to be listening. Clearly as if he were speaking the words the stately melody pierced the night:

> *Oh, God, our help in ages past,*
> *Our hope for years to come;*
> *Our shelter from the stormy blast,*
> *And our eternal Home!*
> *Under the shadow of Thy wing*
> *Thy saints have dwelt secure,*
> *Sufficient is Thine arm alone,*
> *And our defense is sure!*

His heart was singing the words to himself in a young glad trust as he wended his way to his home and thought of the sleeping Patricia for the sake of whom he had just been administering justice.

Thorny Bellingham, draping himself inertly over the picket fence, coming more and more to himself and to the fact that everybody had left him alone and that his assailant wasn't even there to be argued with, contented himself at last with remarking to the country round that he must be a coward, whoever he was. "Coward!" and he called it out thickly several times without effect.

But he was himself enough now to realize that he had several bruises about his head and face and that when he tried to talk his lips were very stiff and sore. He put up a flabby shaking hand and found that his lip was cut and was swelling fast; a tentative finger presently discovered that one eye was swollen almost shut.

Now, what was he going to do? He had had black eyes before and experience taught him that they always had to be accounted for. A pensive survey of the situation showed him that it would be most unwise at this juncture to have to account for this one. In the first place he didn't know just how many people had witnessed his late humiliation, nor who had administered it. If he were only sure of those two things he might be able to manufacture a story that would get by with his father whom he thought of tenderly under the term "the old man." But under the circumstances, perhaps it would be best for him to disappear until that eye was well, and those bruises healed. There wasn't one of those "fool kids" that he had played around with today who could be depended upon to keep their mouths shut. In fact, he wasn't at all sure that the crowd that came home with him were the ones with whom he had gone to the picnic. Better not try to find out anything. Even Della Bright whom he vaguely remembered as a girl who had gone to the dance hall with him was too stupid to trust. She might blat out something that would be awkward. And his father had distinctly said that if he got into any more scrapes before commencement he would see that he got what was coming to him in a good hard job of work, before he ever got to loaf through another school year. And the worst of it was that when the old man really put down his foot he meant it.

Thorny consulted his watch by aid of a cigarette lighter, and found that it had stopped. Whether because time was up or because it had taken the walloping to heart more than Thorny had was a question.

But if he only knew what time it was he could work on his problem to better effect.

He dimly remembered that his mother and father had gone to town to attend a banquet connected with some political organization. That meant that they would return very late, and expect to find him fast asleep in bed. If he only knew what time it was!

Just then the town clock in the old church steeple decided to help him out. It began to chime out a great many strokes. He lost count of them, but decided it must be somewhere around eleven. And that being the case there was time to work out something. The best thing would be to write a note saying he had gone back to school. Of course that would be a little hard to explain since he had made a great disturbance getting his mother to ask for his absence over Sunday, but he could surely get up something to explain it. A telegram! That was the thing. They had called him back to school for some important reason. Sure, that was it!

He wouldn't necessarily *go* back to school, of course. He wouldn't want to appear there with a black eye and a swollen lip and jaw, but he could make the mater think he had gone. His years of experience in putting things over on the mater would stand him in good stead now. Only, how was he going to get money to finance this expedition? After paying for all those girls' dinners, and the drinks, he probably hadn't a cent left to his name, and this bluff would take dough. If Aunt Mamie were only home he could stay with her a few days. He could always put over a tale on Aunt Mamie. But she was abroad. And there wasn't anybody else he dared bully into keeping quiet about his bruises. He would have to go to a hotel somewhere.

He pawed around in his pockets futilely and wavered around tentatively to try his walking abilities. He found not a cent in his pocket and every joint pretty sore. That bird sure had done him up slick. Well, he'd better be getting on to the house and see if he could rustle up some money. His mother had a secret drawer in her desk, the secret of which was an open book to him. If she hadn't taken it all out he might be able to find some.

So he went home unsteadily.

Thorny was not accustomed to as much drink as he had had that night. His experience thus far had been an occasional drink to seem grown-up and large. His head was spinning around unpleasantly, and it was difficult for him to manage a little thing like fitting a key into a lock. But he managed to get into the house at last without rousing the maid, tiptoed softly upstairs, and went cautiously into his mother's room. He hunted through her desk till he found the secret drawer. He opened it and found a little over fifty dollars. This he pocketed with satisfaction, went into his own room and slung his clothes into his bag without ceremony, then sat down at his desk and scrawled a note to his mother.

Dear Mums:
   Just got a wire from school. They want me back in the morning. Something important about a class meeting. Am leaving on midnight train. I got some money—you know where! Will write from school.

So long, Thorny.

Then still stealthily he took his way to the midnight bus to the city, and caught a train to a city not far from his school, reflecting that it would be easy to phone his roommate and get service and a contact when needed, in case his bruises didn't clear up by tomorrow.

The next morning Mrs. Bellingham found Thorny's note pinned to her pincushion, and when Mrs. Prentiss called her up after breakfast and asked to speak with Thorny she answered quite sweetly:

"Oh, I'm so sorry, dear, but Thorny isn't here. They telegraphed him last night to return to school for some important class meeting and he had to leave on the midnight train. He was so sorry not to be able to say good-bye to dear Patricia, and he asked me to make his excuses and to say that he would be looking forward to the summer vacation and he hoped that there would be many more opportunities to have such good times as they had yesterday. He wanted me to thank you, too, dear, for giving him the opportunity to go with Patricia yesterday. My poor homesick laddie!"

"Why of course, Arabella, it was Patricia's pleasure I was thinking of. But it's nice that Thorny enjoys being with her. I'm sure she was the one to thank him. I know it made the picnic a great thing to remember beside what it would have been if Thorny hadn't come. So sweet to see young things enjoy each other, isn't it, Arabella? But I didn't know Thorny was gone. Patricia didn't tell me."

"Oh, he must have found the telegram here when he got back after he left Patricia at home. I didn't see him again, you know. We hadn't got back yet, and he had to catch the midnight train. But what did you want to see Thorny about? I hope he hasn't missed another lovely party or anything?"

"Oh, no," said Patricia's mother, "nothing as nice as that. I just called up to see if Thorny could remember what Patricia did with her new lunch basket. She seemed to think Thorny had it, but she's getting so forgetful and careless, I just know she must have laid it down and forgotten all about it. And I really didn't think I ought to let it go at that. I paid a lot for that basket, it was so pretty, and seemed quite durable and all. But I suppose in the confusion of getting away in the storm she must have left it somewhere in the woods and it is likely ruined."

"Oh, that's too bad! But I don't suppose Thorny would remember anything as useful as that. He has never been domestic in his tastes, you know. However, I'll write and ask him to put on his thinking cap, and will let you know as soon as I hear from him. Meantime, of course I'll look around. He might have brought it home absent-mindedly, though I'm sure I would have noticed it if it had been here!"

"Oh, don't trouble. I'll just call up that place where they were dancing last night. He might have dropped it down there somewhere. Of course if you find it let me know and I'll send Patricia over after it. Sorry your boy has gone again. I know how lonely you must feel without him. But then you must remember vacation will soon be here and there'll be lots of nice times ahead."

The two mothers tore themselves apart at last, and each of them instituted a thorough search for the basket, which was even then lying wet and limp in a copse of sweet fern where Thorny had thrown it in the woods when he had finished the last delectable bite all by himself behind a great laurel bush. Thorny had always appreciated good food, even from his early youth. But for baskets he cared nothing at all.

So the little basket lay and wilted in the rain, while Thorny lay low out of the picture for the time being, and Patricia mourned neither of them. She felt as if she never wanted to see either again.

Eventually a child from the city slums at the annual country-week picnic found the basket and exclaimed over its gay colors; she did not mind that it was limp and slightly warped from the sharp crisp lines it had worn on its first picnic. And so it turned out that Patricia never did see that basket again, for it went to gladden a dark little attic in a city slum and give joy to a little child who had no problems except how to get enough to eat.

But Patricia's mother went on worrying about how much money she had spent on that basket, and nagging at her child to try and locate it, until sometimes Patricia grew fairly frantic about it.

Then all suddenly she didn't care any more, for commencement was at hand.

"I don't see why you care so much," said her mother unpleasantly. "It isn't your commencement. I shouldn't think you'd want to go. I should think it would bore you."

"Oh I want to go!" said Patricia with shining eyes.

Patricia went, and her father went with her.

"You're just encouraging her in all her whims and fancies," said the mother with dissatisfaction.

"Yes," said her father. "I like to. I like it myself. It makes me feel young again."

And so Patricia sat by her father and watched it all. She saw John Worth take his place on the platform filing in with the procession in cap and gown. How handsome he looked, and how manly. How he seemed to be head and shoulders above them all in every way.

And then she saw his father sitting over at one side in a sheltered corner by a door, sitting in a wheeled chair. How nice that he could be there to see his boy graduate!

By and by John Worth's father saw her, and twinkled his nice pleasant smile at her across the room. And she smiled back. Her father looked up and followed her glance with his eyes.

"That's John Worth's father," she whispered, and her father looked again, for John Worth had just finished his valedictory address and had made a deep impression on his audience. "Yes, over in the corner, in a wheeled chair."

Patricia's father studied his face, and then looked back at the boy on the platform who was receiving with heightened color but with young dignity the applause that was still filling the house with pleasant din. Then he looked back at the father again.

"I like his face!" said Mr. Prentiss. "I like both their

faces!" and Patricia's heart sang. But only the light in her eyes and the smile she gave her father told him how pleased she was at what he had said.

Afterward Patricia took her father over to the corner where Mr. Worth had sat, hoping she might introduce them, but the wheeled chair was gone. And John Worth had disappeared too. He was carefully rolling that wheeled chair down the village street and out toward the highway on the long trek home, hoping, praying, that this long ride and excitement might not be too much for the precious invalid. But Patricia did not know that, and was disappointed.

13

AND then the summer came on and the Prentisses talked about going to the seashore. They talked about getting a cottage on the beach, and Mr. Prentiss said that maybe he could arrange to come down every evening and they would have a real time together.

"Lovely!" said Mrs. Prentiss. "Get a good big cottage so we can have guests. I want to have the Bellinghams down. It's high time I repaid some of the nice invitations I have had from them. Mrs. Bellingham has taken me five times to the theater, and twice to the symphony concerts!"

There was a dead silence in the room for a minute, and a grayness seemed suddenly to descend upon Patricia's face. Her father saw it, and looked up quickly.

"That settles it!" he said firmly. "If that female dreadnought is in danger of coming, nothing doing! Pat and I'll stay at home and take our vacation together."

"Now, Mr. Prentiss!" protested his wife. "Why do you have to be so impossible! Don't you understand that you have a young daughter growing up and you've got to think a little about that? Patricia must have some nice boy friends or she won't have a good time at all. She'll want to go sailing and swimming and fishing, and it will be so nice and safe to have a boy who is well-mannered to take care of her. You might get a cottage that has a tennis court, too, perhaps, and not too far from a country club with a good golf course, you know. Then everybody could have a good time and we could feel perfectly safe about our child."

"Not on your life!" said Father Prentiss with a quick look at the ghastly horror in his daughter's eyes. "I don't want any young chump like that Thorny lying around in the way all summer, and I don't believe Pat does either. Do you, girl?"

The young girl lifted expressive eyes to her father's.

"Mother knows I don't want him, daddy," she said in a low tone.

"There!" said the mother indignantly. "Now I hope you see, Mr. Prentiss, just what you have done to your daughter, making her disagreeable and self-conscious, and unable to have any friendships with nice boys. If she ever gets free from that dreadful school I shall have a pretty time training her for her social life."

"I don't see that she needs any training," said her father with a cheering smile and a wink. "I think she's a pretty nice kind of a girl now, myself."

"Yes, that's just about as much as you know about social life," said his wife. "You never had any yourself, you know."

"Well, I've managed to rub along fairly well and get money enough to support you in ordinary comfort and a little over. But I draw the line at those Bellinghams. If you like them, all right. Go and see them all you want to, but don't ring Pat and me in on them, that's all I ask. And if you can't produce any more manly boys than that

Bellingham irresponsible, I think Pat would be better off without any social contacts. Come on, Pat, if you want me to play tennis with you, now's your time before dark. Excuse us, won't you, mother?" and the two escaped from further discussion.

But that was not the last time the subject was brought up, for Mrs. Prentiss had no idea of giving up such a delightful thing as a cottage at the shore, and she kept ringing the changes on it until her husband said he guessed they would have to give up the plan for this time. He wouldn't be able to get away from his business very much and he didn't want his family away from him.

That was before they heard that Thorny must attend summer school if he wished to pass his finals and go on to graduate the next year. When that was told at the table one day Mr. Prentiss looked up with interest. And when two or three days later his wife announced in a grieved tone that her friend Mrs. Bellingham was going to the mountains for a month, he began once more to take an interest in a cottage at the shore. He said very little about it however, till one day he came home and announced that he had taken a nice little place right on the beach for a month, rented it furnished from a friend who was going abroad on business and wanted somebody to look after his house.

Mrs. Prentiss felt very dubious about it. A man, she told him, didn't know how to pick out a summer cottage. However, it was all picked out and she might take it or leave it, so she submitted, and Patricia had a glorious time with her father for playmate and no fear of running into Thorny anywhere. Her mother was fairly happy too, for the house was charming and so near the sea, and the only trouble with it was that there was no guest room. However, Mrs. Bellingham was away, so she settled down really to enjoy her family for once. Of course she did try to get Patricia off to a dance now and then at the hotels on the beach, but her father took her part, saying she needed to go to bed early and get well rested up for next winter's study. "The last year of high school is always the hardest, you know."

"And thank goodness, that will be over at last!" said Patricia's mother.

So the summer was comparatively free from annoyances, and there was plenty of outdoor exercise and play; a boat which she learned to row on the little lake near by, good swimming, tennis, a pony she had the privilege of riding twice a week, and best of all a time to rest in the hammock in the wide wind-swept porch, with a book in her hand and her eyes off to the sea, dreaming of the great things of life that were just beginning to touch her consciousness deeply, thinking of the future and what it might hold in store for her.

Sometimes as her eyes wandered to the far horizon, of an early evening, when the sea was pearly with its myriad lights, and its silver ripples looked like a pathway to Heaven, she got to thinking what Heaven would be like; would she always be wanting to do things up there that her mother did not think were right for her?

Then one day her father flung his evening paper down and left it on his chair when he answered his wife's call to come into the house for something, and the paper slid down and began to blow across toward the hammock. Patricia reached down and caught it in its flight, and as she smoothed its pages down and tried to crease them more carefully her eye caught a name among the death notices. "Worth!"

She caught her breath and stared at the page.

WORTH—John Graham Worth died today after a lingering illness at his home, Braeburn Cottage, Briarwood Road, Waverly Township. Services Thursday at two o'clock, interment private.

Patricia's eyes filled with tears as she read swiftly and then searched the page for other word. Yes, here it was.

Professor John Graham Worth, for ten years professor of Greek and Hebrew at Carrollton University passed away in the fifty-eighth year of his life. He was a graduate of Oxford University, England, and took his degree at Edinburgh University, Scotland. After serving for a time as teacher of Hebrew and Greek in his native land he accepted an urgent call to Carrollton University and was there till his failing health made it necessary for him to take an extended rest—

Patricia's head went down upon the paper and a soft sob came from her lips. She was seeing the fine sweet face of John Worth's father as he sat before the fire in his own cottage and talked with her. Seeing him seated at the table, laughing with his family over their bright repartee. Seeing his head bowed reverently as he prayed that earnest prayer which included her. She was hearing again the kindly words he had spoken to her, hearing his voice as he read those words of scripture.

And she had so hoped to be able to go back there some day and talk with him, ask him questions about the Bible he had started her to reading just by his gentle way of taking it as a word direct from God.

And now she could never talk with him again! He was gone! Up to God Himself, to whom he had talked so intimately in that notable prayer!

It seemed as if she had just discovered a great personal loss! Something that she had hoped was to have come into her life, that would never be hers now.

Oh, but there was eternity! Perhaps she could know him then, in Heaven!

And it wasn't as if it were a loss that she could mourn openly. Her mother, perhaps even her father, would not understand her weeping for an utter stranger of whom they had never heard. Oh, later, when she was a little older and knew how to explain things better she might be able to tell her father all about that storm and that wonderful day in Braeburn, and the gentle-man whom she would have liked to be her father's friend, but now, would he understand? Or was this one of those things that had to be experienced to be understood?

And her mother surely would think she was crazy to weep over a poor man who lived in a cottage among cabbages and lilies, even if he had been a notable scholar once. Her mother would never understand.

If she were only at home she might go to that service and show her sympathy to that dear family, the sweet lady who called him "feyther," he who had gone Home and left them now. And the wise courageous son! What would they do now? Oh, how her heart ached for them! How she longed to do something to show them her sympathy. How she wanted to go to that service. To get the feeling of that family who knew God so well, and to see the radiance she would surely find in their faces in spite of their sorrow.

Her father would take her tomorrow perhaps if she could manage to make him understand how much she wanted it. But her mother would make such a fuss about it, insisting on knowing every detail, how she came to know them, who John Worth was, and what school he attended. Patricia shrank in dread from the thought of the discussion she would bring upon herself if she tried to work that. And not only upon herself but upon her father also. No, she must not try that.

But couldn't she send some flowers? How could that be managed? She had money enough to pay for them, and flowers could be sent by mail or telegraphed. Nobody need know anything about it.

People from the neighboring cottage had come in to call. Her mother and father would be occupied for a little while. It wasn't far down the beach to the little drugstore where they had a telephone. She couldn't do it here in the cottage. Her mother would come rushing right out and demand to know who she was telephoning to, and what about. But couldn't she run down to the drugstore and telephone Mr. Mathison, the florist at home? He knew her, and would know how to get the flowers to the right place.

She picked up the paper again, searched for the date. This was last night's paper. Yes, the services were tomorrow.

Quick as a flash her decision was made. She slipped softly up the stairs to her room without attracting the attention of anyone. They were sitting on the west porch away from the village end of the beach. Quickly she got her purse and noiselessly hurried downstairs and out the side door. Then she flew up the beach in the soft moonlight that was beginning to get brighter every minute. It wouldn't take long. She could buy a box of candy and take it back to pass to them all as an excuse for going if they found out.

So she hurried through the silver brightness with her heavy young heart full of a new kind of trouble she had never known before. Trouble for those dear new friends of hers who were friends of God and one of whom had gone home to Him.

Having done her errand and bought her candy she came back quietly, watching the silver sea where it met the silver-blue sky, as if the gate of Heaven were off there and might possibly open while she looked, and let her glimpse in.

Back at the cottage again she went to the porch where they all were sitting and passed her candy, then she slipped away to her room, and undressing in the darkness knelt before her open window in her soft white robe, and looked across the sea. Laying her head down on the window sill she prayed.

"Oh God, dear Heavenly Father, help them to bear it. Love them and keep them, and make me Your child just as they are. Let us all meet up in Your Heaven. And please—if You don't mind worrying about a little thing, will You let my lilies that I sent tell that dear family how sorry I am for them, and how much I care?"

For Patricia had said to the florist: "Please, Mr. Mathison, if you have any, I'd like them to be lilies of the valley if possible. I know it's late for those, but couldn't you get them somewhere? It doesn't matter if they cost more, and send the bill to me, please, not to father."

So she prayed "lilies," though the florist had only said he would try.

A long time she knelt there and prayed, and when at last she rose and lifted her eyes to the far silver sea where the sky came down and touched, she could seem to see bright angels dimly standing by an open gate to let a new soul go Home.

One day when Mrs. Prentiss had gone down to the city on some errands a letter came to Patricia, forwarded from home:

Dear Patricia:

Mother and I thank you. Father would have been so pleased with the lilies. He liked you.

John.

Patricia was so glad that it came while she was alone. Now she would not have to explain.

The days went on, golden with sunshine, and the silver nights, and Patricia felt as if she were growing up.

"She is really lovely," said her mother to her father one night as they watched her walking down the sand ahead of them. "Too bad she has to spend another year in that silly school!"

But Patricia did not hear and walked sweetly on. She was studying her Bible daily now, and some of the words came gently to her on the wings of the wind as she watched that silver sea and sky: "The heavens declare the glory of God. . . . In them hath He set a tabernacle for the sun which . . . as a bridegroom . . . rejoiceth—" The Hebrew professor would never tell her now on this earth what some of those wonderful words meant in their original setting, but somehow her heart was beginning to know, as if God's Spirit was teaching her. As if just because she had the will to accept them all even before she understood them, the Spirit was graciously leading her to a wider place where she could see farther into their meaning, making her sure that these words were of God.

14

PATRICIA went back to school life in the fall with eagerness and zest. This was to be the best year of all, and she was looking forward to it. Her father had made it distinctly understood that she was not to be hampered in any of her school activities, and her mother with sighs had acquiesced, saying that of course it didn't matter much for just one year more, and then, thank fortune it would be over, and she would have her way with her precious child and try to undo some of the harm that had been done in all these young years.

So there was a different look on Patricia's face when she went back to school, and there was more freedom in her friendships with the other girls and boys, though to tell the truth she usually had very little to do with the boys except in gatherings of the whole class, for the boys were just a little bit afraid of Patricia. They had never quite figured out why she had disappeared from the picnic. Of course the storm had managed to take their thoughts away from the subject to a certain extent, but they had never been able to decide why she was not on hand at lunch time, nor for any of the games. Likely she was high-hat after all, and didn't want to tie up to them. They had not connected her disappearance with Thorny because he had come back complaining of a twisted ankle and a scratch in the face from briars. He had stayed and eaten what was left of his lunch with Della Bright, and had been generally annoying in little ways to the rest of them. But he had stayed with the crowd and had been the chief instigator in taking them all to the roadhouse for a refuge in the storm. It had also been Thorny's influence that had made the whole latter part of the day a riot instead of a time of innocent fun. Most of the quieter boys had taken their special girls and their sisters home as soon as the rain was over, but many of the others had stayed, willing enough to explore a side of life with which they were not familiar.

But now Patricia was eager to make the class feel that she was one of them, and to erase all memory of the unfortunate picnic. So she went faithfully to their parties. However, as the winter wore on she decided that she didn't enjoy dancing. There was too much familiarity about it.

But there were not many parties, and at least for this one year she was not expected to go to many festivities among her other set of acquaintances, which was a relief. Also Thorny was definitely out of things, word having gone out that he was attending a famous school in the far west, and Patricia was greatly relieved that she had not that problem to face.

So the winter went on in a pleasant whirl of work. Patricia loved study. She wanted to be at the head of her class, and she studied hard.

But there was one element missing in the school this year. John Worth was not there. As she looked back upon the past few years, she realized that she had never had much personal contact with him, very seldom even spoken to him for days and sometimes weeks at a time. But he had been there, a quiet presence, a strong influence upon his whole class, the admiration of the whole school, even since he had not been active in athletics. Now that he was only a memory they still boasted about him, as something of the past; but the fine flavor of each day seemed to be growing less and less. At least to Patricia, who had been wont to watch him from afar so long, and to think of his attainments as something to be emulated, to look toward his quiet strength when she was tired or excited, or uncertain—always those lamps behind John Worth's eyes had meant that to Patricia since first she saw them, and now she missed them every day.

Of course, there was now a still more pleasant personal memory to think back to, in that day she had spent in his home while the rain poured down. The day seemed framed in a rainbow at the end, and perfumed by the lilies she had carried home. But school now was just a little less than it had been because he was no longer there. And perhaps she would never see him again!

True, he had promised to come to see her sometime in the dim and misty future, but Patricia, in the months that had passed, had been learning to grow up in her thoughts. To realize that all that young people promise is not likely of fulfillment. That time changes even thoughts and wishes.

Since his father died it was rumored that John Worth was working full time now on Miller's farm. They said he was just going to be a common farm hand. That seemed too bad for the best scholar in high school, never to have a chance to go on and study further. The valedictorian! Imagine it! Somebody ought to have done something for him!

That was the way a few of the seniors talked.

Patricia when she heard it was sure in her heart that John Worth wouldn't have taken help from anybody. His father hadn't brought him up that way. The grand old college professor had not brought up his son to be a "softy." John Worth would help himself. Besides, just now he was probably taking care of his mother.

But Patricia didn't participate in any talk about him, and soon it died away. In time John Worth was all but forgotten by the new class that was coming on.

"But there isn't one in this year's class that is up to John Worth of last year," Patricia heard one of the old teachers say to another. "Not scholastically, anyway."

And Patricia's heart was glad that one worthwhile teacher recognized that.

There was plenty to do all that winter, however, and little time for regretting scholars of the past.

Patricia had a few more or less intimate friends among the girls in her class this year. Heretofore she had felt that she must not be too friendly because her mother would not let her bring the public school classmates to her home to visit her. But now her father's edict had gone forth most decisively and she had been told in her mother's presence that she might bring her friends there, and even have a party for them sometime during the year, so she felt more free and easy with them. She found the girls most eager to come and see her. They had always been curious about the big pretentious mansion in which she lived, and came home with her sometimes with great delight. They seemed to vie with one another to be her most intimate friend. So the days went by pleasantly, and Patricia felt her life was very full and happy.

But in the midst of it all she did not forget that little touch with the Worth family. She remembered how John Worth had told her that she could have family worship by herself, and every morning and evening she religiously read her Bible and knelt to pray, falling little by little into the habit of talking to the Lord as if He stood close by and she could see him. The mysterious beauty of those few hours spent in that consecrated home listening to the conversation of God's saints had made a deep impression, and she did not want to get away from it.

Deeper and deeper grew her thoughts as she went on reading her Bible and asking to be shown the right way in her life. All unknowingly she was more and more surrendering herself to the leading of the Holy Spirit, which makes for the understanding of the Word, until things she read grew always clearer to her mind, and stayed with her as she went through her days, and many a time when she might have made wrong decisions she was kept, and led aright.

But of her growth in grace she was as unconscious as a growing babe is unconscious of its physical development.

Yes though the girl herself knew nothing of the daily working of the Spirit within her, this was not hidden from those about her. Her father saw it first, and one day commented upon it thoughtfully.

"Our girl is getting sweeter and more lovely every day," he said.

He was perhaps only thinking aloud, and did not realize until his wife spoke up.

"She has always been sweet!" she snapped. "I can't see why you haven't understood what a very beautiful daughter you have. Perhaps if you had realized it more you would have been a little more careful how you subjected her to the influences of the common herd."

He was sorry at once that he had spoken, and he closed his lips and said no more about it, but he continued to watch his child from day to day and to wonder over her sweetness and gentleness, and how she patiently bore the nagging of her mother about unimportant matters, till she must have been tried almost beyond endurance. And once he asked her how it was that she contrived to keep her temper so much better than in former years when unpleasant things came, and she looked down shyly with a soft color in her cheeks and hesitantly said in a low wistful little voice:

"Perhaps it is because I asked the Lord Jesus to help me," and her lashes remained down upon her cheeks for an embarrassed moment. It was the first recognition between them of some special preaching they had been hearing together intermittently at their little church without a name, that was so unfashionable.

A great shyness and embarrassment came over the father and he did not answer for a full minute. Then in a low husky voice:

"Yes, I guess that must be it," he said and cleared his throat and looked away off in the distance for awhile. Then he added:

"I guess I'll have to try that way too."

Patricia looked up astonished, a great light coming into her face. Why, he was getting like that other father! Wouldn't it be wonderful if they could have that family worship in their home, too? But—what would mother say? Mother wouldn't hold with such an informal unfashionable thing as father kneeling down to pray at morning and at evening. Mother might be afraid that someone would come in to call.

But Patricia came over eagerly to her father and kissed him softly on his forehead and on his down-drooping eyelids and murmured softly:

"Oh, daddy, I wish you would! Wouldn't that be nice? You and me both! I'd love that, daddy!"

Somehow after that there seemed to be a closer bond between father and daughter that made life sweeter. It was as if the years during which the father had protected her were culminating in this sweeter fellowship, and the two understood one another as they never had before.

It was days after this first word was spoken between them about the spiritual life that the father asked her one night while they were sitting together alone for a little while:

"What started you on this religious line, Pat? Did you just get it from our little old-fashioned church, or what?"

And Patricia blazed out in a sweet bright smile, her eyes full of something lovely and deep.

"No, daddy, not altogether. At least—there was something else. You remember that picnic last year? The day the storm came up?"

"Oh, yes. I wasn't at home, was I? I was in New York. Someone took you you didn't like. Was it Thorny? I remember. Your mother said she would have been so worried if he hadn't taken you, but she knew you would be all right since you had the right kind of an escort. But how did that help you religiously? Were you scared?"

"Yes, I was scared," said the girl with downcast eyes, "but that had nothing to do with this. I was only scared because Thorny got me alone and then he took me in his arms and began to hug and kiss me in a horrid way. I got so frightened that I tried to scream, and he put his hand over my mouth and almost strangled me. At last I got away from him and ran as fast and as hard as I could, and I got away off from the rest, though I had thought I was running toward them all the time, till I found I was really lost. I fell down and almost knocked the breath out of me, and then I was afraid to look around lest Thorny was after me, so I just lay still. And I must have gone to sleep, for I was very worn out and excited, and then all at once I was wakened by a terrible clap of thunder. It startled me so I sat right up, and when I looked around there was somebody standing beside me, and I thought it was Thorny. I was so frightened I did not know what to do."

"The little whelp!" said Patricia's father angrily sitting up. "Why wasn't I told of this before? I would have given him a big horsewhipping! Why didn't you tell me at once?"

"Oh, daddy! Because I knew it would make mother so angry. Because she was so pleased that Thorny was taking me."

"But you should have come to me alone and told me. You poor little girl! Well, go on. What did Thorny do next?"

"But it wasn't Thorny," said Patricia with a sweet hazy look in her eyes at the memory, "it was John Worth. Do you remember him, daddy, at commencement last year? He gave the valedictory."

"I should say I do remember him!" said the father excitedly. "Don't tell me that nice refined-looking boy was unpleasant to you!"

"Oh, no, daddy! He was wonderful! The lightning was flashing terribly, and it had begun to rain hard and fast, and John just took off his sweater and stooped down and put it around my shoulders and then he picked me up like a baby and ran across the plowed ground with me to his own home! Such a sweet dear home with lilies of the valley all around, and a precious sweet-faced mother standing at the door to take me in! And that nice kind father sitting in his wheeled chair by a lovely fire on the hearth. And then John's mother took me in her room and wrapped me up in a scotch wool blanket while she ironed my clothes dry, and we had a lovely time by the fire, with hot gingerbread and milk and then supper.

John and I helped to get it, and it tasted so good. Hot scones and applesauce, and more gingerbread. It was wonderful! And they wheeled John's father up to the table, and after supper John gave him a big Bible, and he read a chapter and then prayed, just as if he knew God intimately. And afterward when John brought me home we talked about it and John said they did that every morning and evening. He called it family worship. And when I said I wished we did that he said of course I could do it by myself if I wanted to. And I do. And I think it has helped me. I understand the sermons at the church now. And it makes me a lot happier, daddy!"

Mr. Prentiss was still for quite a long time, until they could hear Mrs. Prentiss coming up the front walk talking to one of her friends who was evidently coming in to call, and then Mr. Prentiss drew a long sigh and said:

"Oh, little Pat, you ought to have had a father like that! I was brought up that way, and I ought to have kept it up, even if I had to do it by myself! I'm sorry and ashamed, little Pat! I guess your mother wouldn't have stood for it. But I ought to have done it anyway."

Patricia folded her arms lovingly around his neck and kissed him hard, whispering "Dear daddy." He held her close for just a minute, till suddenly they heard footsteps coming down the hall toward the library where they were. Patricia stepped back into the shadow, and her father quickly brushed the mist away from his eyes and said in a husky voice:

"I liked that man, Pat. We'll go and see him some day when we have time. I'd like to know him."

"Oh, but daddy, he isn't here any more. He's gone to Heaven. Last summer while we were away!"

"You don't say!" said Mr. Prentiss looking troubled.

"Now that's too bad! That was an unusual man, I'm sure. I thought when I saw him I'd like to know him."

"He was a professor in a college," said Patricia softly, for the footsteps were very near now, "and they had such a nice picture of the college, and a picture of Mrs. Worth's old home in Scotland. Oh, I wish you could have seen it!"

Then the door opened and Mrs. Prentiss swept in.

"For mercy's sake!" she said. "What are you two sitting in a dark room for? Why didn't you have a light? It's quite dark outside and high time the lights were on everywhere. It must look very queer to people passing outside to see no lights over the house. I wonder what the servants are thinking of."

That was the end of their talk that night, but Patricia and her father felt nearer to one another than ever after that.

15

TOWARD the end of the school year, Patricia, to her great surprise, became popular with the whole class, and three or four of the boys began to show her little attentions. The most daring of them took turns walking home with her, carrying her books, vying with one another to get first place.

She was always gracious and sweet, and most friendly, yet they never got to the place where they felt quite free to go in with her unless she asked them in, and then they would only go as far as the porch. They still didn't drop in at any hour of the day or evening as they did at the other girls' houses. They admired her, but she was still in a class by herself.

Patricia liked them all pretty well, some better than others of course, but none of them enough to want them around continually. She was content with things as they were.

One day her mother happened to be passing through the hall as Bramwell Brown stood at the front steps with her, talking about who should be on the decorating committee for commencement. Afterward her mother asked:

"Who was that good-looking young man with you at the door?" and Patricia answered, "That was Bramwell Brown."

"Do you mean he is from your high school?"

"Yes, mother. He's the prize debater, and sings in the class quartet."

"Really? As good-looking as that? I don't think I ever saw him before. Has he just recently come to town?"

"Oh, no," said Patricia. "He's been in my class since primary days. You probably never noticed him."

"Well, that's strange, as good-looking as that. He's almost as handsome as Thorny Bellingham! Who is his mother? Strange I never met her at the club or somewhere."

"You wouldn't," said Patricia half-smiling. "She's a dressmaker, mother, and lives down on South Street. She wouldn't have time to go to a club."

"A dressmaker! And one who lives on South Street! Well, Patricia Prentiss, I am amazed at you, that you would allow such a young man to attend you home! No matter how handsome he is you could certainly have made some excuse. I certainly am thankful that there are only two or three weeks of that dreadful school left. I don't know what your father can be thinking of to allow you to be exposed to things of this sort. But then of course the poor dear man doesn't understand social correctness, and never will, I'm afraid. Please don't bring that young man around again, my dear. I know, your father said you were to have freedom, but when it comes to somebody from South Street that certainly is the limit. What would my friends think if they saw such a young man attending my daughter? Patricia, I simply *can't* have it!"

"But mother! He wasn't tagged! He didn't have a placard pinned to his back saying he was from South Street, and you said yourself he was good-looking!"

"Don't be ridiculous, Patricia! Well, I suppose we can stand anything for the next few weeks and hope it will all be forgotten next year when you go away to college."

Little brushes like these were only occasional however, and Patricia lived from day to day happily.

Of course there was a big time over her commencement wardrobe. Mrs. Prentiss wanted an elaborate affair of chiffon with hand-drawn work in the waist and profusely edged with handmade lace, or else a lovely tailored white taffeta with a real lace overblouse. But Patricia would have nothing but a simple organdy.

"Mother, we're all dressing alike," she said gently with a smile. "You see, there are some who can't afford elaborate expensive dresses, so we voted to have everything very simple. Then everybody will be happy. And we're not having any lace at all, just simple lines, sort of tailored, with deep hems. Some of the girls are making their own, and we've chosen a very simple pattern, but I think it's going to be lovely. Then each one will wear the kind of sash, or belt she chooses. Some are having white organdy sashes. I'd like a white silk sash, I think. And then for class day we're wearing the class color, light green, or green and white."

"Do you mean you are going to look just like everybody else? *My* daughter going to look just like all the rest? I think that is *terrible!* Look just like some scrub woman's child!"

"Oh, no, mother! I'll have my own face, you know," laughed Patricia. "And we haven't a single scrub woman's child in the class! Betty Low's mother scrubs offices at night, but she is a soph, and won't graduate for two years. Besides, Betty is the prettiest girl in the whole school! Mother don't look so disappointed. It's just like a school uniform, you know, and I think it will look lovely having us all alike!"

"But you only graduate once, Patricia, and I've been planning on your dress all this year."

"Oh, yes, mother dear. I hope I'll graduate from college sometime, and you can spread yourself then, although I don't believe I'll like an elaborate dress even then. I don't think it is good taste. Always in stories I've read a graduating dress is a simple affair."

"Oh, dear me!" sighed the mother. "How simply impossible you have become! If I had known what a difficult child you were going to be I should have been so discouraged I would have given up at the start. Now take this matter of low heels, it's absurd to wear low heels like a child. And this awful party you are going to have. Whoever heard of a party without dancing? What on earth will you do all the time?"

"Oh, we have that all planned. Some lovely new games. I've been hunting them out all the year. They are going to be fun! Some of them are fascinating."

"Games?" said her bewildered mother. "You mean card games?"

"Not a card, mother dear, just cute funny games, and old-fashioned charades and things. Daddy has helped me telling me some of the games they used to play when he was a boy."

"*Daddy!*" said Mrs. Prentiss with contempt. "As if daddy knew anything that would be suitable for entertainment! I declare you two are the most impossible creatures that ever lived. But if daddy has helped you get this up I suppose it is quite useless for me to concern myself about it."

"Oh, quite, mother dear!" laughed Patricia again,

whirling away upstairs to complete her arrangements, and glad to escape further inquisition.

But the evening of the class party Mrs. Prentiss had a new grievance.

"What have you done with all the ash trays, Patricia?"

"Put them away in the closet, dearest," answered the girl promptly.

"Well, get them out, all of them and put them around. I certainly am not going to run the risk of having my lovely rugs and upholstery ruined by cigarette stubs and ashes everywhere. Of course they'll be smoking all the time."

"Oh no," said Patricia, "they won't. It isn't done at the school affairs, not when the teachers are present, and we are having three of our nicest teachers here. You needn't worry about ash trays. Besides, they all know how I feel about it. We'll just forget the ash trays, please."

"Oh, Patricia! You're so difficult! So that's where you get that queer idea about not smoking! You know you're going to have to learn to do it, now and then at least. Simply everybody does it."

"No!" said Patricia, "I'm not going to learn. I don't like it, and I think it is silly. I know daddy doesn't like it when you do it."

"There you go, condemning your mother. You think that is right, do you?"

"I'm not condemning you, mother, but—I just wish you didn't do it."

"But Patricia, if you don't smoke people are going to think you are very queer when you get out into society. You won't be smart at all!"

"I'm not anxious to get out into society," said Patricia, "and I wouldn't care to be thought smart. It doesn't seem a nice word to me. Come, mother, forget it, and let's have a nice time!" Patricia was very happy and her eyes were shining, her cheeks aglow. She was wearing a little pink frock and a pink rose in her hair. She was lovely.

"Nice time!" sniffed her mother. "Nice time at a low-down party, for a horde of children who don't know how to act at a party. But you do look beautiful, darling. Only, I wish you would run up to my dressing table and just put the weest mite of lipstick on your lips. Then you would look all right. Do that to please mother, won't you, precious?"

"Oh, no, please, mother," said Patricia firmly. "I want to be myself, not a prinked up society girl. I hate lipstick!"

"Oh, you perfectly impossible child!" sighed her mother. "Shall I ever be able to make anything out of you after this awful time is over?"

"I sincerely trust not," said her father in a low reverent tone as he came in the door just then. "You certainly ought to be satisfied with her the way she is now, Amelia. I never saw anything lovelier. In fact she looks a little as you did when you were her age," he added grimly. "I used to think you were the prettiest girl in the whole countryside."

"There, mother, listen to that!" said Patricia. "You ought to be satisfied with a compliment like that from our dear silent daddy!" And then Patricia escaped up the stairs laughing.

The party went off "with a bang" as Mr. Prentiss said afterwards, because everything had been so well thought out and prepared beforehand.

When the guests arrived and went down the line in the wide hall, Patricia stood first by the door to greet her classmates and introduce them, first to a grim reluctant mother who had pretended till the last minute that she did not intend to appear at all at the affair, and then to her smiling father.

Mr. Prentiss had his pockets full of little green ribbon bows with cards attached on which were written the names of characters about which they had all studied during the year. After he had laughingly, cordially, greeted each guest personally, he pinned one of the little bows to their backs and bade them go among the rest and find out by asking questions, just who they were supposed to be. Thus was the first awkward moment of stiffness avoided, and the guests made at home at once. So the line went rollicking down the hall, and Mrs. Prentiss watching each one critically failed to discover the bad manners and illiteracy she had expected to find in young people who had not had the privilege of Miss Greystone's Select School for Girls. She was quite surprised. One startling incident that made for her further astonishment was the fact that Della Bright was wearing an exact duplicate of the dress she had wanted to get Patricia for a graduating dress. Patricia's mother was amazed. Why, these girls looked just like other girls! And Jennie McGlynn was wearing the replica of a charming little imported pink organdy; Mrs. Prentiss did not guess that her mother had made it at night after her hard work of the day was over. The evident charm of the young people made Mrs. Prentiss unbend far more than she had intended. Besides, she was quite intrigued to see what was happening next. For her husband and daughter, failing in getting her co-operation, had not confided their plans to her, and she had been greatly distressed to know what on earth they would do all the evening if they did not dance. She had secretly told the servants to be ready at a moment's notice to serve the refreshments, if the interest should lag, and she had asked a friend who was a fine player for dances to be ready to run over and supply the accompaniment for dancing in case Patricia found she had to resort to that after all before the evening was over. Therefore she was amazed at the way everything moved on like a performance that had been rehearsed many times and was letter perfect.

She was even more nonplussed when she discovered by the conversation of the three teachers and the superintendent who had been the last of the guests to arrive, that she herself also was wearing one of those ridiculous name-bows on her back, and they were bursting with information to impart concerning her namesake.

But unfortunately Mrs. Prentiss had not been studying history nor the biographies of famous people that winter, and she found that the whole company were so much better informed about the person she was supposed to be than she was herself that she was in despair. These people all seemed to be remarkably intelligent. Perhaps after all there was something in what George had been reiterating all these years, that public school people were sharp and keen and well-informed. At least it was something she could say when she had to explain that her daughter had attended public school.

The first guest who discovered his identity was to ring a tiny bell. Everybody stopped talking when it rang, and one of the boys announced that his name was George Washington.

With prompt response Mr. Prentiss produced a small hatchet decorated with a bunch of artificial cherries as the prize. There was a good deal of laughter and then the guests turned with renewed zest each to find out who he was. It was great fun as one by one the guests solved the problem of his or her identity and received an appropriate prize. George Prentiss had enjoyed selecting those prizes.

It was all very gay, and the little bell rang over and

over as more identities were discovered, and then there followed other games, fully as well planned and just as happy.

Suddenly a halt was called and the company was asked to sit down. It was explained that ten of them, whose names were called, were wanted upstairs for a few minutes and while they were gone the rest of them were going to indulge in a game of old-fashioned stagecoach. Then each one was named some part of the outfit, and there began gay hilarity again. Even Mrs. Prentiss who had seated herself in a large comfortable chair hoping to rest a little found herself a bandbox, who had to jump up and turn around every time it was named. The story for the game was being ingeniously told by one of the teachers at Patricia's suggestion, and Patricia coming down the stairs to make an announcement about a charade that was to follow was moved almost to tears to see her smiling dignified mother earnestly whirling around as a bandbox, and then joining with the whole company in a common whirl as the word "stagecoach" was mentioned. Patricia felt that her mother was being the grandest sport ever, and was convinced in her heart that never again would she have such a terrible prejudice against the public school. She gave a little quick sigh as she wished, oh how she wished, that this party might have come sooner in her life. What happy years those would have been if mother only had been in sympathy with her school life.

But there was no time to regret anything now. Down the stairs in hastily improvised costumes, some of which had been thought out beforehand and left convenient for the purpose, came the people who had gone upstairs to get ready for their charade, and Patricia had to hurry into the room and shout out, "And the stagecoach tipped over!" Then she told them that a charade was to follow, a word of five syllables, in six acts, the last one portraying the whole word. Everybody settled down to one of the funniest performances they ever saw, with Mr. Prentiss as chief actor taking the part of an old-fashioned country school teacher.

When the word was finally guessed, and it wasn't an easy one either, ten more of the company were sent upstairs, in charge again of Mr. Prentiss as coach, and mysteriously a formation of chairs took shape straight across the room, set in place by alert boys. One of the teachers announced that they were going to play "Going to Jerusalem." Old stuff of course, that they all used to play in their kindergarten days, but it seemed just the thing with which to fill in the two or three minutes till the new set of charaders appeared. Patricia had another laugh of joy as she saw her stout mother, marching around the line of chairs to the gay music, grappling each chair as if it were her last hope of safety, and finally plumping down almost on top of the boy whose mother was a dressmaker. And it came to her suddenly, almost tenderly, that her mother was nothing but a grown-up child, getting back to play again and really enjoying it. So was father! And her heart thrilled again. They were really having a good time, and no Thorny Bellingham in on it either!

It was later, while they were seated at the long, long table in the dining room, eating the delightful refreshments which began with fruit salad and dainty sandwiches and ended with ice cream in molds and delightful cakes, that the door bell pealed through the house. The servant whispered to Mrs. Prentiss that there was a lady at the door who wanted to see her just a moment on some important business.

Patricia saw her mother frown, and look perplexed, and then slide her chair back and go out as quietly as possible. She wondered if the fly in the ointment had arrived at last. It seemed there had always been a fly in Patricia's ointment no matter how carefully she guarded it.

Mrs. Prentiss patted her hair into place as she crossed the living room and stepped out into the hall, brushing a possible cake crumb from her garments. And there it was Mrs. Bellingham! Standing on the porch in the shadow, trying desperately to twist her neck so she could see into the dining room.

"Oh, my *dear!*" she said gushingly. "So sorry to have troubled you. I thought of course you'd be upstairs and the waitress would tell me to go right up where we could talk uninterruptedly. I hadn't an idea you'd be down here participating in the festivities!"

"Oh, why *certainly,* I had to be down. I couldn't let Patricia have a gathering here of her schoolfellows and not be present, you know. Sorry, but won't you come in? I really must go back to the dining room before they miss me."

"Oh, no, I couldn't, thank you. I just ran in to tell you that we're expecting Thorny back next week and I'm arranging to give him a welcoming dinner. I wanted to ask if Patricia will be the hostess for me. I think it would be so precious to have one of his old girls for a hostess, and I had to be sure Patricia would do it before I go ahead. I want to send out the invitations early in the morning and I thought I'd put her name in the paper as hostess. Just some of Thorny's old friends, you know. People darling Patricia knows well. She will, won't she?"

"Oh, my dear! That's so sweet of you, but—what night did you say it is? Thursday? Now, that's too bad! That's the night of Patricia's commencement, and of course as she's graduating it's most important to her. I know she will be heart-broken, but she really couldn't, you see. If it was only the next night, you know—"

"It couldn't be the next night," said Mrs. Bellingham coolly. "Thorny is going on a fishing trip up to Nova Scotia and he leaves early Friday morning. Couldn't Patricia possibly get excused from that commencement? It's only a public school and I know you don't think much of it. I don't suppose Patricia would care about staying for the exercises, would she? She'd get her diploma just the same, and the exercises wouldn't matter, would they?"

"Oh, my dear! Patricia would be utterly heart-broken to miss her commencement. It is the goal for which she has striven all the years, and besides, they are really very nice young people indeed. We have been having a delightful time with them. Just come in and meet them, won't you, and you'll understand."

"No, really, I couldn't," said Mrs. Bellingham, quite coldly. "I didn't suppose you felt that way. I supposed of course I would be doing you a favor to get her out of it. I thought you didn't approve of the public school."

"Well, I didn't *choose* it, of course, but since Patricia has been working so hard through all these years, it would be quite disappointing to her to be unable to finish in the regular way. And, I must admit since I have come to know the young people, they really are quite charming. Sorry to disappoint you, darling."

"Yes? Well, I think Thorny will be deeply disappointed in your daughter if she refuses the highest honor I could give her at his coming-home party. I'm sure he has counted on Patricia. But people change. As I said when I heard you had consented to letting that sweet little girl attend a public institution, people change. And environment has a great deal to do with it. Well, goodbye. I won't detain you any longer."

Mrs. Prentiss went back to the dining room with a troubled mien. She was distressed that she had had to refuse her friend, and dear Mrs. Bellingham didn't seem to understand!

After she got back to her seat in the dining room and was finishing her ice cream which was in the form of a great white dove with a leaf of green in its yellow bill she began to think it over. That would have been a wonderful chance for Patricia to shine, being hostess at Thorny's party. But of course there would have been a terrible uproar if she had tried to put that over in the face of all her husband had said. Besides, it would be a pity to disappoint Patricia, she seemed so fond of all these nice young people, it was the last time she was to be with them. And really if Mrs. Bellingham wanted Patricia so much she could have managed it so that Thorny would stay over another day. Surely she would do something about it. Anyhow tomorrow would be time enough to think up a solution.

So Mrs. Prentiss enjoyed her ice cream and laughed with the rest over the comical after-dinner speeches. For Mr. Prentiss was acting the part of the toastmaster now, and calling on different ones to make speeches. And George was really very clever! His wife had never had a chance to hear him, when he went out to business dinners and banquets, though she had heard now and then that he had to speak and she had often wondered what he would find to say. But now she could see he was quite versatile, and it surprised her for he had been so silent through the years, except when he now and then broke forth in argument. She looked up at him in wonder and admiration. She almost fancied she saw in him some semblance to the George she married. Why hadn't he ever been willing to go out with her in her set, attend dinners and shine among the people she liked?

So she watched in wonder as George little by little got a speech or a funny skit of everyone present. Even the shyest girl among them sang a frightened little song. Several of the boys made good extemporaneous speeches on subjects he gave them. They really had a nice time and Patricia's mother beamed around on Jennie McGlynn and Della Bright and all the others, and quite enjoyed the admiration they gave her as Patricia's mother and the mistress of this lovely mansion. Mrs. Prentiss couldn't remember when she had had as good a time. It was just as interesting as a bridge party and one didn't have to think half as hard nor worry so much about whether one was doing the right thing.

So the evening went on to the last half-hour when the young people gathered around the piano and sang school songs, till even Mrs. Prentiss began to see why they loved their school. Patricia stood in the doorway with her father's arm about her and sang with all her might, and her father was singing too, some of the old songs that he used to sing when he was young; and how he enjoyed them.

They trooped out into the night under a bright moon, and after calling good night they stood in front of the house and sang:

> *Good night, Patricia, Good night!*
> *We've had a lovely time, Patricia,*
> *We like your people fine, Patricia,*
> *Good night, Patricia, Good night!*

The words rang out sharp and clear in the still moonlight and echoed all along the street, and even Mrs. Prentiss felt a thrill of exultation, during the instant of

stillness after the last note had died away. And then sharp
and clear there came:

> Pat, Pat, Patricia!
> Rah, Rah, Rah!
> You're the real thing
> And that is why we sing!
> Pat, Pat, Patricia!

Patricia stood there with her eyes shining and tears
very near the surface. When they began "Pat, Pat, Pat,"
Patricia winced. She was so afraid her mother would
object to their calling her that.

But Mrs. Prentiss with her head high and satisfaction
in her eyes only said:

"There! I hope Mrs. Bellingham heard that!"

16

THE actual commencement was almost a heart-break to Patricia. Now that she had just come to the place where they loved her, and seemed to believe in her and understand her, it was the end, and she would see them no more. But she went quietly, sweetly through the rest of the days. The class day had its sadly gay pleasantries, when all of them felt their relationship together in a class as they never had before, looking into a new, strange, almost awesome future and wondering what it was to hold for them. College for some, business for others, teaching, and perhaps homemaking for most of them. They realized as they gathered for the final evening affair that they were standing at that strange place between childhood and grown-up life; that tomorrow, when though they might look the same, act in the same way, even feel the same, they would be different. Life would be all changed for them. They would no longer take their way in the early mornings down the wide pleasant street to the great spreading brick schoolhouse to spend their days, happily working and playing, learning and being merry. They would no longer meet one another day after day, knowing pretty well what was to be in the next hour, the next day, the next month. The future was all untried for them, and Hope stood wide-eyed at the door to lead them on, to joy or disappointment.

Patricia had an essay to read on the meaning of life. She had written it with much care, finding many things in her Bible reading that helped her to write. Her English teacher had looked at her curiously after reading it, and asked her if she really believed in God as she had said in her essay, or whether that was just imagination. Patricia looked at her with earnest eyes and said that she really did believe, that God had seemed to be very near her as she wrote, and she honestly believed that God had a plan for each life, and if one missed it by wanting one's own way instead of His, it was harder in the end.

The teacher looked at her almost wistfully, and said:

"Well, Patricia, it is very beautifully written, and since you really believe that, we'll leave it as it is. I wish I could believe that myself." And she sighed heavily and looked very sad. Patricia prayed about her that night when she got home, but at the time she only answered:

"Well, it's only what the Bible says. It's all there. I think if you will look for it you will find it yourself. It makes life a lot lovelier for then you find out it's all true." And then with a smile she had slipped away with her paper. But she had studied over her essay a great deal and prayed over it too, and when the time came for her to give it she did not need to read it. With her wide eyes upon that unexpectedly large audience she simply spoke those words that were written from her heart, for somehow she had a feeling that she must bring them all her message and convince them of its truth.

And once as she looked about upon that sea of faces, she was sure she saw John Worth's face, away at the back under the gallery in a shadow. He was tall, and a good deal thinner, as if life had taken hold upon him, and there were grown-up trials he had to face. But the lamps were in his eyes, lighted, and shining straight into hers for a single brief second as their glances met. It was just as she was giving her last-few words, and somehow she knew he liked what she had said. Then she was done, and had to bow and go back to her seat while the hushed audience suddenly broke forth into applause. She didn't want that applause. It seemed so out of place. Their silent listening had been so much better.

And then when attention was taken from her and she might look for John again, he was no longer there. Afterwards she heard one of the sophomore boys say:

"John Worth was here. Did you see him, Sam?" And Sam replied, "Yep, I saw him once, but then he disappeared."

"Yeah, he said he had to go back to stay with his mother. She wasn't well and he didn't like to leave her alone away out there near the woods."

Patricia was glad that he had been there that she might speak to him in that way, since there was no other. Their paths would probably meet no more, but she had let him know she was doing her best to walk God's way, the way his father had started her on that day last year when it rained and the rainbow shone over the garden walk.

But there were other pleasant things to think about also. Patricia's father and mother had both been at commencement, and had enjoyed it. Mrs. Prentiss had been very proud of her daughter, even if she was arrayed in an absurdly simple frock, with a soft white sash about her waist and a wreath of tiny white rosebuds binding her hair. Perhaps it was just as well she was simply dressed. It gave her even more distinction! And on the whole it was a rather pleasant thing to look back upon. The common school had been a trial but it was over now, and she need have no further thought about it. She must begin on Patricia at once and get her ready to go into the social world in the proper manner. Perhaps she wasn't so harmed by the school as she had feared. At any rate she would say no more, and likely Patricia would be all the more tractable now this ordeal was so beautifully over and she had nothing to regret.

Alone together the next day Mr. Prentiss told his daughter how pleased and proud he had been, and shyly commended the subject of her address.

"I liked it, Pat. I'm glad you had the nerve to say those things about God and trying to serve Him. It made me feel I'd done right after all to insist you should go to that school. I used to worry about it sometimes when mother would rave so. I would get to thinking maybe it wasn't important after all to keep you out of that nonsensical world your mother had got into after we began to have money. But now I'm glad. I wouldn't choose anything better in all the world than to have you feel that way about life, and I mean it. I don't want you ever to forget how I liked that, Pat! And I'm glad you've had the discipline and training of that school. I feel you've got hold of something that makes you see things in their proper values. I'm glad we stuck it out, Pat, and I think your mother doesn't feel so bad about it now, either. Especially since she got acquainted with some of the scholars."

But Patricia in her heart knew it was not any school that had taught her the things her father was glad about. She knew it was that day in that sweet home with the man who knew God, and talked with Him so intimately. She knew it was the sweet Scotch mother, and the boy who loved the Lord too, who had led her to study the Bible and pray for guidance. Though if she hadn't gone to that school she probably never would have known

John Worth, and would never have gone to his home that day in the rain to hear the truth. So in a way the dear old school that she loved so truly had been a strong element in the shaping of her life thus far.

It was quite late the next afternoon before Mrs. Prentiss came back to the daily order of life enough to remember about Thorny and his party which did not seem to have materialized. At least Thorny had not appeared on the horizon so far. What had happened? Perhaps she should call up her friend and find out. It might be that she had been unpleasantly hurried when Mrs. Bellingham came in to give the invitation, and she was hurt. She must apologize, but first she must tell Patricia and get some adequate expression of regret from her and of gratitude for the honor, and so on.

But even the possibility of Thorny in the offing could not dim Patricia's happiness. She had accomplished her aim. She had graduated with honor from the same school her father had attended, and he was pleased. Whatever lay in the future did not so much matter now. There would be a way out of hard things, and she was learning to trust unpleasant things to God. He always helped when she called upon Him.

"Oh!" she said looking blankly at her mother when she told her. Then her face cleared and shone radiant. "Oh, mother dear, I'm so glad you didn't tell me before. It would have spoiled everything to be afraid all the time that Thorny would turn up and ruin things the way he spoiled the picnic that day. I could hardly have stood it. I'm so glad it's over and you didn't try to make me go. That would have been awful!"

"Of course, dear, I understand that," said her mother with an appearance of always having been right in her judgments and decisions. "But you just must get over that idea about Thorny. You know it was really my fault he went that day. I was afraid to have you off there in the woods without anybody to guide you. You must understand that, little girl. Of course I didn't realize that these other young people were as nice as they are. But you will feel differently about Thorny when you get a little older and realize how truly fine he is and what a family and station in life he has, and all that. So do be polite to Mrs. Bellingham and tell her how honored you feel that she wanted you for hostess, and how sorry you are that it wasn't possible for you to come."

But Patricia shrank back.

"I couldn't, mother, really. You don't know how I feel. And if you had been there for just a minute and seen how Thorny hugged me up and—oh, mother, I can't tell you. It was too horrible—! It was so much worse than any snakes or tramps or anything could have been."

"Silly little girl!" said her mother indulgently. "Some day you will understand that that was only admiration and real liking that made Thorny want to kiss you. He is growing up himself, you know, and you really are a very beautiful girl. I'm sure it won't make you proud for me to tell you so. You are foolishly backward and have quite an inferiority complex. Some day you'll get over that and want Thorny to show you attention. Now, dear, go tell Mrs. Bellingham!"

"No!" said Patricia sharply. "I will not talk to Mrs. Bellingham. I don't feel honored and I am not sorry, and I can't say what isn't true. You'll have to tell her what you feel, or else let it go as it is. I wish you would do that. I don't want to have anything more to do with the Bellinghams."

"Well, all right, dear," said her mother fondly, "have it your own way for the present. You are all wrought up anyway with all the excitement. Never mind, I'll talk to Mrs. Bellingham myself."

So Patricia went up to her room and took her turbulent young heart to the throne of God where she was learning to find quietness and peace. And her mother went to the telephone and discovered from the maid that Thorny Bellingham had not come home at all. He had gone straight up to Nova Scotia and had telegraphed his mother he would not be home till fall. Mrs. Bellingham, the maid said, had gone into the city shopping, to send Thorny a lot of fishing tackle and sports clothes he had ordered her to get.

Mrs. Prentiss hung up the telephone. Well, that was that! Now she had gone on record calling up, and a few days later she would invite Mrs. Bellingham over for tea, and everything would be all right.

That evening Mr. Prentiss came home and suggested that they take a trip somewhere. They could go to the mountains and get a real rest for Patricia for a few days, and then they could drive around in the car and stop wherever they liked. How about day after tomorrow? Could they start as soon as that? He wasn't sure yet that he could make it but he would try and if they couldn't go then they would start the next morning, though late afternoon was a nice time in hot weather to start on a trip. A short drive the first night, then dinner in some hotel, and a nice quiet night in the mountains.

Patricia's face shone. That was so nice, and no one around to have to go along. Mrs. Bellingham had gone west to visit her sister. She had called up to say good-bye.

So Patricia began the next morning to get ready. There was a little shopping to be done, at least her mother thought so, and Patricia loved to shop.

They got home late that afternoon, and Patricia was pleased with all her purchases. Her mother hadn't insisted as much as usual on dressy things. Patricia really was more of the ingénue type, she decided, after meditating on commencement and its simple tailored styles. Perhaps those things really suited her best.

So Patricia was allowed to pick out the things she liked best, and came home delighted with her new clothes.

A couple of the girls from her class ran over that evening to make a party call, and just as they were leaving, as the three walked slowly down from the house to the gate, one of them said:

"Oh, Pat, you remember John Worth in last year's class, don't you?"

"Yes," said Patricia quietly. They were passing by the spot where John Worth had planted the valley-lilies and she felt as if they could hear.

Well, had you heard that his mother died? You know she wasn't well the night of our commencement and he had to go back home after just a few minutes."

"Yes," said Patricia, "I heard he was there a few minutes. When did she die?"

"This morning. Jim Tanner heard it and told my brother. He said she had some heart trouble."

"Oh, I'm sorry for John," said Patricia trying to keep her voice steady. "She was such a sweet woman!"

"Oh, did you know her?" asked the other girl looking at her curiously.

"Yes," said Patricia. "She helped me get dry after I was out in that awful storm. She was a dear lovely lady. She was Scotch and had such a pleasant voice. His father was a college professor. Did you know that? They had a picture of the college, and a picture of his mother's home in Scotland. It was a lovely place."

"Say, that's tough luck for John though," said one of the girls. "They say he was just devoted to his mother."

"Yes, I guess he was," said Patricia. "His mother loved him very much too."

"Well, he was some kid. My brother says he was the

best all around man our high school ever had," said the girl Jennie. "Well, I've got to get going. I promised my parents I wouldn't stay late. Hope you have a lovely time, Pat. Give my love to all my friends you meet," she giggled, and then they went away.

And Patricia, with a sudden heavy load of sorrow upon her heart went softly in between the trees and the hedge and knelt down by the broad dark leaves of the valley-lilies, laying her hand upon one leaf as if it had been a child's head, and prayed softly:

"Dear God, comfort John, and help him in this hard time."

Then she went into the house and up to her room.

A long time she lay there in her bed before she went to sleep, thinking about the sweet Scotch mother who had gone home to Heaven and had left her wonderful boy all alone. What would John do now?

The next morning she went down to the village quite early. She told her mother she had an errand she wanted to do before she went away. Her mother was busy with the dressmaker who was altering a dress she had bought the day before, and didn't pay much attention, so Patricia slipped away without any trouble.

She went down to Mr. Mathison her florist friend, and bought a great box of madonna lilies and blue delphiniums the color of Mrs. Worth's eyes. Then she took the box herself and walked up the long dusty road to the place where she and John had climbed the fence. Would she know the way to the house again? Oh, she must find the way! If daddy hadn't had to hurry away so early this morning to make the arrangements for them to leave on their trip that night she would have asked him to take her. Or would she? Somehow she felt she might be embarrassed to go with her father, and she hadn't any idea how to reach that cottage where they lived except across the meadows. So she plodded on, soft tears falling now and then, and great pity growing in her heart for John who was alone now, with his own life to shape and his own way to make. What could she say to comfort him if he was there?

But he knew the place of comfort, better even than she did.

Perhaps he would not be there, and then she would just leave the flowers to speak for her. She had brought a card with her name written on it and just the words, "I am so sorry for you. She was dear and I loved her." But she had hidden it shyly in her pocket where she could get it if he wasn't there.

She found the fence where they had crossed that evening under the rainbow. She tried to climb, and found it more difficult than when he was helping her, but at last swung her feet over, and clambered down into the soft grass. She had dropped the box over first. Then she picked herself up, and took her box, starting toward the brow of the hill over which they had come from the house. The distant gray chimney against the sky guided her.

But she walked slowly, finding tears in her eyes continually. What was she going to find in the little gray house over the brow of the hill? Death was there, and she had never seen death. In all her sheltered life death had not come her way. When it touched her family, or sometimes her acquaintances, her mother had always been there to decree that it wasn't necessary for her to go to funerals yet. Life was sad enough later on, and the young should keep away from the thought of death as long as possible.

So as she walked slowly over the uneven ground she was trying to prepare herself for the dreadful phenomenon of death.

It was very quiet as she at last reached the garden and walked up the path from which her own lily-bells had come. The house seemed still, as it would be of course when it had to entertain a guest like Death.

And yet the sun was shining and there was a quiet homelikeness about the place, the dear place that had seemed so sweet and charming that one afternoon that she had spent there. Her heart suddenly smote her that she had not come sooner. She had fully intended to come again of course, but the winter had been so full, and she had felt shy about going, almost as if that other visit had all been a dream. But why hadn't she come right after commencement, after she heard that John's mother wasn't well? Oh, why hadn't she come then to see if there was anything she could do? How sweet it would have been to see her once more, and get a little word from her to remember.

So she came to the door, the plain little cottage door. There was no crepe on it, no elaborate wreath of flowers. It did not need that sign to tell that the house mistress was gone Home. There were perhaps very few friends to come away out there. Nobody but John to see after the tender rites!

How her heart ached for John. Would the lamps in his eyes have gone out, quenched by his sorrow? For she seemed to know his sorrow would be very great, especially coming as it did a little less than a year from the death of his wonderful father!

And now she was standing before the door! She felt uncertain what to do. Did one knock? There was no doorbell.

While she hesitated, puzzling over what to do, the door opened, and there stood a rugged-faced woman with toilworn hands. She knew at once that it must be Mrs. Miller, the farmer's wife, where John worked. She had seen her once when she came to school to see about why her son Charlie didn't get promoted. Patricia was sure it was the same one.

The woman eyed her with a stolid glance, taking account of her dainty garments, wondering. Patricia felt suddenly confused. She lifted a pleasant wistful look to the woman's gaze.

"I've brought some flowers," she said gently. "Is—can I see—? Isn't John here?"

The woman gave her another searching glance and stood back.

"They're in the living room," she said drearily. "You c'n go in ef you like."

The girl hesitated. Should she venture to go in without being announced?

But the woman had no notion of announcing her. She wiped her hands on her apron and went back into the kitchen, turning as she closed the door to say:

"Just go right on in!"

Patricia felt a great awe upon her, but she walked slowly over to the door and turned the knob, opening it just a crack, and then a little wider.

The casket was in the middle of the room, almost where the table had been spread that night. Just a plain wooden box with a scant black drapery put about it by the undertaker. Beside it knelt the boy, his head down on his hands that rested on the edge of the casket. The fire was out on the hearth, and there was a desolate emptiness about everywhere. Patricia noticed that the pictures were gone. It gave her a sad lonesome feeling as she drew near to the casket and stood looking down at the sweet face that lay there, so still and lovely, like an angel. Did death always do that to people, make them look like supernatural beings? She stood silently before the evidence of death, and saw in it more than death.

Life! A new kind of life, eternal life, that could never fade away.

Then as she continued to stand gazing at that sweet dear expression, that she would always remember, after a moment John raised his head and looked at her. And suddenly the lamps in his eyes lighted for her.

"You have come to her!" he said in a great wonder. "She will be so pleased—if she knows—and I think she does!"

"Oh, how I wish I had come before!" said Patricia, coming closer. "I loved her, and I thought about her a lot, and how sweet she was to me. I always meant to come, but I wasn't quite sure whether—that is—if she would like me to."

"She would," said the boy earnestly. "She often spoke of you. She thought you were very lovely. She enjoyed that day you were here. She loved getting supper for you."

"Oh, and how I loved being here and having her doing nice sweet things to help me. I shall never, never forget her."

Patricia was weeping now, the tears plashing down her cheeks.

"How sweet she looks," she said huskily, "just as if she were walking into Heaven."

"She did!" said the boy, and his voice choked. "She knew she was going. She said good-bye, and she said 'I'll tell feyther all aboot ye, laddie!' She was a wonderful mother!" The boy's face suddenly went down upon his folded arms again on the edge of the casket, and his shoulders quivered with his sorrow.

Patricia came over quite near to him and laid her hand upon his bowed head.

"Yes, she was!" she said softly.

The boy reached up his hand and laid it gently upon

hers, pressing it lightly as if to show her that it comforted him.

They stood so for an instant and suddenly he lifted his tear-wet face and smiled at her.

Then Patricia gravely stooped and laid a kiss softly on his forehead. It seemed a right and holy thing to do.

Suddenly into the silence there came the distant sound of the woman's footsteps. She was coming toward the room.

"I brought some flowers," said Patricia quickly. "I thought perhaps we might put them about her, if you'd like to."

The boy arose and stood beside her. When the woman opened the door they were taking the flowers out and laying them about the edge of the casket, great white lily branches, framing her sweet face, and blue flowers in between. The boy had taken a single lily and was folding it in her hands.

"How she loved them!" said her son as he gently turned the lily so it seemed to be looking up at her.

The woman watched them curiously for a moment, the lovely girl and the sorrowing boy working together. Then she said in a voice that seemed to have lost some of its harshness:

"They've come! The car is at the door and the undertaker is in the other room."

"Oh!" said the boy as if an agony were torn from him. Then with a great effort controlling himself he turned to the girl and said:

"I'm taking her down to our old home to lay her beside father. Her old pastor is there and he will have the service down there. She planned it that way for father."

"That is nice," said Patricia softly.

She stepped to the side of the casket again and bent over to the sweet dead face among the flowers.

"Good-bye," she said softly, "I'll see you again in our Father's House."

Then she turned and went quietly out of the room. A man was standing there waiting, the undertaker she supposed. John went with her to the door.

"I never can thank you enough for coming," he said, "and for the flowers. And I'll be seeing you—sometime!"

Then the man claimed his attention, and Patricia went quickly down the hill, and across the meadow. When she had climbed the fence she looked back and saw the funeral car start away from the door, out upon its long journey. And the next time she looked back she saw a great moving van leaving the house. What did that mean?

As she went on her way, the long walk in the sunshine toward home, she pondered on life and death, and the wonder of the peace upon that sweet dead face.

When she got home her mother was in a great to-do about her.

"Why, Patricia, where in the world have you been? I can't understand your being so inconsiderate today when we have so much to do to get ready to go! Your father has telephoned that he thinks he can start about five, and I need your help."

"I'm sorry, mother."

"But where in the world have you been?"

"I went to take some flowers to that dear lady who took care of me in that storm the day of the picnic."

"Now, how silly, Patricia, when you could just as well have sent them to her from the florist's, or you could have taken them to her yourself when we get back. Having waited so long a few weeks more wouldn't have mattered."

"But she is dead, mother! I wanted to say good-bye to her."

"Patricia Prentiss! You haven't been alone to a house of death, have you? You didn't go in a bright dress like that to a funeral? You have no sense of the fitness of things at all."

"But she wouldn't have minded, mother, even if she could have seen, so what did it matter? And it wasn't a funeral anyway. They were taking her away to her old home. I was in time. That was all I cared."

"Well, if you're not the strangest child. I don't know where you get your peculiarities. You couldn't have dragged me to a house of death when I was your age. Now, hurry and get your suitcases packed. Daddy said he might come any minute if he got through what he is doing, so we've no time to waste."

So Patricia packed her things, and then went back and repacked, putting in more things which her mother thought she might need. She went patiently through the day, and got gravely into the car late that afternoon beside her father, silent for the most part, thinking of that brief lonely funeral train winding down the hillside, and the boy with his heavy heart sitting beside the driver. The boy she had sent on his way with a tender little kiss of sympathy.

Tomorrow she would tell her father all about it. But not now. Mother wouldn't understand and would ask so many questions. But daddy would understand. When he and she were all alone she would tell him.

17

THAT was a happy summer for Patricia.

The unwonted vacation in the company of her father filled her with delight, and the entire absence of Thorny from the scene did much to help her forget the unpleasant happenings of late which had made his company so offensive. She had a joyous time and was more unhampered than she had ever been in her life, mainly because her father had plenty of time to be around watching, and kept so in touch with her that there was no opportunity for her to be forced into social obligations that she did not like.

She played tennis and golf; she went swimming and canoeing and rowing and hiking; she climbed mountains, and exulted in the great out-of-doors.

And when her mother would reproach her about not dancing with the other young folks in the evening in the hotel, her father would say, "Let her alone, Amelia! She knows what she wants to do. Why force her? She has been exercising all day, and is healthy and happy. Let her get to bed early if she wants to, and be ready for another gay wholesome day. Why insist on dancing?"

And Amelia would say petulantly, "Oh, George, you don't understand. Patricia will grow up without any poise or social training. She won't have any friends, and won't be invited anywhere, and will just be a social flop."

"Let her flop, Amelia, if that's what she wants. She's having a good time. And as for friends, she appears to have plenty of them. I hear them calling for her all over the place."

"Oh, George! How impossible you are! Haven't you noticed they are all girls, or else children? Not a young man among them. And Patricia is quite grown up. All of sixteen, and going to college in the fall. She isn't a child any more."

"Then let her be a child as long she can and will," sighed her father. He wasn't relishing the thought of his girl going away to college. The house was going to be very empty without her.

"There'll be boys enough around before long, goodness knows, mother, and I'm not in a hurry to see them! At least not the kind you seem to admire. So let her alone!"

And the days went on happily enough, with plenty of time to rest and read her Bible, to dream a little over the past, and to catch her breath over an unknown future of college which she wasn't at all sure she was going to enjoy. Not that she did not enjoy study. It was the college life she wasn't sure of. Would she like it, or would there be a lot of girls like Gloria and Gwendolyn? The college was one her mother favored. She was going there because there was no point in just refusing to go where her mother wanted her to be merely on general principles; and she knew very little about any of the colleges. Of course several of her class in high school were going to college, but they could not afford the high class institution Mrs. Prentiss had chosen. Most of them were going to a small cheap college nearby where they could come home every night or at least for week-ends.

So Patricia had acquiesced in her mother's decision, and let her mother revel in selecting curtains, cushions, and adornments for her room. It was almost as if Amelia were going to college herself, the way she was planning things. Patricia smiled and looked on, though in her heart she was a bit troubled. It seemed to her as if she were leaving everything she loved behind.

Often at the hotel that summer when she went up early to her room while gaiety was going on below-stairs, she would sit and read her Bible for a little while. Then, turning out her lights would drop down beside her low window sill to gaze off to the eternal hills, and think of some of the pleasant days that were past. Quite often a vision of John Worth came to stay with her a little while; she thought of the day in the rain, how he had sheltered her, wrapping her in his own coat, carrying her to safety; how he had hovered in the shadow the day of her commencement; how he looked kneeling there beside his mother's coffin; the kiss she had put on his forehead. They all seemed holy memories. And then that small funeral procession vanishing down the hillside. How she wished there had been a way for her to go along to that service, but of course there wasn't. Unless she had dared to tell her father. He would have done something. But she hadn't even asked where they were going. And mother would have made a terrible fuss. Just to a funeral of an unknown person. Mother didn't approve of funerals. Not for her, anyway.

Then she would sigh and think of the brightness in that sunset after the storm. She thought the heavenly city would be like that in the distance when one was going Home.

These were not morbid thoughts. To her, going to Heaven was something beautiful to anticipate. Something sure in her dim uncertain future, something that could never be a disappointment.

Then she would kneel and ask God to teach her, and softly, shyly, ask Him to keep John Worth when he had to come back to a lonely house. Would he stay there? She wondered that often. Would he have to keep house for himself? And go on working on Miller's farm always?

The next morning she would get up early with glad eyes and plunge into the delights of another glorious day in the woods, or on the stream, or flying about the tennis court.

One day her mother called her up on the porch to meet two young men who had just come in on the train that morning.

"Archie Dunwoody, and Harold MacCardy, darling," she said, as if Patricia ought to be overwhelmed with just the mention of them. "They are the sons of two of my very best girl friends when I was in college the way you will be in a few days now, you know," and she gave Patricia a warning smile. It was a smile so like the one she had worn the day she brought Thorny on the scene for the picnic that the daughter took warning and looked sharply from one to the other. Patricia wasn't particularly impressed with either young man. They seemed too sophisticated for her simple taste. But she obediently went with them down to the tennis court and played "a smashing good game for a girl" as they condescendingly told her, the while they mopped their sleek foreheads and toiled up the slope to the hotel for lunch. But Patricia still did not care for them. They smoked too many cigarettes and said contemptuous things about the people she liked best. Then they informed her that they were going to show her a good time that evening in return for giving them such good tennis that morning, they were going to see that she had either the one or the other of them for a partner at every dance that evening.

Patricia turned unenthusiastic eyes on the two and observed them coolly. She was looking very pretty herself, with her hair in little careless rings about her forehead from the exercise, and a fine natural color in her cheeks. She always had a cool look even on a hot day, and she smiled distantly.

"Thank you," she said calmly. "I'm sure you're very kind. But I'm not especially fond of dancing, and I'll not be down this evening."

"Oh, but you must come down," said the one called Harold. "I'll guarantee to teach you to like dancing. I can show you all the newest steps, and we'll be the talk of the evening."

"Oh," laughed Patricia, "I've been to dancing school all my life and I probably know as many steps as you do, but that doesn't make me like it. And I really shouldn't enjoy being the talk of the evening. I think you'll have to excuse me. But dad and I are climbing the mountain tomorrow morning, starting at five. I think he would be glad to have you join us if you care to."

"Climbing!" exclaimed the two in unison.

"Now don't be unkind!" said Harold. "Dance all night and then climb a mountain at daybreak! If that's your idea of a good time it isn't mine."

"Nor mine," echoed Archie. "If I get down to breakfast by nine after dancing half the night, I'll be surprised."

"Sorry," smiled Patricia. "I hope you have a pleasant evening," and she walked airily off toward the elevator. The two young men stared after her in astonishment.

"Well, now, how do you make her out?" asked Harold. "Her mamma said she was just a little school girl not yet in society. But she sounds like an old hand. Is she deep and experienced, just taking us out for a ride, or is she merely honest and blunt?"

"Search me," said Archie. "I only know she's the best girl tennis player I ever met, and I don't care to have to play her again, not in vacation. I'm absolutely all in, and that isn't what I call a vacation."

Wearily they dragged themselves to their rooms, and rested awhile before they came down to the dining room. But Patricia washed her hands and face, smoothed her hair a bit and hurried down with a good healthy appetite.

"Well, did you have a good time, dearest?" beamed her mother, already seated at the table with her husband. "How were the boys?"

"Not so hot, mother. Dad can play all around them."

"Patricia! What an expression! 'Not so hot!' I am surprised. Will you ever get over the effects of that school?"

"Excuse me, mother," said the girl smiling, "I didn't realize you would object to that. It is so expressive! But speaking more classically, the young men were not very good players. They didn't seem to care to exert themselves, and I had a terrible time holding myself back to be polite and not beat them too badly. Dad, we'll have to get in a set sometime this afternoon just to relieve the tension. Mother, were those boys' mothers like them?"

"What do you mean, Patricia?" asked her mother severely. "Are you trying to be unpleasant? What was the matter with those boys?"

"Oh, no, I'm not trying to be unpleasant, but mother, they seemed sort of sissyfied to me."

"There, George, you see. Patricia thinks that all boys who didn't go to the public school, and had the misfortune to be brought up gentlemen, are sissies."

"Oh no I don't, mother," said the girl quickly with a

warning look at her father. "We had a few sissies in the high school too. I suppose they are everywhere. But you don't have to play tennis with many of them, thank fortune!"

"Now, Patricia, I do hope you'll be polite to my old friends' children."

"Of course, mother. But say, mother, why don't you get dad to drive you up to the mountain he and I climbed yesterday? It's gorgeous! You won't see anything as beautiful as that till you get to Heaven, really, mother."

"Oh, for pity's sake, don't be so gruesome, darling. No, I don't want to climb mountains, even in an automobile. It gives me the creeps. By the way, Patricia, I wish you'd run into the little dress shop just off the lobby right after lunch. I want you to try on that little green dance frock they have there. It's a perfect confection, and I've had it laid aside for you. I thought it would be nice if you could wear it tonight, now that you'll have two really good partners to dance with."

"Oh, but mother, I don't need another dance frock, and I'm not going to dance tonight, or any of the nights here. I'm tired of dances and I'm having a grand time. Daddy and I are taking a hike in the moonlight tonight, aren't we daddy? We're getting acquainted all over again. Why don't you try that with dad, mother? He's awfully nice. Just go out and do some of the things you used to do together when you first knew each other. I think that would be fun!"

Mrs. Prentiss looked up and met her husband's questioning eyes upon her.

"Would it, Amelia?" he asked searchingly.

She colored and dropped her eyes, and then looked up again embarrassedly.

"Why—I guess so," she answered hesitantly.

"All right, Amelia, just think it over, let me know the time and I'll be on hand!" he said.

Amelia sat back in astonishment and said nothing for one whole minute, while Patricia was slipping out and away to her room, and then she said: "All right, I'll think it over and let you know."

Mr. Prentiss smiled a slow smile and sat thoughtfully waiting for his wife to finish her cheese and coffee.

But the two young men watched in vain for Patricia to appear in the ball room. She was on a delightful hike with her father, up a long bright hill in the moonlight. It was then she told her father about the sweet lady lying among the lilies, and the sad brief funeral train.

Patricia went home to an orgy of shopping and fitting in preparation for her winter in college. It distressed her greatly. She had a feeling that her mother's idea of college was a place where she was to attend continual dances and dinners and card parties, and the "dear little morning dresses" as her mother expressed it, were extremely elaborate sports clothes that the girl felt would be unsuitable to wear to attend daily classes. But she submitted to it all sweetly, and then begged the privilege of getting a few little things for herself, just plain common things for rainy days and such, she said. Her mother willingly consented to that and let her go unattended to pick them out. The other things were being carefully packed in the very latest model of wardrobe trunks and shipped ahead of her, so that when Patricia arrived everything would be there ready for all possible occasions.

So Patricia bought her a few plain dresses and packed them herself in another wardrobe suitcase, and felt far more comfortable than if she had only the elaborate outfit. She was being launched into a world of her mother's choosing, but at least she had enough sensible things along to make her feel at home.

Of course this season of outfitting was a busy one, and there was very little time to visit among her old friends, but Patricia got bits of news here and there. Jennie McGlynn was going to college too, just a plain cheap college where she would work for her board and tuition, but she was radiant about it. Della Bright had been taking a summer business course and was going into somebody's office the first of September. Two of the boys had bought a little service station and gone into business. One had joined an archaeologist's expedition and was going to Egypt to dig up lost cities. Most of the rest were just hanging around forlornly trying to get jobs, and looking sad and disappointed about it. But nowhere did she see or hear of John Worth, though she kept her eyes and ears alert for any news.

It was Della Bright who told her at last about him. She came shyly in to tell Patricia that she was going to be married a little after Christmas. She was marrying the boy that used to bring the groceries from one of the chain stores. He was being promoted at Christmas to be manager of the store. He was four years older than Della and quite dependable. Della's face was radiant. She seemed to have forgotten the glamor of the day when she had all of Thorny Bellingham's attention and reveled in it. She was evidently very happy indeed. She had picked out her little new bungalow where she was going to live, and was making curtains and getting her "hope chest" well plenished. She actually looked down on Patricia as if she was a poor little rich girl who had to go away for four years to college and play at lessons again, while she, Della, was going to be grown-up at once and begin housekeeping. She told Patricia grandly that she was to have an electric refrigerator, and a piano. Jim was buying them on the installment plan.

Patricia looked around on the elegant furnishings of her mansion-home and realized for the first time in her life that there were people who had to get things like these one at a time, and work hard, and sometimes suffer a little to get them, but they enjoyed them a great deal more than she had ever enjoyed or even thought of all the accessories of her luxurious life.

It was just as she was going out the door that Della told about John Worth, that he had gone away somewhere. Patricia caught her breath and listened to every word that Della said.

But, isn't he coming back any more?"

"I don't know," said Della disinterestedly. "I 'spose not. He doesn't work at Miller's farm any more of course. They've got a new man there."

"Oh!" said Patricia, thinking of the dear little house on the top of the hill, with the glowing fireplace and the valley-lilies by the door. "But what have they done with his house where he lived?"

Della laughed.

"Oh, I 'spose that's there yet. He couldn't take that with him. I 'spose the new man lives in it. He comes from over near Morgantown. He has seven children. The oldest girl is in high school. There'll be a lot of changes in school this year, won't there?"

Patricia said yes, there would, and swallowed hard and tried to look gay when Della tripped away to her happy cheap little future. But after she was quite gone, and had turned out of the street into the next block, Patricia went slowly down the steps and walked down the old path between the hedge and the tall hemlock trees where grew her lilies. She stood there and communed with those broad green leaves awhile and remembered how a boy with lights behind his eyes had planted them, and had said that he would come back some day and see her. Would he remember that through the years, now that he was growing up?

The next day Patricia went away to college.

18

PATRICIA went in a daze through the first year of her college life. It was all so utterly different from her former life. Here her days were marked out for her in a way, and there were certain things she was supposed to do at each hour, but she was on her own, and not under the dictates of her mother concerning the little matters of life, like dress and companions. She might choose her own ways and she did to a large extent, but she found herself harking back constantly to the influences of her past, and sometimes she found them conflicting so hopelessly that she was all at sea to know which way to turn. So one day she took her Bible on her lap and sat down by herself when she knew there would be no interruptions, to face the situation and see just what she should do.

In the first place as she thought it out it seemed there were people and principles to which she had always deferred; one of the strongest things ingrained in her being when she was little was that she must do as her mother told her to do. For a long time she had felt that mother must be pleased no matter what anybody else thought, and this habit had a strong power over her yet.

It was right, too, one's mother should be deferred to and pleased, of course. The Bible made that plain. She turned over the leaves until she found the old law "Honor thy father and thy mother." She sat studying it for a time, and then bowed her head and asked that she might be guided in this study of her duty and the plan of life she ought to follow.

As she thought about it she realized that she had usually done what her mother wanted because her mother would have made such a disturbance for everybody if things did not go the way she wished; was that altogether a right reason for obedience? It wasn't usually loving obedience either. There had been a great deal of heart rebellion with it all. Was that altogether her fault? Wasn't it perhaps that mother didn't always see things in their right light? There, for instance, were the times when it made father unhappy!

Then it came to her that she had always obeyed her father because she loved to do so. It pleased her to please him. Could it possibly be that he wasn't always altogether right in every case, either? What then should be the criterion?

She turned the pages of her Bible again, and searched in her concordance under the word "Obey." Ah, here was a verse! As so often when she was searching for guidance in this book, it was just as John Worth had told her it would be when she came to it with a will to believe, and a desire to be guided; it seemed just as if the words were written straight to herself. They stared out at her from the pages: "Children, obey your parents *in the Lord.*" Ah, there was her answer. There was One Other, higher than either of her parents, the Lord! And suddenly she recognized that that was true. She had accepted the Lord as Head over all, and whatever she did had to be first pleasing to Him. Beyond that she would have to trust to Him to help her make the other pleasings fit.

She put away her Bible at last and knelt to pray, to tell her Lord that He was to be her Head, and show her just which way to turn as day after day opened up a new way.

As she finally arose and sat down to think again, it came to her that there was one other who had influenced her a great deal, more perhaps than she had realized, and that was John Worth; and back of him his family. When she thought about it more she realized that it was certainly John Worth and his wonderful father and mother who had made her see her Lord and want to follow Him.

After that it was easier to settle questions. She just took them all to her Lord in prayer, and somehow each was worked out. So day by day the problems were presented and settled, and she went on taking her place in that college life, making her own firm young mark on those about her, letting them see that she had her own pattern to follow, and there were certain things she would do and certain things she would not. There were no compromises with her, except in those things that did not really matter, and only affected her own pleasure. In those she was always ready to give up.

With a standard of life like that it was not surprising that presently her companions and fellow students came to recognize in her the likeness of the One who was her Guide.

It was so a student approached her one evening, coming to her room to talk a few minutes.

"You're one of those they call Christians, aren't you?" she said with something like a sneer.

Patricia looked at her in surprise.

"Why, yes, I'm a Christian."

"Why?" she asked.

"I never stopped to think," said Patricia. "But I guess it was because I needed Christ, and when I found He had loved me and died in my place for my sins, I just accepted Him, and it's been good." There was a look in Patricia's face that the other was amazed at. She had never seen that look in anyone's face before. She looked at this new girl in a puzzled way.

"You believe the Bible, then, don't you, Pat?"

Patricia had been called Pat in college almost from the start.

"Oh yes, I believe the Bible," she said brightly.

"I wonder how you can," mused the other. "They say it's full of contradictions! And don't you find it very hard to understand?"

"But you see you have to have the key before you begin to understand," said Patricia. "There's no trouble when you unlock it with the key of willingness to believe what it says. I was told when I began reading it that I must accept it with a willingness to believe what it says. I was told when I began reading it that I must accept it with a willingness to believe it and let it prove itself. That was the way I took it from the start, and it has always been made plain to me so far. Of course I don't pretend to be very wise or great, but I have been satisfied that it fits my need. It is only the people who have decided not to accept it who can't understand it. They aren't willing to take it, therefore God has let them have a strong delusion that they should believe a lie. That's what it says. And in another place it says: 'If our gospel be hid, it is hid *to them that are lost.*' I guess the people who are really anxious to find the truth won't have any trouble."

"But you can't make yourself believe something you don't, can you?"

"Well, you can trust a thing till you try it, the way you

trust people and things, and prove them. And besides, I think believing is something you *decide* to do, not something you *understand* all about and are sure of beforehand. It has to be tried to be proved. But—I've tried it, a little that is, and it proves! It really does."

They talked a little longer, and the other girl went away at last with a wistful good night.

"I'll come and talk to you again if you don't mind," she said. "I like the way you talk. It sounds sensible. And I've got a rotten deal ahead of me when I get through college. I'll need something to help me through, even if it turns out to be just religion!"

After she was gone Patricia got down on her knees and began to talk to God about that other girl. It was the first time the thought of praying for another's salvation had come to her, and now she wanted with all her heart to have this Rose Sheffield find her Lord, and know the sweetness of fellowship with Him as she did.

How she wished she were wise in the Bible. If only she had known the Worths for a little while before they went to Heaven, and could have gone to their home often and asked them questions and listened to their wonderful way of explaining the Bible! Oh, she knew so little! Just what she dug out for herself.

After she was in her bed for the night, and her head resting softly on her pillow, it came to her to wonder where John Worth was. If she only knew where he had gone she would write to him and ask him where she could get some books that would answer some of the questions Rose Sheffield had asked. Maybe John Worth would come back next summer while she was at home, and she would get a chance to talk to him sometime. She would ask him a great many questions. Of course it might be the young minister who had recently come to the little church where she and her father went, could give her help, but she didn't know him very well, and she wasn't sure he would talk as the Worths had talked. She would just ask God to lead her, and then perhaps He would send some message to her from someone who understood as John had done. She would trust God and wait.

But after that night she began to pray for some of her classmates. And there were plenty whom she saw were under that strong delusion that they should believe a lie. She didn't know how to do anything for them but pray, but she presently found her ministry in prayer, and things began to happen quietly. Someone came to the college and gathered half a dozen among the students who were Christians and got them started praying for others, praying that a witness for Christ might be established in that institution. And before the year was over there were a little group who gathered quietly without any stir or notice, in one another's rooms, to pray for themselves and for each other. And the witness that went out in various directions in that non-Christian institution all started from quiet Patricia Prentiss and her sweet unobtrusive witness.

So when Patricia went home for the summer vacation she found herself refreshed in spirit. But she was longing for more teaching now. She had not found much in the environment of the college. The churches were mostly cold and formal like the one her mother attended spasmodically, and she was glad to get back to the old-fashioned church and Sunday School where she had grown up. She found, too, that the new minister was preaching answers to some of the questions that had often troubled her, and her heart rejoiced to have them voiced and explained.

Mr. Prentiss had found that his daughter had a longing

to learn to ride horseback, so when she had been home a few days he bought her a horse.

"Now, Mr. Prentiss," said Amelia, "you know that was a very foolish thing for you to buy. You might much better have rented a horse if Patricia has to ride. She will go back to college after a couple of months and what will she do with a horse, at college? She can't take it with her of course, and if she could I would just worry every living minute lest she had been thrown off and killed."

But the horse was bought and remained, stabled in the old barn far behind the Prentiss mansion, and cared for by a groom who knew how to care for horses and who knew and loved that particular horse. The light of delight in Patricia's face had settled the question for her father. If his daughter wanted a horse, a horse she should have.

"Why, if the horse doesn't care to attend college," said George Prentiss whimsically, "she can stay at home here and play around with Peter till Patricia gets back."

"But it would have been so much better for you to have got her a car," mourned Amelia. "All young girls have cars nowadays, and she could have taken me around a lot on my errands."

"You have a car of your own, mamma," said George Prentiss, "and a man to drive it. If Patricia wants a car too she shall have it, but we're going to keep the horse."

So the horse stayed.

It did not take Patricia long to learn to ride, and she was soon off around the countryside, with Peter well out of her sight, but keeping a careful vigil riding an old cob of his own.

So the summer passed quietly and most happily for the girl who was enjoying her home more than she had ever enjoyed it before.

Her mother of course made a great attempt to bring

her into the social eye, inviting a few of her old dancing class informally to tea or dinner, or trying to get up various festivities but constantly Patricia begged her not to do so, saying she wanted the time to rest and get acquainted with her family again. Nevertheless, Gloria and Gwendolyn and a number of the other girls whom Mrs. Prentiss favored were often running in, and getting up this or that, and Patricia found it very hard to escape all their invitations. Often her father was inveigled into borrowing Peter's horse in the evenings and taking a ride with her so that she might escape something she did not want to attend. Still, there was one thing that she was fervently thankful for, and that was that Thorny was not at home, and there was no reference to him in any of their conversations. Always she took good care herself not to mention him. From a few casual words she happened to overhear now and then among the friends of her childhood, she gathered that Thorny was abroad, having passed brief careers in two or three minor colleges; but nobody seemed to know just where he was now or what he was aiming to be. His absence removed an old source of much argument, however, and when it came time for her to return to her own studies, she told herself hopefully that she and her mother seemed to have come a little nearer to one another; there had not been as much discord between them as when she was a child. She told herself that probably a good deal of the trouble in the past had been her fault. Or perhaps, now that she took her troubles to the Lord in prayer He was helping her to bear little annoyances more patiently.

So passed another year, with only the brief homegoings at Christmas and Easter, and by the time she came back for the second summer at home Thorny had almost faded out of the picture, for no one seemed to know much about him.

One thing that distressed her however was that though it was now two years since she had seen John Worth drive away on that sad funeral train, there was no word of him from anyone. No one knew anything about him, and no one seemed to care. And of course a girl who hadn't been supposed to have any contact with him whatever couldn't go around asking questions about him.

Only down in the sheltered little path between the hemlocks and the hedge, where somehow his presence seemed to linger, she could go sometimes at night, and stoop and touch the faithful green leaves he had planted. Looking up to the stars she would pray her Lord to bless him and keep him safely.

And then one day Thorny came riding into her life again.

Patricia was sitting in the hammock on the side porch reading when he came cantering showily up the drive on his lovely bay horse. Stopping under the porte cochere he flung himself off with skillful grace, looking his handsomest in expensive riding togs.

Patricia looked up from her book when she heard the horse coming, and for the first minute she didn't know him at all, he seemed so grown up and mature, so altogether a finished man of the world, though with a jaded look about his eyes, as if he had gone far and seen much.

She had arisen quickly and was studying him as he caught sight of her before he was quite up the steps. Then his face beamed into recognition.

"Oh, hello, Patty, old friend!" he exclaimed graciously, and sprang up the remaining steps to greet her. "Say! you certainly have changed a lot, Pat, haven't you? I had no idea you would ever be as beautiful as you are. Why, you're rare! You're *mar*velous! Say! You take my breath away!" and he suddenly came nearer and took both her hands in a close grasp, looking down at her in sudden admiration, as if unexpectedly he had come upon a jewel of great price. Dramatically, with his characteristic quick reaching out for whatever pleased him, he took possession of her as if it were his right.

"Why, Patty, you are precious!"

Patricia, at his voice, quickly recovered from her astonishment and smilingly drew her hands away from his insistent grasp.

"Oh, hello, Thorny!" she said with easy friendliness, which was by no means too cordial. "What a surprise! I didn't know you were in this country. And I didn't know you rode. When did you take that up?"

"Oh, I've been abroad for the most part of the past year. Been specializing in horses, polo, racing and so forth. I just ran home for a few weeks to rest up a little and look into the possibilities over here. Of course I shall be in college somewhere this fall, either here or abroad again, but the main thing is my polo, which college will give me the best offer."

Patricia watched him curiously. So this was what Thorny had become, a horseman, specializing in polo at present.

But there was a new kind of poise, almost dignity, about him. Was it real? She hardly knew how to take him. The indignities that he had put upon her in the past were still keen memories that stifled any impulse she had to be friendly, so she turned her eyes to the spirited horse that stood with fiery eye champing his bit and stamping a dainty foot on the hard drive.

"That's a beautiful horse you have," she remarked, turning the subject from his own personal career.

Thorny's eyes lit up with satisfaction.

"Yes," he said coolly, "I'm rather proud of him. I got

him in England. Pedigreed of course." He launched into a brief detailed account of his horse's ancestry.

Patricia listened politely and knew her mother would think she ought to ask him to sit down. She didn't want to, she was deeply interested in her book, yet she knew she must.

Perhaps he saw her indifference for he brought his discourse to an abrupt close and looking at her again with that amazed smile remarked almost irrelevantly:

"My, but you are lovely! And by the way I understand you are a great horsewoman. When I heard that I came right over, for I thought we would at last have something in common. I understand you have a wonderful horse."

Patricia smiled.

"I enjoy my horse," she said pleasantly.

"I thought so," said Thorny dramatically. "Then we shall have some wonderful rides together."

"Why, I usually ride with father," she said coolly.

"Never alone?" he asked with lifted meaningful brows.

"Oh yes, alone sometimes. But then I am *alone*, not with anyone," she laughed.

"Ah! but you and I will ride together!" he announced as if it were a fiat gone forth. "Now that I have found you again as it were, I am not sure but I shall linger longer than the few days I had planned."

"Well, I'm rather busy this summer doing some extra studying."

"How about *now*? Go get ready and I'll bring your horse. He's in the old stable, is he?"

"No, I could not go now. I have something else to do."

"Then how about tomorrow morning?"

"No," said Patricia decidedly, "I have other plans. Excuse me a minute and I will call mother. She used to be a great friend of yours and she would not like to miss your call," and suddenly Patricia slipped inside the screen door and upstairs.

Mrs. Prentiss came down at once all smiles, but Patricia did not return for some minutes, and when she came she was very cool. But somehow this only made Thorny more eager to gain her attention.

Of course Patricia had known that to call her mother into the matter would mean a return of some of the persecution she had suffered when she was younger, but at least, she reasoned, the conversation would not be too intimate. However she had not been seated again three minutes on the porch before she realized that it had been a mistake to call her mother down. Of course sooner or later she would have found out that Thorny was at home, but she might have managed to delay the knowledge for a day or two.

For Mrs. Prentiss sailed right in as if her daughter were still a small child and said how nice it was that Thorny was at home, and how wonderful that he rode, and what a relief it would be to feel there was some competent person to go riding with "dear little Patty."

Patricia's heart grew heavy as her mother enlarged upon the subject and she saw herself in bondage once more. Then she remembered that she had a refuge, and silently her heart cried out to God to help her with this situation.

That was the beginning of Thorny's constant attention. Patricia was so filled with the horror of the past that she could not imagine it possible for her to endure riding alone with Thorny, so she got her father to promise to go out with them some mornings, and he did.

"He's not so bad, Pat," he said when he came back. "Just a dumb bunny that likes to show off. But I'm game to go with you whenever you say."

So Patricia rode less and less that summer, and almost always her father was along. Though she did have to own that Thorny was not so bad as she had feared. Thorny was finding out that here was a girl who could not be won by flattery, nor cave-man stuff. He must take her seriously. And so he set about being serious, though there wasn't a serious fibre in his whole being. He succeeded however only in making her feel that he was a bore.

Patricia was glad when it was time for her to return to college, because she was weary of Thorny's constant attendance wherever she went, and her mother's happy purr over the state of things.

Not that she hated Thorny now the way she used to do when she was a child. He seemed to have given up his tormenting ways and love of cruel teasing, though she sometimes suspected him of acting a part, because he had never before let any girl snub him.

As for Thorny, he was really exerting himself now to be courteous, and to make his attentions so unobtrusively necessary to her well-being that she would fall into the habit of getting used to him. And then, *then,* he reasoned, when she once was his he could bend her as he would.

So Patricia went back to college and another year began.

But Thorny had ways of being extremely attentive even at a distance. He was getting a name for himself in the polo world, getting his handsome picture and his name in the papers. He wrote to her constantly, though her replies were few and far between. She told him that she was studying hard and intimated that it was time he did so also. Yet still he went on with his career, bombarding her constantly with photographs, both portraits and snapshots, and begging for one of her. To this request she made no reply except that she had no time to have her picture taken. And then of course he begged one from her mother. It really was of no use to try to get rid of him. She just must settle down to the fact that he would stick whether she wanted him or not. More and more she let his letters go unanswered for long periods. Only when he sent great boxes of roses and orchids and other lovely flowers, or enormous boxes of expensive candy, she felt she had to reply, and then she made her notes most brief and cool, and often gave the flowers and candy away to her fellow-students.

But the winter passed, and the summer came. Patricia had accepted the fact of Thorny's inevitability with a kind of apathy. She didn't enjoy his presence, neither did she ever miss him. He never gave her a chance. When she was at home he was always there. Always on hand to take her anywhere that she had to go. He had become a habit. He was taking it very much for granted that he was wanted. He never asked if he might go, he went. And any other admirer she might have had must stand by and let him have all privileges, for he took them anyway. Well, Patricia had no admirers that she cared anything about, so what did it matter? There were pleasant young men who called sometimes, but inevitably Thorny was always there also, and whatever calling they had to do must be done under the shadow of his presence.

Patricia was tired. She didn't tell anybody, but she was fearfully tired of it all, this espionage by Thorny. Her father saw it and tried to help. He took time off from his business and went with her everywhere, until his wife called him to account for it.

"Don't you realize what you are doing, Mr. Prentiss? Don't you know that those two young things don't want you along all the time? Don't you see that you are giving them no chance at all for courting."

"Courting!" roared Patricia's father. "Why should they want to court? You don't suppose that our Pat is going to take up with that poor simp after all these years of hating him?"

"Now, George, don't be silly! Don't you know that the strongest love often begins with great dislike? Look at us. I never disliked anybody so much in my life as you when I first met you. I thought you were the homeliest man I'd ever laid eyes on!"

Her husband looked at her with keen tired eyes.

"And you think our love is that kind, do you? The strongest kind there is?" His honest eyes pierced her fussy little soul. She got a little red and fidgeted around, and then answered:

"Well, George, I supposed you thought it was."

For answer her husband watched her silently a minute and then said with a deep sigh, "All right, Amelia, you win! I'm sure I don't know anything about it, only I intend to go wherever Pat wants me."

"What makes you so sure she wants you?" asked Amelia in a superior tone.

"What? Well, because I am, that's all."

But sometimes when Patricia got very tired of it all she used to think away back to the young boy in high school and wonder if she would ever see him again. He was a man grown now, and he probably had other interests. Very likely he had forgotten that he had promised to come back. And if he came he might not seem the same to her as long ago. Oh, life was hard, and it seemed to grow more complicated as one grew older.

But she went back to college again and worked faith-fully.

That winter Thorny came to the college to see her several times. Just brief calls he made, took her down to a wonderful concert in the nearby city. Took her to dinner at a famous restaurant. Never urged her when she declined to go to a night club. He was biding his time.

And all the time she was just suffering him, neither liking him nor entirely disliking him as the days went on, and he seemed to be fairly trustworthy and devoted. Yet no more than in the days gone by did she want his devotion. There was not anybody, now that the vision of John Worth was fading and growing so dreamlike and impossible to her maturer mind, not anybody she wanted to have devoted to her.

And then commencement came on apace, and now and then when she had time she wondered vaguely what she was going to do with herself when college was over and she was supposed to begin her life.

Her mother's idea of course was that she should have a great coming out party and be presented to society. She had spoken of her plans and ideas about that several times. She had also suggested that they go abroad and Patricia be presented at court. But Patricia didn't want all that. It might be interesting perhaps, to meet a king and queen, but what was that to being presented to the King of Heaven some day when all this mixed-up disappointing life was over? And she was twice as interested in the little prayer meetings they were having regularly at college, or in gathering in a shy new soul now and then who was troubled about life, and death that might be lurking along the way, than she was in planning a marvelous wardrobe for her coming-out days.

The commencement came at last, and all the hard work was done. But when she herself stood up for the very honorable part she had in the program of the day, in spite of herself she lifted wistful eyes to the far corner of the great auditorium back under the gallery, much like the old high school gathering place, to see if there were quiet brown eyes with lamps behind them watching her.

Of course they were not there, and she had known they would not be when she looked, but still she looked, and sighed when it was over, and turned away from Thorny's classic face with that smug assurance upon it as he watched her. It was only her father who really cared, and was looking at her with love in his proud eyes. Her mother was looking at her dress and thinking it might have been a shade more elaborate if only Patricia hadn't been so silly, still clinging to that old idea of being a child. Well, at least her education was done now, and she could have clear sailing to establish her in the right circle of life and give her a good start. And of course, there was Thorny, so the stage seemed to be already well set.

19

AND then at last it was all over, the good-byes said,
the baggage packed, the flowers stowed in the back of
the car; the graduating presents, the tears, the smiles,
the last little prayer-meeting up in Patricia's room with
the door locked even against her family whom she had
bribed to let her alone a few minutes; and then the
going home.

Her father's gift was a tiny jeweled wrist watch and she
loved it. Her mother had persisted in getting her a
diamond necklace and she shrank from its glitter.

Her mother of course had tried to make her ride with
Thorny in his car, for he had driven up with that in
mind, but Patricia said no, she was going home alone
with her parents. She didn't want anybody else along
either. No, Thorny must not crowd in and hire someone
else to bring his car home later. No, she wanted to rest
with her family for the drive home.

Strangely enough this kind of thing only made
Thorny more devoted, more determined to win her
finally.

And then at home after the first quiet days, there was

the coming out party that her mother was so determined about.

"Better let her have it, Pat! She tells me she's just lived for that ever since you were born," said her father with a sad little smile. "She wouldn't understand if you didn't."

So Patricia sat obediently down day after day and helped her mother write out lists of people to be invited, and saw her turn down any of her old friends from high school that she suggested, even though some of them had married into very respectable families and were doing well. Mrs. Prentiss meant to have this party one of the grandest affairs socially that their town had ever known.

They discussed whether it should be held in the house, or whether they would hire a big hall in the finest hotel of the city. How Patricia hated it all, the tiresome question of what "they" would think about this or that, and no thought of what her Lord might think. But there wasn't anything that she could do about it. Her mother was having the time of her life, and why not let her have it? Of course there were questions of worldliness that were involved. Patricia had had opportunity in college to come to certain decisions about them. There would be liquors. Her mother would insist upon it. Her father wouldn't like it, and she hated it, and yet it would be. And there would be dancing. Patricia had not enjoyed that for a long time now. Never had she heard discussion of it but her own feeling was against it. Patricia prayed about that party a good deal in those early fall days, that the Lord would take control of it, and somehow direct it the way He wanted it.

Mr. Prentiss watched his daughter's face from day to day and saw shadows gather there. He knew without her saying anything that this great coming out was not happiness to his little girl.

And then one day when the hotel was all but hired, the decorators and confectioners were all but arranged for, he came home and suggested that the party be put off and they take a year in Europe first.

He knew by the great light that broke on Pat's face that it would be an intense relief to her tired young soul.

"Why, papa!" babbled Amelia bewilderedly. "We couldn't! How could we? The party, you know. Patricia's coming out party."

"Put it off," he said quickly, "or chuck it altogether!" and he laughed.

"Papa!" said Amelia aghast. "When Patricia has her dress all ready!"

"She can wear the dress to church or somewhere, can't she, mamma? Or to a garden party. Any old place. I'll tell you. She can use it to be presented at court in. That'll settle it all fine! Then you can chuck the party altogether and no harm done!"

"George!" reproved his wife severely, "is it possible that you don't know that young women are not presented at court in garments of their own choosing? Surely you know that the fashions for such presentations are all prescribed by the court!"

"To heck with the court then! To heck with the king and queen, I say. Any old king and queen that aren't satisfied with a dress my daughter picks out to come and see them in can go to thunder for all me. She doesn't have to be presented to any old court either if they're that particular!"

"George!" said Amelia almost in tears. "I'd be afraid, positively *afraid,* to take you over to Europe lest you might express some such ideas and be overheard and get arrested."

"Well, Mrs. Prentiss, I didn't know that you contemplated taking me over to Europe. I thought I was taking you. In which case I can readily promise that I won't get me arrested, not while you're around anyway. Now is that all settled? What do you say, Pat? Shall we go?"

"Oh, daddy, that would be too beautiful!"

"Well, then get up and dance with your old daddy, and mamma, Pat, and let's celebrate. We'll put away the whole kit of plans for that bloomin' party and get us ready to trip off to Europe on the next desirable boat." He danced over to his wife and pulled her to her feet, making her dance over to their daughter, and pull her to her feet, and together they three whirled around the room, with joined hands, till poor Amelia was all out of breath and puffing like a porpoise.

And so they sailed for Europe the next week, while Thorny was away playing polo.

But Thorny came trailing after them on the very next boat, and turned up everywhere they went, until Patricia again grew quite used to him and altogether indifferent to him. There were so many other things to see and do that she didn't have to think much about him. Mrs. Prentiss enjoyed his constant presence immensely and was always inventing excuses to call her husband away and leave Thorny with Patricia. She followed them with fond eyes when they went anywhere together, and felt that she had her daughter very well placed in spite of all the trouble she had had.

Patricia was living in a world of wonder, getting acquainted with the reality of things about which she had studied. That Thorny was her constant attendant made very little difference to her. It kept her mother satisfied to have someone along with her.

Thorny wasn't in the least interested in the historic or literary value of the things they were seeing. He trailed around with her making very little response to what she said about them. He was watching Patricia, rather proud to be with her, for he saw that she made an impression wherever she went. She was a beautiful girl, her family was all right, and she dressed in exquisite taste, though rather plainly when one considered her position as the daughter of a moderately wealthy man. And their fortunes were well matched. Of course Thorny hadn't any fortune just now, for his father had him on a strict allowance, but he was sure if he should marry, his mother would make his father "come across," and any way dad wasn't very well and he would inherit a lot when he passed on. That was the way he reasoned.

Of course Pat wasn't exactly his style, a little too sober, but if he once got her in her place as his wife he could remedy all that. Then, too, her mother would be an awful pill to have around, but he'd take good care to locate pretty far away from her. He wanted no relatives of his own or hers to do any curbing to his plans.

So he went patiently around between his several affairs in the world of horses, trailing Patricia, watching her, studying her, and when his gay nature was too bored with her quietness and her determination not to have the kind of good time he wanted, he would fly off for a day or two and find some kindred spirit, either some old acquaintance, or one he could pick up anywhere. For Thorny had never been particular about his casual acquaintances. His chief object was a good time.

But he managed to keep fairly sober. At least he did not return to the vicinity of the Prentisses until he was thoroughly in command of himself. Thorny could carry a good deal of liquor by this time without being visibly affected. Sometimes when he considered it seriously he told himself it was ridiculous to think of marrying a girl who would not take even a glass of liquor. But that, too, would be one of the things he could change in her when he got in control.

And so, watching her carefully, and going gaily with her everywhere she would let him, he came gradually to the decision that he would marry Patricia.

It never seemed to occur to him that she might have a mind of her own about it. Thorny had been admired so much that he thought of course any girl would be glad to marry him if he decided to ask her. True, she used to have a nasty little temper, but she seemed to be pretty well over that. She was gentle and sweet most of the time, only now and then when he proposed that they should go to some night club or something of that sort, then she was adamant with her refusals. He'd change all that when they were married, but just now it didn't seem wise to make much protest, not since he had guyed her one day about her old-fashioned tastes and her father had appeared casually on the scene with a stern glance in his eyes. Thorny didn't want to get in bad with the old man before the thing was a foregone conclusion.

As for himself, he considered that he had been very docile, going almost everywhere she wanted to go. Of course she never asked him to go with her, he just trailed along. If he hadn't he wouldn't have seen much of her. And of course if he had been too indifferent her mother would have supplied an invitation. But he preferred to trail. That way he was freer. There was only one place where he did not go often with her, where he knew she liked to go best, and that was church. He couldn't understand why she liked to go to church so much. All kinds of churches, the more old-fashioned they were the more she liked them. Stuffy, queer churches where the preachers believed a lot of old-fashioned things that Thorny had never even heard of, and preached them hard so that you almost felt uncomfortable, as if they were being preached right at you. That was the impression he had drawn from the few times he had swallowed his distaste and gone with her.

The first time that Thorny proposed to her they were sitting on a lovely hillside overlooking the Mediterranean sea. It was where Patricia loved to come and spend some time with the marvelous view every day while they were in the vicinity. Views bored Thorny, but he always knew where to find her when she wasn't available anywhere else. So with his plans fully matured he came gaily into the picture and dropped down beside her on the grass. Boy, but she was beautiful sitting there against the background of those trees, with light and shadow flickering over her lovely hair! Even without lipstick or rouge she was angelic, and if she were just touched up a little the way women of the world knew how to do it, she would be simply stunning. No, he was making no mistake. The trifles that were not just according to his mind he would set right when he had her for his own.

So with some of his old time assurance he began, half laughingly:

"Pat, why don't you and I go get married? Wouldn't it be a lot more sensible than all this hanging around and waiting that we are doing now?"

Patricia turned astonished suddenly worried eyes toward him and answered coolly:

"Are we hanging around waiting, Thorny? I didn't know it."

"Well, you certainly must be blind. What did you suppose I was sticking around for? You know I'm crazy about you and the natural conclusion is that we'll be married sometime. Why not now? We can have just as good a wedding over here as we can at home any day, if that's what you're stopping for. Or, if you're sentimental and have to be married at home, let's all fly over and get the affair out of the way, and then come back and hike around where we like?"

Patricia gave him a quick troubled look, and then lifting her chin a bit haughtily said:

"But you see, Thorny, I'm not in the least crazy about you, and I have no intention whatever of getting married now, or perhaps not at any time, so, let's go back to the hotel. It's almost time for dinner!" Lithely she sprang to her feet and started slowly walking away from him.

That was the way most of his attempts ended, either by Patricia turning them down utterly, or else laughing at him. She simply wouldn't take him seriously.

"You're nothing but a boy yet, Thorny. You don't really know what you want out of life, and perhaps I don't either, only I'm sure of one thing. I don't want to marry you. So let's forget it and see everything we came over here to see."

"To heck with the sights!" said Thorny. "I can't see anything but you!" and he said it in such a flippant way that Patricia looked him in the eyes and said:

"Oh, no, you don't either, Thorny. You see every pretty girl that comes by. Don't try to put that over on me."

Then he would go away for a couple of days and come back and start trailing her again.

That went on for almost two years, while the Prentisses lingered in Europe. As long as there were plenty of new wonders to see Patricia stood it all right, ignoring him time and again, or putting him off with a laugh.

But when they came home it was a different matter. Thorny grew more and more impatient, and Mrs. Prentiss grew more and more worried.

Patricia began to adopt a new method now, for there seemed no other way to get rid of Thorny who parked on her trail on all occasions. The people at home had begun to couple their names inevitably, to invite them together, to place them side by side at dinners. It was beginning to get on Patricia's nerves mightily. And so she suddenly began to cultivate the acquaintance of this and that man whom she met here and there among her friends, or at the club, or out at some house party which her mother had inveigled her to attend. And when she began to go out with other young men than Thorny, and to flit from one to the other in her attempt to keep her name from being constantly associated with Thorny's, then her mother was fairly frantic. How did they know who these other young men were? Outsiders, strangers in the town. When everything seemed to have been so satisfactorily arranged, why did Patricia have to upset it all and be so difficult? Thorny was becoming restive under this treatment. Why didn't her daughter see that herself?

And it wasn't as if Patricia was a babe in arms yet. It took time to know people, and find out all about them, meantime Patricia was almost twenty-four, yet apparently as carefree and gay as when a child. When her mother protested she frankly owned that she did not want to be tied down. She declared she was not sure she would ever care for any man enough to want to live her life out with him. And when her mother asked aghast, "Mercy! Patricia, what else could you do? You couldn't get a divorce. You know your father would never stand for that!" Patricia only laughed gaily and replied:

"Why, I hadn't thought about that, dearest. I'm sure there would be plenty of other things to do besides getting married. There always have been."

"But," said her mother, "there has always been Thorny!"

"Yes," said Patricia with a sigh, "that's the trouble!

There has always been Thorny. I never can stir without Thorny and I'm getting fed up with it."

Then she flitted away to a golf game with a perfectly new young naval officer whom she had just met.

Sometimes she wondered to herself whether after all she had a haunting fear of a possible truth underlying her mother's words, that had prevented her so far from cutting Thorny entirely out of her life. It could be done of course if she really went at it in earnest. Why had she not done it? Would she miss him? Had Thorny become a habit? Or was it just that her apathy concerning him was because she dreaded the combat with her mother that would surely come if she sent Thorny away absolutely.

Well, and why couldn't she give up and marry Thorny? He seemed to care for her. It would satisfy her mother, and in a way she would be much freer than she was now, having to account for every breath she breathed. Or would she? Her memories of Thorny still haunted her. Had he really changed?

But they had nothing in common. And that vague longing of her soul that had never been wholly satisfied, could that find satisfaction as Thorny's companion? It wasn't thinkable. Must she just surrender and take life as it came, giving up all the sweet dreams of a home some day where God would be honored and life be an ante-room of Heaven? It wasn't thinkable that Thorny would ever be one who would be willing to have family worship every day. She almost laughed at the idea. Wasn't that a pretty good guide? Or was she just what some of her friends called her, a sentimentalist?

But she didn't love Thorny. She never felt happy when he tried to make love to her. She remembered too vividly that time he kissed her so violently in the woods. She would never let him touch even so much as her hand. Always when he tried to be affectionate, she turned away, laughed pleasantly, suddenly asked him a question about something utterly irrelevant, and managed to get out of the room as soon as possible.

20

THORNY of late had been exceedingly restive under Patricia's continued indifference and one day he broached the subject before her mother.

"I say, Mrs. Prentiss, what's the matter with your daughter that I can't get any answer out of her when I ask her to marry me? I'm about fed up on being put off. I think she ought to say yes or no, don't you?"

"Why, Patricia, how rude of you!" said Mrs. Prentiss.

"Mother, I've told him no a great many times!" protested the girl quickly with a light laugh. "The trouble is he won't take no for an answer."

"Now, Patricia, I think you ought to be serious about this. It's time you sat down and really considered the matter. Thorny has been very patient, and it isn't fair for you to act this way. Everybody knows that probably in the end you will marry him, and you are getting yourself unnecessarily talked about. I don't like it. It is time to end all this and know just where we stand. Patricia, I am serious. I ask you to set a definite day when you will answer Thorny. A good young woman does not play around with the leniency of the man who wishes to marry her. She does not lead him on, and yet go with this one and that, and leave him to wait her pleasure. I am ashamed of you. It looks as if you were trying to make Thorny jealous."

"Mother! I haven't been doing that!" protested Patricia stormily. "And I have never led Thorny on. He knows himself that I have told him no time and time again, and then I finally settled down to just consider him a good friend. But that doesn't suit either."

Her mother eyed her in scorn.

"It does seem, my child, as if you were crazy. Acting this way to such a wonderful boy as Thorny. I'm afraid, my dear, you will bitterly regret this some day. And for your own sake I am going to ask you to set a definite time, a day, when Thorny may expect a real answer from you, and you will begin to plan your life and end this suspense."

Patricia looked at her mother in despair, then her eyes went down for a minute thoughtfully. At last she looked up.

"All right!" she said huskily. "Call it one month from today."

"Very well," said her mother firmly. "Put that date down, Thorny, so we won't forget it," said Mrs. Prentiss with satisfaction.

"All right, Mother Prentiss, I'll do that little thing. Although I don't really have to, you know. That's a date I don't forget. May the fifth. That's the day I came home to go to the picnic with Pat. Don't you remember? I had the dickens of a time getting off from school that day. I was supposed to be cheerleader in the biggest game of the season that year. And that was the day I first discovered what a little beauty our Pat had become. That was the day my devotion to you first began, Pat."

Patricia looked at him wide-eyed. That day! The day

her real torments from him had begun! Not the day she went to that dear home on the hillside! The day the lilies of the valley were in bloom and John Worth had walked home with her in the twilight! Oh, not that day! Not that!

"Wait!" she said suddenly. "Suppose you make it May fifteenth. That will be better."

"No!" said Thorny stubbornly. "I prefer the fifth, and you gave your word, you know."

"Yes, Patricia," said her mother, "we can't have any backing out nor hedging. That is just what you have been doing for a long time, and I won't have that going on any longer. We'll call it the fifth of May and we'll give a party. We'll give a party to all your friends and you shall announce your decision to them. Now, that's decided. We won't talk any more about it. The whole thing is settled and I'm going to send out invitations."

"Oh!" said Patricia in a stricken voice. "Am I to have no voice in who shall be invited?"

"Well, of course if there's anybody else besides the ones we want you can have them, I suppose," said her mother, "but I don't fancy there'll be any trouble about that. There is, of course, just our regular group of friends."

Patricia looked at her mother with stormy eyes, and then huskily agreed. But she walked out of the room and upstairs. She stayed by herself while Thorny and her mother took council from which they emerged, Thorny with a possessive look of triumph on his face, Mrs. Prentiss with the brightness of worry in her eyes.

All the rest of that day she stayed by herself and faced her future, trying to look ahead and see just what was the right thing to do. At last she prayed a sad little prayer, asking the Lord to show her just what was wrong with herself that she didn't want to decide a matter like this.

Asking Him not to let her do anything that would make her unhappiness and wrong in the future. Asking Him to take out of her heart the things that made her unhappy and restless, to show her a right way clearly ahead.

When she crept to her bed at last and tried to see if any answer had been given her it was all just as mixed-up as ever. There was her mother and Thorny on the one hand, and her own uncertainty on the other. Personally she would have been just as content to go on and live from day to day without considering marriage at all. But that didn't seem to be what was considered the right thing for her to do at all, and she wanted above all things to do right. There seemed to be no question of her own pleasure in the matter, and shouldn't people be happy, be really in love when they married?

"There!" she said at last, unhappily, one day about a week before the party, "I'll just go ahead to the time, and the Lord will show me what to do then, I'm sure He will. If He doesn't I'll be sure He wants me to marry Thorny. But somehow it isn't at all what I thought marrying would be. I thought it was supposed to make people happy, and this only seems to me like a kind of slavery."

During the days that followed she tried several times to think of an engagement with Thorny calmly, as inevitable, a foregone conclusion, but something in her continually rebelled.

She tried to tell herself, as her mother had often told her, that all girls felt that way about the man they were going to marry until they were married, and that he was probably her reasonable mate, her "fate," as she put it to herself. But the future as Mrs. Thornton Bellingham looked dark indeed to her, and she shrank from it inexpressibly.

Day after day went by, and still she had not finally

faced the question with herself, had not even told herself whether her answer was to be yes or no. She doubted sometimes, if even when she stood upon her feet to announce her decision, she would be any clearer in her mind about it than she was now in her present distraught state.

And day by day as the night of the dinner approached, she found herself wildly hoping that some Power, greater than her own, would intervene and save her, or that somehow there would be given some light upon her way.

But now the day was almost upon her, and she was breathless over the thought of it.

She felt as if she were blindly walking into a trap. She was vexed with herself that she had promised her mother and the young man to settle the question on the evening of the party. If only she could go on being free and not be heckled and nagged to make a decision. If only she could be a little girl again and somehow begin life over, like a bit of knitting that could be raveled out to be knit up right once more without a mistake. There seemed to have been some stitch dropped in her life, some loop of life's thread left out that made all of her young span look wrong. Something that might have changed it all to joyous living.

She blamed herself for being weak, and unable to stand against her mother's bitter sarcasm, her hints that she was growing older every day and that she wasn't treating Thorny in an honorable way. There was something about her mother's persistence that wore her down to utter discouragement, and made her feel that anything, even marriage with Thorny, might be better than being continually blamed and nagged and managed.

And yet—well, there was still a brief period in which to think this thing out. She had hoped that somehow she could get a saner view before the time was actually upon her. Perhaps by talking to someone, even that flier she had just met. He seemed a sensible person, with a clear brain. Perhaps she could put a hypothetical case to him, and get him talking about generalities that would help her. That had been her hope when she impulsively invited him and decided to seat him beside herself. At least he was someone to hold off Thorny for a little while at the last minute until she could be sure, could think just what to say when she was called upon for her decision.

To that end she had seated Thorny far down the table by her mother's side. It was her own dinner. She had arranged all such details herself. But she felt as if the walls of a great stone prison were slowly closing about her heart to crush her. As each day rushed on she felt more and more desperate.

Twice she had tried to talk to her father about it but it always seemed as if some evil power were trying to prevent her.

The first time she broached the subject she got only as far as one sentence:

"Dad, do you think that people ever should marry when they are not sure they love each other?"

She asked it anxiously one evening when they were sitting on the porch alone for a few moments to watch the sunset.

He looked at her keenly, yearningly; but before he could answer a servant came up respectfully.

"Mr. Prentiss, you're wanted on the telephone."

And then before he was through telephoning, all suddenly there were callers, just neighbors, who stayed and stayed, and there was no more opportunity to speak to him alone that night. Nor for two whole days following. There wasn't a time when she could see her father alone without exciting her mother's curiosity.

At last another brief time came, and she plunged into her trouble once more.

"Dad, is it ever right to marry unless you are sure you love the man?"

Again he looked up sharply.

"No, *never!*" he said almost fiercely. And then, still watching her keenly, "Do you mean that slick Thorny Bellingham?" he asked suddenly.

All at once there was a footstep in the hall and Mrs. Prentiss came to the door, pausing to look suspiciously at the two.

"What are you two having a secret conclave about?" she asked sharply. "Why do you always have to hide in corners to do your talking?"

Before either could answer the doorbell interrupted, and a telegram for Mr. Prentiss broke in upon their plans for the evening.

"I must leave for New York on the next train!" he announced annoyedly. "Something important in the business world has gone wrong and I have to see a certain man tonight before he sails for a foreign land. I hope I'll be back in the morning, but I can't tell how things will turn out. It may take longer than I think, perhaps several days."

There was no time to talk farther. He was gone in a rush, and Patricia, almost sick with worry, wept alone that night, and prayed. Oh, if her father would only come back in the morning! Why hadn't she talked to him about it before?

But day after day came telegrams instead, that he was detained still longer.

And then finally he didn't come till a few minutes before that awful dinner the very night of the party. It was grotesque! It was unbelievable, that he should be kept away so long! And she had prayed so much that

God would help her, guide her, send her some definite word, and nothing had happened! Oh, she still believed in prayer of course, but it must be some wrong attitude of her own somehow. But, oh, why didn't God send her some help?

There wasn't a minute to talk to her father after he came. She didn't have even an instant alone with him. She had meant to tell him all about her perplexity, and the foolish promise she had made to Thorny and her mother. But now it was too late. She had only time for a hasty kiss as her guests were arriving and a hurried whisper:

"I'm having a party tonight, dad, and you're the guest of honor. Hurry up and get ready!"

It was just then the telephone rang and she was called for. Her father was upstairs hastily arraying himself in evening garb, while she was receiving the apologies of the recreant flier. And she was in such a tumult. If she only could have talked with her father for just five minutes and got his calm view of things, she might have been strong to face the evening. But there wasn't an instant.

And then she suddenly took in what her flier was saying, that he could not possibly get there, and her heart almost failed her. Here was even this brief respite from Thorny torn away from her!

Her brows were drawn with annoyance, her eyes were full of trouble. She hadn't realized how much it was meaning to her to get away from Thorny for that last hour before she had to give her final word. It seemed as though there had been no time to think for the last two weeks. Her mother had been cheerfully going ahead preparing for this night, getting every last detail just as she wanted it, and there had been too much tumult in her heart for her to reason things out in the calm right way they should be reasoned. Even yet, though she had done her best to think of an engagement with Thorny, marriage with Thorny, as a foregone conclusion, she had not frankly told herself whether she would say yes or no when the moment came. Perhaps she was hoping that they would not press her at the last minute to keep her word, though she ought to have known them both better than that. Her mother's cheerful determined mouth, Thorny's possessive eyes, told her there was no hope from that quarter. And on the other hand if she should dare to assert her independence and say no, what catastrophe she would bring down upon the house. It would be too unpleasant to stay there after that. She shivered at the thought.

Oh, of course dad would help her to get away from it all somehow if she made him understand what terrible pressure she was under, but that would be misery for dad. She couldn't do that! Oh, how silly it all was anyway. Why did she have to be married if she wasn't ready?

But yet, suppose this was God's plan for her life and she was trying to frustrate it? And suppose that by and by after it was too late to right things she would sometime understand that and have to suffer all the rest of her life for what she had passed by in her vague uncertainty? Would God let her do a thing like that? "Oh, God, I'm yours. Won't you please make haste and help me to know what to do. Make me certain! Don't let me go frightened into this!" That was what her heart was crying out as she turned away from the telephone.

It was just then that the servant approached with John Worth's card, and as she saw it her hope of a few moments' reprieve sprang up again in spite of her.

And then, when she had read that card, suddenly the thought of John Worth seemed wonderfully steadying. A little talk with John, even if it were but for a few breathless moments, would be like a breath from a fresh mountain breeze to her fainting soul!

So, her face clearing, her eyes bright with sudden hope, she gave the orders to the servant, and turned swiftly to go to John. He had promised to come, and now he was here! What would he be like after all these years?

She went through the library door to the porch and made her way by an outside entrance to the room where he was waiting. As she went memories flocked around her, memories of things of the past that she thought had long been put by. They came like dear old friends as if to rescue her from her trouble of the past few weeks. Silly, when of course they could not help her now, and she was but making more trouble for herself with this delay. But she had to see John!

Memories! Ah! A pleasant school room and a lad with lights in his eyes! A voice that made her listen even when he was just reciting commonplaces! A rainbow and the breath of flowers, the smell of newly washed earth, and a walk in the gloaming! A sweet dead face with lilies about it, her lips softly touching his brow!

She passed her hand over her eyes and drew a deep breath of mingled pain and exultation. He was come! Would he be the same?

She paused an instant with her hand on the latch before she opened the little door beside the chimney place in the small reception room. "Oh God," she breathed, "Help me!" Perhaps this had come to show her that it had all been a dream that meant nothing. Perhaps it had been this dream which had stayed in her mind and hindered her from accepting other things that might have been satisfying if her heart had not set up an ideal that perhaps was not so fine as she had thought. But no, that could not be! What crazy thoughts she was thinking! She must be going to be very sick, and was even now beginning to be a little delirious! How silly! She must get control of herself.

Then girding up her heart she opened the door and went in. As she entered she thought she caught the fragrance of valley-lilies on the air, and wondered. Was it just her imagination?

21

JOHN Worth had been waiting there what seemed to him an age before he heard her footsteps coming along the tiles of the sun porch. Was she coming, or had she sent someone to say she could not see him?

He could not help but hear what was going on on the other side of that velvet curtain beside him, the throng in the other room clamoring away, and his heart had been going down, down, into a deep despair. This was not his world. Why had he come here? Why had he presumed to think he could ever fit into an atmosphere where this girl belonged, or that she would care to fit into his?

But oh, she didn't seem, in his memory of her, to belong here. She had always seemed to be of finer clay than any of those who were shouting their gay nothings back and forth to one another.

Momently others were arriving and swelling the gathering into a noisy clamor. What a fool he had been to come in when he found there were guests! But perhaps it was just as well that he should have come here to see for himself, for there would have been no other way to get that vision of her out of his heart. He wasn't sure even that was going to do it. She had seemed such a true, such a wonderful girl, even when she was but a child.

But now surely his eyes were open wide! Would it not be better for him to slip away before she came and end this business, now while it was possible? Or must he stay and make some excuse? Say he had just dropped in to call, and as she had guests he would go with just a greeting, and perhaps come again sometime?

No, it would be better just to silently disappear before the whole gang discovered him. That is, if there was a way to get out. He felt guilty of great folly.

He studied the door beside the fireplace. Did that open to a coat-closet, or the sun porch? If so could he get out the porch door before anyone discovered him?

"Where's Pat?" cried Thorny raucously just outside the curtain. "I say, Barker, get me another cocktail, can't you? That was only a sample."

He rose impatient to be gone, and just then the door into the sun porch opened.

She dawned upon him at that instant and held him breathless. She was all in silver, slim dress and little slippers, and her dark hair wrapped about her small head. He thought he had never seen anything so lovely.

"John!" she said softly, out of the shadows that were beginning to grope in the corners of the room. "John!"

She came toward him shyly, all her worldly manner dropping from her like a cloak she had cast aside, and she stood shyly before him as if they had been again on the hillside together.

"Patricia!" He took both her hands in his and spoke her name reverently.

"Another cocktail, Barker, don't you hear?" shouted Thorny just outside the curtain.

John Worth quivered at the sound as if his palace of dreams were shivering at atoms about him.

"John, you have come just in time for my dinner!" said Patricia, rousing to the present with a new lilt in her voice. "Come, I *need*ed you! Someone has failed at the last minute, and to think it should have been *you* that came to fill the place! Come, we are just about to sit down. Your place is beside me. We can talk at the table." Her voice was happy and her lips were smiling, but her words were like a cold draught from another world. He drew back.

"No, Patricia, I would not think of intruding. I will not keep you from your guests but a moment. I've come a long way to tell you something—"

"Won't it keep till tonight after they have gone—? Or after dinner, perhaps, in the garden? You won't mind staying a little late—?"

"My train leaves at midnight."

"Well, then you will tell me at the table—"

John Worth took one step toward her and caught her hands gently but firmly in both his own.

"Listen!" he said and there was something arresting in his voice that made her pause and look into his eyes.

"It won't take long to tell. It is just this. I've loved you all these years and I've always meant to come back some day and tell you as soon as I was in a position to honorably do so. At last I have reached that place but I am afraid I am too late. I've been called to take a position of great honor over in Europe and I sail tomorrow noon. I must leave here at midnight to catch my ship. I'd have given you more time and myself a bigger chance if I had known sooner, but I came the first minute I got the word. This is all horribly abrupt I know, but when I found you had guests I could not bring myself to go away without at least telling you. There! I've been fool enough to lay bare my heart before you! Now, do you see why I cannot come out to dinner with you?"

Said Patricia, after just an instant's pause, lifting her eyes filled with a lovely light:

"No, I don't, John. Please come out. I really mustn't keep my guests waiting any longer."

He gave her a puzzled look, wondering, his heart sinking.

"Do you want me under those conditions?" he asked, searchingly.

"I do." Patricia's voice sounded almost as if she were responding to a question in a ceremony, so solemnly she said it.

John stood hesitating, studying her. What did she mean? Was this just her way of sweetly putting him off?

Outside the curtain Thorny's voice rose clamorously:

"Where's Pat? Where has she gone?" he babbled, his hand pulling back the velvet curtain as he peered into the room where the two stood.

"Here I am," said Pat in a steady voice, stepping out from the folds of the curtain, one hand lifted to push it back. Then turning her glance back to John Worth she said with a smile, "Come John!" and slipped her other hand through his arm.

So they appeared suddenly in the doorway.

"See!" she called in a clear voice, her eyes starry, "I've a surprise for you all. A surprise-guest. Thorny, you remember John Worth?"

Afterwards she was glad she had not even remembered to notice whether John Worth wore evening clothes or not. He *did*. She noted with satisfaction later that his attire was faultless, and that he wore his garments quite as if he were accustomed to such apparel. Indeed as she caught a better glimpse of him in the lighted room she thrilled to the fact that he was even distinguished-looking.

There was a moment's tense silence after Patricia's announcement. The guests were thinking back, trying to identify the newcomer.

There was utter astonishment, amid a dead silence, as if a bell had sounded, calling them all to attention. There seemed something almost electric in the air.

Perhaps the eyes of all would not have been quite so bewildered if it had not been for that whispered hint of a surprise in store. They looked and were puzzled.

There was nothing wrong with the distinguished man standing beside Patricia, watching them with grave aloof eyes. Nothing wrong at all. He was even most interesting. But somehow he did not fit into the picture. He was not of their world. Was it that he was of a world *above* theirs? Why was his presence somehow like a dash of cold water when one wanted wine?

"Who is he?" whispered the coral one of the jade.

"Oh, some grind she's picked up somewhere. Someone who has done something intellectual I'll bet! Pat gets those complexes at times. I've often wondered if it isn't just to get in the limelight some more. But what a bore tonight when we're all set for something else. And what will Thorny say? Look at his face. Now he'll get into one of his tantrums and drink a lot. I don't see why he cares. There are plenty of girls just as good-looking as Pat, and just as rich!"

For Thorny had come about-face with battle in his eyes.

"Worth?" he said. "John Worth? Why—ah—yes, seems to me I do remember him. You worked at Miller's farm, didn't you? Looked after the cows or something, didn't you, and barged into high school between times when you got done being nursemaid to the cows?"

There was a sneer on Thorny's handsome lips and scorn in his angry eyes.

Everybody stared, but John Worth only grinned pleasantly, till Bramwell Brown called out:

"Yes, but remember the time John Worth rescued you and me from Miller's old blind bull in the pasture!"

Then the whole fickle company burst into wild mirth. The laugh was on Thorny now.

Then Patricia was aware of her mother suspiciously watching the stranger from the length of the room. She had just entered, and perhaps had not heard Thorny's hateful fling, but there was iciness in her glance and haughtiness in her bearing. When Patricia introduced him she said coldly:

"Oh, you are the flier Patricia told us about, aren't you?" and looked him over, a puzzled sharpness in her glance as if something about him perplexed her. Or was she just appraising him to see how much of a hindrance he might prove to her plans for her only child? "Did you fly down here?"

"Yes," said John Worth easily, "I flew down, but I'm not the flier. He couldn't make it and I came in his place."

"Oh!" said Patricia's mother, and then gave him another piercing glance. This was someone altogether new, was it? Well, Patricia certainly was a difficult girl, and it would be a real relief when she was safely married to Thorny.

But Patricia's father came to the front just then, stepping up with the first gleam of interest in his eye since he had come into the room.

"Why, it's John Worth, isn't it? I'm glad to see you again. Where have you been keeping yourself all these years? I haven't seen you since you disappeared into thin air just as I had my eye on you for a job in my office as soon as you got through high school. I couldn't get trace of you."

George Prentiss' voice was big and hearty, and boomed into the noisy clamor of the gay company. His wife turned astonished eyes at him, and then quickly searched the face of the young man. Who was he? Had she seen him before? And was George in on this? Were he and Patricia trying to put something over on her, now at this last minute, when everything had been going so nicely?

The other guests seemed to sense something significant in the atmosphere, for they suddenly ceased talking and turned to look at John Worth, hushing their voices just in time to hear what he was answering to his host's question.

"Oh, I was away at college, you know, then Tech two years, and after that I taught in Tech until I took my present position. I thank you for thinking of me."

There was a quiet self-possession about the young man that prolonged the silence, as they studied him and tried to classify him. And in that instant of silence the servant approached and announced dinner.

Patricia swept a quick glance over the guests and took command.

"Thorny, you're to take mother out, you know," she said in a clear voice, smiling over her shoulder at the scowling Thorny.

Thorny was standing just behind her, obviously expecting to take her into dinner.

"Where the devil did you raise him, Pat?" he growled under his breath, nodding contemptuously toward John Worth. "For Pete's sake get him out of here quick or there'll be murder. I always hated that guy. You didn't *invite* him, did you? He certainly had his nerve to dare to come here—!"

But Patricia, ignoring him, turned to John.

"Come, John," she said in a clear voice, slipping her hand within his arm. "You're to take me out."

The coral one was at John's right as they sat down, and engaged his attention for the first few minutes, despite his best efforts to withdraw. She was burning with curiosity, but John Worth knew how to answer questions without giving forth much information, and at last she turned from him in despair.

"Now," said Patricia turning to John when they were well started on the first course. "What time did you say you have to leave?"

"One minute after midnight."

"And it is half-past eight now," said Patricia briskly, lifting her eyes to the ancestral clock across the room. "We haven't much time, have we, John?"

She spoke in a low conversational tone as if she might be talking about the weather, or old school days.

"It doesn't look as though we were going to have any," gloomed John sadly. "What time do you hope that this jamboree will break up, if any?"

Her face sparkled into smiles, but she gave undivided attention to the soup course that had just been brought.

"No, it doesn't," she said in a matter-of-fact tone. "But we can get quite a little across. Tell me—all about it—please."

She might have been making any commonplace remark, and his manner was equally as cool as he said:

"You have some white flowers down by the hedge."

She flashed him a look of deep comprehension.

"Oh, had you noticed them?"

"They called me in. In fact I might not have had the courage if they had not been there."

"They are my favorite flowers." Again her voice and

manner were most casual. "In fact, I believe I prefer them to any others."

"Tell me about them, please."

John Worth's manner was perfect, as if he were quite accustomed to dining out.

"They were given me by a very dear friend," volunteered Patricia.

"A *friend?*" enquired Worth calmly, though his heart was filled with radiance.

"On the happiest day of my school life—" continued Patricia.

Cryptically they talked on. Occasionally the coral one broke forth and interrupted, and now and again Patricia as hostess remembered the man on her left and graciously dropped a few words his way. But magically the conversation pursued its fairy way beneath the frivolity of the table talk, and thus they drifted from course to course, scarcely noticing what others were doing, toying with the food upon their plates, but not distinguishing one course from another. Patricia was unaware of the radiance that sat upon her face like a cloud of glory, unaware of her mother's icy stare that swept down the table toward her until all in its path felt it and shivered into silence. Most fully unaware of Thorny, eating almost nothing and having his wine glass filled from time to time. She had forgotten Thorny completely and her own brief reprieve which was drawing swiftly to a close. She was altogether absorbed in the enigmatic conversation which she and her dinnermate were carrying on under the guise of polite conversation. They were knitting up the years in terms of symbols, of which the little white lilies were the key.

Suddenly a silence descended upon the table. Just how it started or who was the instigator perhaps no one was quite sure. It was most skillfully wrought, and psychologically perfect. All voices were hushed in an instant, and then, before she had spoken a word, all eyes were turned to Mrs. Prentiss.

"Friends," she said in that well-modulated voice of hers that could always command attention, "perhaps you never suspected it, but we have invited you here tonight for a very special reason."

Patricia looked up suddenly, startled back to reality by her mother's voice, and that odd thrill that always went down her spine and ended in a choke, whenever her mother disapproved of anything she was doing, took possession of her.

She grew cold about her throat now, and her lips set firmly as her mother went on:

"But I am not going to tell you what it is," she said playfully, with a swift meaningful glance at her daughter. "You may, or may not, have guessed our secret, but now our dear Patricia is going to tell you with her own lips!"

Those lips which had never known lipstick, much to her mother's disgust, were white now and set in a thin little line of purpose. White were her cheeks too, and her eyes dark with feeling, but shining with a sudden glow as joy broke over her face. She had a keen realization that there was no need for her to be afraid any longer. God had answered her prayer and shown her a way out. Well, she would give them what they asked, then. It was not her fault that things had come about thus.

There was a quick little tilt of confidence to her chin, and a set of triumph to her lips as she rose from her chair and looked about upon them with a smiling challenge in spite of her white face. In the soft candlelight of the room with the flicker of the waxen flames across her lovely face, and her silver garments, she looked more than ever like a thing of moonlight, and John Worth looked up at her, his heart bursting with the beauty of her. Then she flung her challenge, sweetly, simply, almost carelessly, as if it were a matter of course.

"I'm just announcing my engagement—" she said calmly, looking them starrily and collectively in the eyes for an instant while she hesitated for breath to finish. She saw them sit up greedily for more, saw the relief and proud satisfaction beginning to dawn in her mother's face, saw Thorny, leaning forward with a voluptuous look in his eyes and on his full red lips, saw his white matched teeth gleam almost with a snarl of conquest. Then she finished her sentence with a clear voice:

"to John Worth!"

22

JOHN Worth had been sitting there in white anguish, like one who had suddenly been brought back from Heaven to die a second death. He had thrust one hand into his pocket where a little cool crushed blossom lay withering. He held it tightly in his fingers as if it would again help him through this trying ordeal, for he must not shame her now by letting others see his misery.

And as his shaking fingers gathered up the frail flower, another cool hard object touched him and stabbed him with a deeper pain.

Then suddenly Patricia spoke his name in that dear lilting voice, putting him on the throne of her heart before them all, and turned to him for confirmation of her words.

His soul sprang into his face. John Worth had no need for anyone to tell him what to do. His hand with the little wilted flower, and the other little cold hard round object still firmly clasped, came forth from his pocket. Reaching for her hand he slipped upon her finger a glorious ruby set in delicate platinum tracery.

It was all as if it had been carefully planned and

rehearsed. But the look on Thorny's face, and the white dawning horror and chagrin on the aghast, amazed countenance of Mrs. Prentiss were utterly lost on the assemblage. They were not looking at them, not yet. They were like a mob following the latest lead, and that lead was Mr. Prentiss, for he was on his feet now, and his face was full of unrestrained joy.

"Here's to their health!" he cried lifting a glass of water, and amid the clapping and uproar of the astonished company Mrs. Prentiss had time to bring her face somewhat into subjection and readjust her tactics.

She was utterly cornered and she knew it! She was caught in her own trap and must make the best of it, at least for the time being. Could it be that the whole thing had been arranged beforehand? She must carry it off with that idea at any rate. Of course later, when they had time to reason with Patricia, they could take her off on a trip to Alaska or the north pole or somewhere, and the engagement could be broken. But that would have to be adjusted. Just now she simply must show people that she was in hearty accord with it all of course. She didn't want them to know that it was all a surprise to her.

Thorny, aghast, unable to believe his own senses, hastily tossed down his glass of wine, and handed the glass to the waiter to be refilled. Then he turned with bitter tongue toward the lady who was to have been his mother-in-law. It was with the utmost tact however that she evaded him, and engaged in earnest conversation with her neighbor on her other side.

Of all this Patricia was unaware for the moment, for she was back in her seat now, with starry eyes and flaming cheeks looking at her ring.

"Oh, John!" she breathed softly up at him. "Where did you get it? How did you happen to have it here?"

She was glad that there was too much noise going on about her for the moment for others to hear.

"I've carried it with me for the last few years," he answered quietly. "It was mother's engagement ring. It came to father from his great grandmother, and farther back than that. It has been an heirloom in the family for years, the one thing my mother would not sell when my father was so sick. He would not let her part with it. She gave it to me the night before she died—for *you*."

"For *me?*" wonderingly.

"Yes, hush, they're listening. I'll tell you later."

Patricia sat up straight and remembered she was on exhibition. Then after a minute or two she leaned over and whispered:

"How soon do we leave?"

"Leave?" asked John wonderingly.

"Yes! Aren't you taking me with you, John?"

"Would you *go?*" he asked with a great light of wonder in his eyes. "*Could* you?"

"Why, of course," said Patricia with an answering light in her own eyes. "Didn't you want me to go?"

"Oh, my *dear!*" said John, and the lamps in his eyes spoke as his words failed him.

Patricia sprang into instant action.

"Mother, why don't we go into the other room?" she called gaily, and amid the general confusion of rising she escaped into the servant's hall, motioning John to follow her.

She drew him along to the telephone booth.

"Get in there quick and call up Mr. Ripley, dad's minister," she whispered. "Tell him to come right over and you meet him at the door of the sun porch and bring him back here. Tell him to be here in a half-hour at the latest. And, doesn't something have to be done about a license? I think Lawrence Seeley would fix that up for you. He's in something over at the court house. You remember him, don't you?"

"Oh, yes. I guess we can get that part fixed up all right," said John as joyously as if he were singing peans over the past.

"Well, get inside the booth quick. Somebody is coming! And when you get that telephoning done, hunt up dad! Talk to him about five minutes and then bring him up to my room. Tell him I want him. You can tell him anything else you want him to know, of course, but I think he's satisfied about you now. I know the look in dad's face."

John hesitated.

"But—your mother—?" he began.

"Never mind mother, she'll be all right when it's over. Don't say a word to her yet. Nor to any of them but dad. I know mother, too. Get in there quick! Someone is coming!"

Patricia dashed down the hall after one of the servants.

"Barker, find Marie and send her to my room as quick as you can," she said breathlessly, and flew up the back stairway.

Up in a great old carved chest in the attic there lay a wedding veil, of finest handwrought lace, yellow with age, and rich with ancestral lore. It was straight to that chest that Patricia Prentiss flew. Down on her silver knees before it she went delving, till she found the box where it lay, wrapped in folds of satin paper.

She met Marie as she reached her own door.

"Get me my white satin dress, Marie! The one with the high neck and long sleeves, and some white satin slippers," she ordered, still breathlessly.

"Oh, Miss Patty, you didn't spill something on that lovely silver frock, did you?"

"No, Marie," laughed the girl. "It just isn't suitable for the next act. You see, Marie, I'm going to be married!"

Patricia had opened the box and now was unfolding the precious filmy veil with its frostwork of handmade lace on the border.

"Oh, Miss Patty, *dear!*"

"It's quite sudden," laughed Patty, "Nobody knows it yet. Can you pack my traveling bag and get my trunk ready for a steamer trip? I'm leaving at midnight, Marie."

"Oh, my dear Miss Patty!" said Marie pausing in her swift moving among the well-ordered garments in the closet and bureau. "And am I to go with you?"

"Not just yet, Marie, but perhaps later."

"And will Mr. Thorny—" the girl paused apprehensively, as if she scarcely knew how to finish her sentence.

"Mr. Thorny isn't in the picture, Marie," said Patricia with satisfaction. "His name is John. You don't know him yet, but you will sometime, and you'll like him."

"Oh, Miss Patty, I'm that glad! I never did like Mr. Thorny! He wasn't good enough for you."

While they talked they worked swiftly. Patricia in a flash changed into the white things that Marie brought to hand, and then Marie arranged the wonderful veil, and without more ado the bride stood ready.

John Worth had not only telephoned the minister, and arranged with his old friend Lawrence Seeley for the license, but he had also telephoned the old family florist, Mr. Mathison, for a quick-order bride's bouquet of lilies of the valley, and it was already on its way, the handsomest bride's bouquet the old man knew how to make for his old friend Patty. But John Worth, at the last minute, was down behind the hedge in the moonlight groping with careful fingers for the little cool crisp stems of the valley-lilies that he had planted there so long ago. John wanted a few of his own blossoms for his dear girl.

And when he sent them up to her she fastened them, a little wreath like a coronet, about the edge of her veil to frame her face in place of orange blossoms.

Mr. Prentiss came tiptoeing to the door stealthily, and whispered eagerly:

"Great work, little Pat! You've chosen a real man! I don't believe there's any doubt that you love him. And the best thing about him is that he knows and loves your Lord! You have all my blessing, little girl!"

It was a great deal for her shy father to say, and Patricia folded her arms about his neck, regardless of her lovely old veil, and kissed him tenderly.

"No doubt at all, daddy dear! I've loved him ever since I knew him, only I didn't think he would ever come back, and mother was so set on Thorny."

"Mother will be all right," said her father with a smile.

Then came John with the bride's big bouquet all of lovely lilies of the valley.

Mr. Prentiss laid a fatherly hand upon John's shoulder and said in a low voice:

"I'm glad to trust my little girl to you, John! I know you'll take care of her! I didn't hope for anything as good as this in her life, and I'm thanking God for you!"

Then Patricia took her lovely bouquet and held it up near her face where it almost touched the coronet of lilies, and looking at John said: "See how they match, John?"

The waitress knocked at the door.

"Miss Patricia, your mother says are you sick or anything? She says you must come down right now! She says people are all asking where you are. They think it's awful queer you've disappeared. She says you must come *at once!*"

And Patricia sang out in her gayest voice:

"All right, Nellie! Tell her I'll be right down!"

Then to her maid:

"Marie, go down and tell the orchestra to begin playing the wedding march as soon as they finish this number!"

And in another minute or two they heard the familiar strains of the wedding march begin.

Patricia swung her bouquet over her left arm, and slipped her hand under her father's arm.

"Go down the back stairs, quick, John, and come around to stand in front of that bank of palms at the foot of the wide staircase. You are sure you told the minister where to meet you?"

"He's waiting for me at the foot of the back stairs. We're going in together," said John. "Good-bye! See you later!" He grinned, waved his hand and was gone. Mr. Prentiss and his daughter stepped out into the hall with measured tread and began their slow walk down the stairs together within the sudden view of a greatly astonished assembly below, who had just begun to sense what it was that the orchestra was playing. They looked up with amazement written in every face.

John and the minister had slipped in from the back hall unnoticed, and were standing at one side in front of the screen of palms that hid the orchestra. Nobody even seemed to glance their way, nor to notice that a stranger was among them. If they had they might have thought the minister was the delinquent flier.

Not till the bride and her father came into sight at the wide stair landing and the guests began to back away from their path and stare in bewilderment, casting about for a possible bridegroom, even thinking perhaps it would be Thorny after all, did they see the two standing there beside the palms looking up.

A bright beautiful light was in John Worth's face, and the lamps in his eyes were lighted and glowing.

The guests gasped audibly, and then turned their gaze in a quick questioning look toward Mrs. Prentiss, who was utterly unable to keep her countenance from expressing her bewilderment, horror and indignation at the sudden turn events had taken—at least for the first instant. But to give her due credit it was only for an instant, and then she hurried on a beam of complacency and fitted it over her frown with the greatest adaptability. Of course, since there was no chance of a long engagement to adjust matters she reflected that there were such things as divorces, although she knew her husband didn't approve of them. Then she lifted her eyes and saw Thorny's furious countenance on the other side of the room, his gaze charging her with having deceived him. It was evident that he would hold her responsible for this, and she quickly adjusted on her face a look of utter delight and turned her attention to admiring Patricia, her child, coming down those stairs with such an easy measured tread. And George! Really he was doing himself credit. How did he learn to walk with such ease? She couldn't help but feel a little proud of them both. And she hadn't imagined Patricia had it in her to plan and carry off a thing like this so well! Really, she was a credit to her upbringing, even if she had introduced a son-in-law into the family about whom they knew absolutely nothing. Who in the world was he anyway? He really was good looking, though she wouldn't have expected her child to care about looks. Patricia had always been so queer, and liked such common people. However, his appearance was very good, and he certainly did look as if he could be trusted. It would probably be best to insist that they live at home, at least for the present, till they could look him over and see if he really was going to be able to take care of Patricia in the way to which she was accustomed.

And who was this minister who was presuming to perform a wedding service right in her house without having gone over the service with her! He had rather a nice voice. It couldn't be the minister from George's ridiculous little old-fashioned church, could it? Well, he wasn't so bad. Perhaps she would go to church with George now and then just to make it seem that they were all in perfect accord.

And now suddenly the ceremony was over. They were pronounced man and wife. It gave her a shudder to think that all this latest spectacular part of Patricia's life had been taken right out of her hands and she hadn't managed a thing about it. But it had been very pretty and she must let people think she had done it of course.

And now the bride and groom were kissing each other. They made a very pretty picture she thought. Only she wondered how her child felt so free to kiss an utter stranger. Patricia who had been so ridiculously squeamish about a childish kiss from dear little handsome Thorny. But then Patricia had always been difficult, and done the thing she had least expected her to do.

And suddenly Mrs. Prentiss realized her duty and bustled up to enfold her child and give her the most tender motherly kiss she could muster on the spur of the moment this way. Then she took her stand in a line that she at once took command of, and waved into place, while the whole party of guests fell into line and gaily congratulated the bride.

"You always did do everything in a different way from anybody else," said Gloria as she gave Patricia a wicked little kiss edged with lipstick, and then flung off to find

Thorny. Since Patricia had put herself out of the running, why shouldn't she take over Thorny herself?

But Thorny was in the butler's pantry getting himself several drinks, and she stayed so long trying to cajole him that she entirely missed the bride's bouquet as she flung it down from the stair landing when she went up to get ready to leave.

"Oh, are they leaving at once?" somebody asked of Mrs. Prentiss, and with quick adjustability that lady smiled and purred:

"Isn't it too bad?" although she had as yet no idea whether they were going away or not. But she didn't intend to let anybody suspect that.

Patricia in her new Spring suit of a lovely soft green with a bunch of the lilies from her coronet at her throat slipped downstairs with John and said good-bye quite informally to her unready guests. Some of them were searching the kitchen for rice which Marie, being requested beforehand, had hidden utterly, and some others of them were preparing to take off satin slippers to throw after the car. But Patricia kissed her mother softly, slipped into the kitchen to say good-bye to the cook, leaving them all on the front porch tying Gloria's white satin sash to the back of the waiting car, and then, all in a jiffy she was out the back door, and hand in hand with John rushing through the garage to a waiting car where her father stood to give her another kiss. And then they were gone, while Mr. Prentiss went in grinning and told them it was too late.

Just a quiet moment the two had together before they reached the station and the train which was almost due, and this they spent in each other's arms.

"Patricia, my wonderful girl! Are you sure you ought to have done this so suddenly?" asked John, as he held her close. "I'm—only a plain man, you know."

"John," said Patricia, lifting her happy eyes to his, "it isn't sudden! Maybe I didn't always understand, but it's what I've always been waiting for. I've loved you ever since that day in the rain—or,—maybe—even before that!"

About the Author

Grace Livingston Hill is well known as one of the most prolific writers of romantic fiction. Her personal life was fraught with joys and sorrows not unlike those experienced by many of her fictional heroines.

Born in Wellsville, New York, Grace nearly died during the first hours of life. But her loving parents and friends turned to God in prayer. She survived miraculously, thus her thankful father named her Grace.

Grace was always close to her father, a Presbyterian minister, and her mother, a published writer. It was from them that she learned the art of storytelling. When Grace was twelve, a close aunt surprised her with a hardbound, illustrated copy of one of Grace's stories. This was the beginning of Grace's journey into being a published author.

In 1892 Grace married Fred Hill, a young minister, and they soon had two lovely young daughters. Then came 1901, a difficult year for Grace—the year when, within months of each other, both her father and husband died. Suddenly Grace had to find a new place to live (her home was owned by the church where her husband had been pastor). It was a struggle for Grace to raise her young daughters alone, but through everything she kept writing. In 1902 she produced *The Angel of His Presence, The Story of a Whim,* and *An Unwilling Guest.* In 1903 her two books *According to the Pattern* and *Because of Stephen* were published.

It wasn't long before Grace was a well-known author, but she wanted to go beyond just entertaining her readers. She soon included the message of God's salvation through Jesus Christ in each of her books. For Grace, the most important thing she did was not write books but share the message of salvation, a message she felt God wanted her to share through the abilities he had given her.

In all, Grace Livingston Hill wrote more than one hundred books, all of which have sold thousands of copies and have touched the lives of readers around the world with their message of "enduring love" and the true way to lasting happiness: a relationship with God through his Son, Jesus Christ.

In an interview shortly before her death, Grace's devotion to her Lord still shone clear. She commented that whatever she had accomplished had been God's doing. She was only his servant, one who had tried to follow his teaching in all her thoughts and writing.

Don't miss these Grace Livingston Hill romance novels!